THE
GLASS
BOTTOM
BOAT

For my dear friends
Sam & Deanna~
Blessings & Joy!

Laura Thomas

The Glass Bottom Boat by Laura Thomas

ANAIAH EDGE
An imprint of ANAIAH PRESS, LLC.
7780 49th ST N. #129
Pinellas Park, FL 33781

First Anaiah Edge print edition March 2019

Edited by Candee Fick
Book Design by Eden Plantz
Cover Design by Laura Heritage

ISBN 978-1-947327-49-8

Anaiah Press
Books that Inspire

For Lyndon: my Welsh Prince Charming and hero-husband, always. Here's to many more glass bottom boats...

ACKNOWLEDGEMENTS

There are certain individuals to whom I owe special thanks for their support, patience, and grace. I am exceedingly grateful to the following:

My publisher, Anaiah Press—thanks so much to the Anaiah "family" for helping to fulfil a dream (or three), and a special thanks to Kara Leigh Miller, who saw something in my writing and "couldn't put it down." You will never know how much that meant to me.

My phenomenal editor, Candee Fick—you certainly came through on your promise to "help tighten or tone any flabby, saggy prose"—and so much more. Thank you for being my writerly personal trainer!

My children: Charlotte, Jameson, and Jacob—you never fail to inspire me, make me proud, and give me the greatest belly laughs. I learn so much from watching you all. Also, be grateful Dad has a real job...

My husband, Lyndon—imagine if we had actually made it onto the glass bottom boat? There would have been no room for my crazy imagination. Thanks for indulging me with unending patience and being my greatest cheerleader. I couldn't do any of this without you.

My Heavenly Father—for giving me life and light and words.

CHAPTER ONE

Life will never be the same again.

Madison's gaze flitted across the table of the oceanside restaurant toward Chloe, her baby sister. The bride-to-be. She attempted a smile and tried to ignore the ominous churning in the pit of her stomach. On top of the massive change occurring in their family dynamics, Madison sensed someone watching her, even here. She shivered in spite of the balmy Caribbean heat, and familiar fear crept up her neck.

"You okay, Madi?" Chloe's concerned face came into focus, and Madison sat a little taller in her chair.

"Sure, I'm fine. Just a little anxious, which is ludicrous, considering you're the one getting married tomorrow. But that's me—completely irrational and a nervous wreck." Her laugh fell flat.

Chloe clasped her big sister's hand. "Everything will be great—you'll see."

Madison breathed in the salty ocean air and concentrated on the sound of gentle waves lapping the shore right in front of them—soft, safe, rhythmic waves with no hint of danger. A gourmet dinner on a tropical beach shouldn't feel this stressful.

Why am I such a mess? Am I being paranoid?

They were safe here with Chloe's fiancé, Nathan, and his missionary brother, Luke. Of course, Chloe was matchmaking, hoping some whirlwind romance would occur between her and Luke, but it wasn't going to happen. No way. That would take a miracle.

Madison glanced around the beach. Other diners were enjoying the spectacular sunset in this picture-perfect outdoor restaurant, engrossed in intimate conversation and delicious cuisine. Some wandered hand in hand down the beach toward the wooden docks and a live band. Everything was fine. There was no logical reason for anyone to stalk her in Jamaica—come to think of it, even back in Seattle, there had been no cause for alarm in months. But prank phone calls and random stalkers left their mark, and the haunting memories crashed over her afresh.

Deep breaths. I'm being ridiculous. I have to pull myself together for Chloe.

Chloe giggled at something Nathan whispered in her ear. Madison smiled even though her heart twinged. Life was changing for them all. She picked up the half-empty glass and took a long sip of ice-cold water. Would her days be half-empty at home without her sister? The last couple of years, it had been just the two of them coming to terms with their parents' tragic death. The Grey sisters survived together, doing their best to navigate the unfamiliar territory of inheritance issues, legal procedures, and taking over the family home throughout their season of grief. Such a nightmare. And now a new transition stared Madison in the face, forcing yet another major upheaval.

Only, this time, it was a joyous occasion—her little sister was getting married right here in Jamaica. But was it so wrong to wish their straightforward, comfortable life in Seattle could stay the same forever?

"So, how do you like the resort?" Nathan winked at Madison as he helped himself to a spoonful of his brother's decadent dessert. "I think I found a little bit of paradise for my beautiful bride."

Madison took a bite of the chocolate bomb she selected from the dessert tray and sighed. Bittersweet chocolate collided with cool, creamy coconut, creating an explosion of bliss in her mouth. "It's fabulous. I know I've only been here one day, but I'm smitten." She took her time with every delectable mouthful and scraped the plate clean.

Chloe pushed her half-eaten passion fruit cheesecake toward Nathan. "I can't eat any more if I'm going to fit into my wedding dress tomorrow. It's all yours." She kissed his stubbly cheek and clung to his bulging bicep as if it were a life preserver.

Madison shook her head. "Good grief, you two, anyone would think you're on your honeymoon." She grinned. "Wait. One more day and you will be."

Chloe wiggled her engagement ring, the diamonds dancing in the candlelight. "I can't believe we're here, sitting among palm trees the night before our wedding. Honestly, I was almost waiting for something to go wrong." She reached over and patted Luke's hand. "And with you here for Nathan, it couldn't be more wonderful."

Madison followed Chloe's gaze across the table to Nathan's older brother. In the hazy orange light, she couldn't help being drawn to the guy. Even though it was their first meeting, there was something special about him—like an aura of peace. How could he seem so confident and humble at the same time?

Not that she was interested. Her broken heart remained off limits to anyone. Period.

Luke was a missionary in Mexico—that much she knew. And from their brief visit so far, it appeared he had a genuine, vibrant faith. That was most likely the reason Chloe thought they were perfect for each other.

Her eyes flitted from one brother to another. Yes, Luke was handsome, even more so than Nathan in a natural, rugged way. Where Nathan was stocky and blond and spent way too much time sculpting his physique at the gym, Luke was dark and lean, maybe a runner. The brothers did share their eye color, however—an extraordinary deep shade of green, exactly like the dazzling emerald in her mother's engagement ring…

"Have you ever been, Madison?" Luke's rich voice broke into her thoughts.

Madison's cheeks heated. She had missed half a conversation while assessing those fathomless eyes. "Sorry. I didn't hear you above the crash of the waves. Have I ever been where?"

Chloe stifled a chuckle and shot her sister a mischievous look.

She could quit her matchmaking right now. Madison reached one hand under the table and pinched through the silky fabric of Chloe's dress before giving Luke her full attention.

He hid a smile as he sipped from his water glass. "Mexico. I was wondering if you'd ever been? I guess I'm a bit obsessed with it."

4

"Just a bit." Nathan licked his spoon clean. "Along with every other country he's backpacked across."

"No, but I'd love to explore Mexico one day." Madison leaned in. "It's on my bucket list, especially as I love the Spanish language so much."

"Right, Nathan told me you teach Spanish. Maybe you could point out all the bad habits I've picked up by learning the language from kids instead of taking a class." He grimaced.

"I'm sure you have a better grasp of Spanish than I ever will. A true conversation is not the same as using it in a classroom with my less-than-enthusiastic high-school students."

"Your students love you." Chloe turned to Luke. "This sister of mine gave up her dream of going to Spain so she could stay with me as I finished college after our parents died. Teaching Spanish at high school in Seattle isn't quite what she had planned."

"I'm having a blast. Really I am. Some days are tough— I'm not going to lie—and I have to admit I was counting the days until summer break began yesterday. But I love my students, even if they're not particularly enamored with learning a second language. And I'm sure one day I'll visit Spain."

"Or perhaps Mexico?" Chloe winked.

Madison's cheeks burned. Again.

"So, you enjoy traveling?" Luke's green eyes sparkled.

"Yes, it's kind of a passion, I guess, although I haven't ventured far from home these past couple of years." Madison glanced at Chloe. "This is only the second time we've flown since Mom and Dad's accident, isn't it?"

Chloe's big blue eyes brimmed. "Yeah, I think it is. Other than Christmas in Hawaii last year, we've just taken road trips. I wish Mom and Dad were here with us now." She smoothed the linen tablecloth in front of her. "They loved Jamaica."

Madison squeezed her sister's hand. "It was their favorite place in the world. They would be so thrilled to know you were getting married here." She looked at Nathan. "It's very understanding of your family. Are your parents okay with it only being the four of us here for the ceremony?"

Nathan folded his napkin and set it on the table. "Sure. They're cool with it. I wasn't interested in having a massive wedding, unless that was what Chloe wanted. But she roped Mom into helping with the reception in Seattle, so it's all good."

Chloe took a sip of sparkling water. "Sylvia is such a sweetheart. And you know she doesn't have any daughters of her own, so she was more than happy to organize our party at home."

Madison turned to Luke. "Are you flying to Seattle with us?"

He leaned back in his chair. "I sure am. Believe it or not, I crave the rain and need a Seattle fix at least once a year."

"He's weird." Nathan punched his brother in the arm. "Loves any kind of water, whether it's coming down from the heavens or in the lakes and oceans. I think he might be half fish."

A water lover? Deal breaker right there.

Madison's shoulders slumped. No way was she ever going to end up with someone who was "half fish"—not with her overwhelming fear of drowning. Yet another major frustration to add to the list of insecurities.

Not that I'm remotely interested…

Luke caught her eye and didn't look away. He cocked his head and rubbed his chin. Surely, he couldn't read her mind. Was she being that transparent? She plastered a smile on her face and cleared her throat. "I think I'll stretch my legs and walk off some of that fantastic food."

She stood, pushed the chair out from the table, and slipped her leather purse over her shoulder. Wait. Where would she go? Along the shore all by herself? What if someone was watching her? She hadn't thought this through.

"Umm, Chloe, want to come for one last stroll as single sisters?"

Chloe raised her eyebrows at Nathan, and he nodded.

"Go ahead, girls. I have a feeling my brother wants to try to impart some older-sibling wisdom to me this evening anyway. Shall we meet up in half an hour or so in the lounge? I think the pianist is there right until midnight."

"Sounds lovely." Chloe planted one last kiss on her fiancé's cheek. "See you later."

Madison scanned the area for suspicious-looking stalkers and turned in the direction of the steel band playing farther down the beach. It looked relatively safe with a scattering of vacationers dancing and relaxing in cabanas. She linked arms with Chloe and compared her sister's spray-tanned arm with her own. Even in the dimming light, she could see the contrast. "Wish I'd thought of a spray tan, too."

"You don't need any help—you inherited Dad's olive skin. I'm the one who naturally glows white."

"Hmm. I look peaky next to you right now."

"I thought your cheeks were quite pink back at the table with the guys."

Madison nudged her sister. "It's glaringly obvious you're trying to fix me up with Luke, but please don't waste your time. You know I have absolutely no desire for my heart to be broken again anytime soon."

"Okay. My bad." Chloe pretended to zip her lips shut. "But you look amazing, and Luke must have noticed, unless he's blind. You always look stunning in red."

Madison looked down at the full-length dress her sister had picked out for her. "Thanks. I'm going to have to steal you away from Nathan for our shopping trips every once in a while."

"I think that can be arranged."

Madison slipped off her flip-flops and carried them, the sand silky beneath her feet. It felt like old times when they used to vacation as a family and she would spend hours having a heart-to-heart with Chloe as they strolled along the shore of a tropical beach. Sweet memories. But that was before.

They passed the main dock holding a number of resort speedboats, which Madison chose to ignore. *Deep breaths.* Palm trees, yes, she would focus on the palm trees swaying in the balmy breeze. The band's island music was behind them now and just a few couples strolled along the shore. But they should be safe. She had already checked and the hotel had security along this stretch of sand.

Madison exhaled and let the sound of the waves wash over her, clearing the jumble of thoughts in her mind. Funny how something that held the power to paralyze her with fear also had such a calming effect on her soul. As long as her feet were firmly planted on dry ground.

Chloe pulled her wavy blonde hair over one shoulder and broke the silence. "You're doing so great. I know this can't be easy for you after everything that happened with Sam."

Aware of a second smaller dock on her right, Madison watched her toes sink into the sand with each step. "It helps that you kept the wedding so low-key. We both know you could have put on a magnificent, gigantic celebration if you'd wanted to."

"Yeah, but that's not really me. I'm twenty-one years old. I wanted simple and fun. When I told Nathan about Jamaica being Mom and Dad's favorite place to visit, he was eager to have the ceremony here. He's such a romantic. And this is perfect. Without Mom and Dad, it didn't seem right to marry in Seattle. And after watching you plan a big wedding last year, I knew it wasn't what I wanted anyway."

Madison winced. The pain of Sam's betrayal was still fresh.

Chloe sighed. "I'm sorry you had to go through that mess. But I'm serious. Look at you now."

Madison raised a brow. She must be doing a convincing job at cool, calm, and collected. Clearly, Chloe was oblivious to the skittish sideways glances, clammy palms, and out-of-control heart rate. "Let's sit for a while, shall we?"

After surveying the area, Madison faced the water and dropped down onto the sand, which was still warm from a day baking in the sun. She tucked the hem of her dress beneath her legs and noticed Chloe had followed suit. They both leaned forward with chins on their knees, taking in the magnificent Caribbean Sea and the final glimpse of a kaleidoscope of colors in the most breathtaking sunset.

Madison lifted a handful of white sand and watched it flow through her fingers in a steady stream. Her life was like this, cascading through a giant hourglass, and she couldn't do a single thing to slow it down. Or control it. *Lord, I don't know if I can keep up with all the changes. Please help me not to have a meltdown. Not here, not when my sister is so happy.*

"That's strange." Chloe pointed back at the second dock they had passed. "It looks like there's a glass bottom boat tied up to that dock. Yes, it is. I can just about make out the sign on the side."

Madison shuddered. Boats of any description made her skin crawl. She averted her eyes and chose to concentrate on the silvery moon shimmering on the water. "Why's that so strange?"

"When I asked at the hotel earlier today, they said theirs wasn't available. Something about it being away from the resort for repairs and that it would be out of action for at least several days."

Madison spun around, scanning the area. Her stomach clenched. *Why does this feel so creepy? I have to get a grip, for Chloe's sake.* She forced a smile. "I guess they were wrong. But we already discussed this—please don't ask me to come out on it with you. You know I would walk through fire for you, but don't ask me to go on a boat, particularly one with a glass bottom. You *do* remember my nightmares, right?"

"How could I forget? You told me every one in vivid detail." Chloe put a hand on Madison's bare shoulder and looked deeply into her eyes. "I hate that you're still freaked out by the ocean. It's been so long." She bit her lip.

"I know." Madison pulled at her hair. "I thought I'd managed to put it behind me, but then it all came back with a vengeance after Mom and Dad's accident. The thought of them going down in Dad's plane into the lake..."

Chloe's eyes clouded with tears. The memories were still excruciating for them both.

"I'm sorry. I shouldn't be upsetting you on the night before your wedding. But I still have stuff to work through, including my fear of the ocean."

"Can't you pray about it or something? You and God are pretty tight, right?" She arched a brow.

Ouch. Did Chloe think she hadn't prayed a thousand times about it? Her shoulders slumped. How could God ever use her for anything great? She couldn't even handle her own insecurities. "Yeah, I know. Give me time. And tomorrow...I promise we'll find a whole bunch of other fun stuff to do before the wedding in the afternoon, and then you'll have Nathan to go boating with once you're married."

Chloe wrapped her in a hug. "Don't sweat it. I won't make you do anything you don't want to. And you're right— tomorrow we have until the ceremony at four all to ourselves. But right now, I think we should make our way back to the guys, don't you?"

"Sure." Madison stood and pulled Chloe up, too. She dusted the sand from the back of her dress and dropped one of her flip-flops. As she picked it up, she caught sight of the mysterious white boat, and her gaze lingered. Was that someone *in* the boat? She froze. A man's silhouette. There was something hauntingly familiar about him. The figure stopped moving and melted into the encroaching darkness as if he sensed her attention. Madison couldn't breathe.

"Madi? Are you coming or what?" Chloe grabbed her hand. "Are you okay? You don't look so great."

Madison blinked and pointed to the boat. "Do you see that? In the stern of the boat? I think someone's there. He's watching us—I'm sure of it." She squeezed Chloe's hand.

"Where? Your eyesight must be better than mine because I can't see anyone in there. But if there is, I'm certain it's nothing to worry about—probably the owner checking stuff out or something."

"But he looked like—" Bile stung her throat.

"Looked like what? Looked like a guy in a boat? It's not exactly suspicious even if there is a guy out there." Chloe planted a hand on her hip.

"But it's starting to get dark now. Don't you find it suspicious that he doesn't even have a flashlight?" She braved one more look at the boat. "He didn't count on it being a near-full moon tonight, where he could be seen."

"Or maybe he *was* counting on a bright moon so didn't bother with a flashlight. You are *so* overreacting. I'm sure there's nobody in the boat, and even if there was someone, it's no big deal. There's a beach full of people close by. Relax."

Madison struggled to keep her breathing even as she glanced around again to make sure they weren't being watched. Chloe had no idea how much Madison had sheltered her from most of the crackpots and sleazy guys who had stalked them after their parents' death when news of their inheritance leaked out. She was also blissfully unaware of the fact that someone had followed Madison around after the disaster with Sam. She would continue to look after her little sister with every protective bone in her body, until she could rest easy that Nathan would take over the role. And even then, she would always be her watchful, somewhat paranoid big sister.

Chloe threw back her shoulders and marched toward the wooden jetty. "I'm going to check it out to prove to you there's nothing to get all freaked out about."

"No!" Madison barely recognized her own garbled scream as she rushed to grab Chloe. "Please, don't go out there. I can't let anything happen to you. Let's leave it and get back to the guys. It's nothing, and I'm overreacting and seeing things in the shadows, like you said. I'm sorry. Please don't go—I can't follow you. Not onto a boat." *And not if someone's out there.* Hot, silent tears coursed down her cheeks.

"Whoa, calm down there, sis." Chloe held her tight. "You're getting hysterical on me. It's okay. I'm not going anywhere near the boat. Come on now. Let's go back to the lounge." She grabbed a tissue from her clutch and offered it to Madison. "Dry those eyes and take a deep breath."

"I guess I let my imagination get the better of me. And now you're the bossy big sister." Madison dabbed at her eyes. "Better for me to be an emotional wreck tonight rather than at your wedding, though. But please tell me you're not saying your vows on board a vessel?"

Chloe smiled. "No, of course not. And like you're not going to cry at the ceremony." She linked her arm through Madison's, and they walked back in the direction of the resort lounge, following the glow of lit tiki torches. "Look. There are plenty of people around, and we're perfectly safe. Feel better?"

"Yes. I'm fine now." A bout of nausea churned Madison's stomach, and her arms prickled. The shadow was no figment of her imagination. And the mere thought of the little white vessel bobbing against that dock made her shiver. What could be more frightening than being able to see down into the depths of the ocean?

13

A glass bottom boat was most definitely her worst nightmare, with or without the creepy shadow of a man. And there was no way she was going anywhere near it.

Ever.

CHAPTER TWO

"HERE THEY ARE, THE MOST stunning sisters in all of Jamaica." Nathan waved from the corner of the luxurious lounge. Madison followed Chloe to their table, relieved that it was in a quiet corner where she could observe her surroundings. The subtle music of a pianist added to a sophisticated ambience in this indoor-outdoor area. Nathan grinned and pulled a plush chair out for his future bride. Madison claimed a seat of her own before Luke felt obliged to do likewise.

Luke chuckled and stood. "Can I order the 'stunning sisters' something to drink?"

"I'd love a piña colada." Chloe slid her chair closer to her fiancé. "Nothing says tropical more than the combination of pineapple and coconut. It doesn't get any better than that. How about you, Madi?"

"Sure. I'll have the same." She looked into Luke's eyes and couldn't help smiling. Those emerald eyes had a calming effect like nothing else—and after that little fiasco with the boat, she needed calming. "Thanks."

"No problem."

She watched as Luke sauntered over to the ornate bar. Did he even want to order drinks at a bar, considering he was a missionary? How comfortable was he at a glitzy gathering like this? He looked great in his smart khaki pants and white collared shirt—his overall appearance fit in, but he'd probably feel more at home around a beach bonfire.

At that moment, Luke turned back, and their gazes connected. She gave a pathetic wave and panned the area with purpose. Hopefully, he would think she was taking in her surroundings and not watching him like a hawk.

Madison's attention was drawn to the accomplished pianist, who was engrossed in playing a jazz number for the audience. A smile tugged at her lips. The piece he played had an unmistakable Jamaican lilt to it, as did every genre of music on the island. On previous visits, her family would always remark on it. The white grand piano stood out proudly from the surrounding mahogany furnishings, all oozing opulence. Crystal glassware, shiny marble floors, and intimate seating areas worked together to give an elegant, inviting atmosphere. Nathan had chosen well with this resort.

"This place is so perfect for a wedding." Chloe sighed as she leaned her head against Nathan's chest. The besotted couple held hands while they sat and admired the grandeur of the rippling ocean against the bejeweled night sky.

Tears welled in Madison's eyes, blurring her vision. She blinked several times and focused on the long white candle on the table. Would she ever share sunsets and beach walks and full moons with someone who loved her unconditionally? How could she ever trust a man again after she had been fooled and the trusting element she once owned was ruthlessly ripped from her? *I won't be fooled again.*

Madison coughed and got up from her chair. "I'm going to give Luke a hand."

Chloe winked. "Good idea."

Madison gave a big-sister glare and spun on her heel in search of Luke. En route to the bar, she wandered over to the windows. They weren't actual windows, just wide glassless openings allowing the view of the ocean to dominate the room. She paused for a moment, enjoying the gentle breeze against her skin, and inhaled the magical scents of coconut, sea salt, and spice.

If only that fateful day had never happened. She missed the thrill of sailing—the way the wind whipped through her hair while the fine, salty spray of cool water chilled her as she sliced through the ocean...

"Stunning, isn't it?" Luke's voice caused her to jump. "I'm sorry. I didn't mean to scare you."

"Don't mind me." Madison broke into a nervous giggle. "I'm afraid I'm a wreck these days. And I was miles away."

"Anywhere nice?" He handed her an umbrella-topped drink from a small tray holding all four glasses.

"Nice place, bad memory."

Concern etched Luke's face, and he looked down at his feet. "I didn't mean to pry. Forgive me?"

"Nothing to forgive." Madison took a sip of her drink and closed her eyes. *If I'm going to start living again, I think I can start by striking up a civil conversation with a missionary.* "I'm petrified of the ocean." She looked up at his frown.

He set the tray on a table and leaned against the marble pillar alongside Madison. "That's a shame. I have to admit, I'm quite the opposite. I love it. Even wish I had gills sometimes." He smiled. "What happened, if you don't mind me asking?"

She took a deep breath. "My family and I were in Barbados for my twelfth birthday. I was an absolute water baby growing up, but a freak windstorm transformed a fun-filled afternoon with my dad on a catamaran into a near-drowning experience for me." She cringed at the quiver in her voice. She had to face these memories if she held any hope of getting past them.

"Wow, that's terrifying—for both of you."

"Yeah, I truly thought it was the end for me." She looked out to see whether that second dock was visible. No, it was farther along the beach than she thought. She moved closer to the pillar for protection. Just in case. "The storm was wild, and I remember something hitting my head and then not being able to breathe underwater." She closed her eyes for a moment. "Dad thought I had died, but when he managed to haul me back onto the boat, he did mouth-to-mouth and somehow revived me. It finished my sailing days forever, much to the chagrin of my family, and I've never been able to get over it." She glanced back at the ocean. It had taken so much from her, yet she yearned for it. "Well, I *thought* I worked it all out and dealt with it until our parents' plane went down into a lake…"

Luke groaned. "That's devastating." He paused for several heartbeats. "If you want any help while we're here, I'd be happy to try to renew your confidence in the water. I'm patient, and I'd never push you further than your comfort level. Think about it. After the wedding tomorrow, I have no huge plans for the week." He shrugged. "Just some thinking and planning."

Madison's cheeks burned. This was beyond embarrassing. A handsome hunk teaching a nervous Nellie how to not have a meltdown in the ocean. She would have to find some other plans. Fast. "Thanks. That's kind. I don't think I'm quite up for it, but I'll let you know for sure."

"No problem. We're here for a week, surrounded by water—it might be the perfect opportunity." He looked from Madison to the water and back to her again. "I see the way you look at the ocean, and I would hazard a guess you miss it."

She chewed on her thumbnail. "Yeah, I do." *More than you can possibly imagine.*

"Thought so. Hey, we'd better get these drinks to the happy couple before they get unhappy. Coming?"

"Sure." Madison caught a hint of musky cologne when Luke walked away, and she couldn't help but follow.

"Finally, dude." Nathan took the glasses from Luke's tray and handed one to Chloe. "Cheers, sweetheart." They clinked drinks and giggled. "Can you believe you're going to be Mrs. Alexander tomorrow?"

"I can't wait." Chloe turned to Madison and Luke with her glass raised. "Here's to bright futures for us all."

Madison nodded. "A bright future sounds wonderful about now. Cheers, everyone." She settled into her chair and set her glass on the table. *A fresh start, a clean slate, the past behind me—no more fear of water or of stalkers...* Something felt off. She whipped her head around to the piano area. Was someone watching her? No, the pianist was quite alone.

Madison gulped and turned back to her sister and the boys. She needed a distraction. "What's the order of events for tomorrow? I know the actual ceremony is at four in the afternoon, so that's when we need to be at the arbor on the beach, right?"

Chloe's eyes twinkled, and she put down her drink. "Yes, but we have all day to get ready. I have us ladies booked in for mani-pedis and hair appointments at midday, so I think we should relax in the morning. Maybe we'll get some sun but not too much. I don't want us looking like lobsters in the wedding photos. We can have coffee, look around the fabulous boutique in the lobby, and chill out." Chloe was bouncing on the edge of her chair. "What are you boys going to do?"

"Can't we come with you?" Nathan asked with wide eyes and a smirk, which earned him a slap on the arm.

"You must *not*—I repeat, *not*—see me before I walk down the petal-strewn aisle at four o'clock. It may be a sand aisle but it's a tradition. Do you hear me?" Chloe stabbed her fiancé's chest with her finger. "I'm serious."

Luke placed his hand on Chloe's tense arm. "Don't worry. I'll keep this one out of trouble. We're scheduled for a round of golf in the morning, even though I've played about three times in my entire life. I think it's my brother's way of boosting his own ego."

Nathan laughed and clapped Luke's back. "Prepare to meet your doom."

"Thanks, Luke. You're the best future brother-in-law ever. And please keep him away from the spa area for the afternoon, okay?"

"Yes, ma'am."

Madison stifled a chuckle. "So, what about after the ceremony? I know you have the private dinner organized for the four of us... " *It could be a really long week—but what did I expect? To be hanging out with my sister on her honeymoon? How needy am I?*

"Nathan and I have the honeymoon suite booked, of course. That means you'll have the room all to yourself. "

"And it'll stay tidy all week long." Madison winked. Their hotel room currently looked like a tornado had hit. And it was all on Chloe's side of the room. "And then I guess we won't be seeing much of you two until we all fly home next Saturday?"

"Are you going to be okay? I hadn't thought about you being bored."

"Hey." Madison squeezed Chloe's hand. "Don't be silly. This is your honeymoon. I'm in Jamaica with no work, a ton of books to read, and a fabulous resort to be pampered in. This is paradise. You know where I am if you need me, but you guys have to enjoy this week and not worry about me."

"Or me." Luke glanced at his brother. "Not that you were in the least concerned about my well-being." He brandished a killer smile. "This is my vacation, too. I haven't had a break in ages, and as much as I love the kids at the orphanage, I'm looking forward to relaxing with a few good books of my own and doing the resort thing."

Nathan wiped his brow. "Phew. I was worried you were going to get all needy on me."

Chloe's face lit up. "Don't forget I've booked for us all to climb the waterfalls together and see the dolphin show later in the week, too. I've always wanted to swim with dolphins. And then next Saturday we'll fly back to Seattle together to party with our friends and family. But we'll always treasure this week. Right, babe?"

"We'll never forget it."

A waiter dressed in a tux collected their glasses. "Can I bring anyone fresh drinks?"

Madison checked her watch. "I think we should call it a night, don't you? Kind of a big day ahead."

Luke thanked the waiter anyway and helped him clear their table.

21

Nathan kissed Chloe's hand. "Hey, can you guys give my fiancée and me five minutes? It's the last time we'll see each other before we say 'I do.'"

"Of course. We'll meet you in the lobby. Take your time." Madison collected her purse from the table and led the way from the piano bar across to the lobby, closely followed by Luke. She almost felt comfortable around him. Almost. She hid a grin as he guided her out of the path of someone who had consumed one too many piña coladas. Yes, he had that protective-yet-not-overbearing quality.

There were numerous seating areas to choose from, and Madison spotted an empty leather sofa, right next to a gigantic fountain. "There okay?" She pointed to the corner. Corners were good. She could view the area well, and no one could creep up from behind.

"Looks great to me."

They settled on opposite ends, and Madison turned to face Luke. "Does this whole experience feel surreal to you?"

He took a moment before answering. "You mean your sweet little sister marrying my crazy little brother in tropical Jamaica—tomorrow? And after dating for six months?"

"Yes, that's what I mean. It's been such a whirlwind romance and Chloe's so young. But the realtor and the interior designer—they are a perfect fit. It's just that I barely feel like I know Nathan at all."

"I understand."

"Don't get me wrong—what I do know of him is great. He treats Chloe like a princess, and she deserves that. I'll admit I'm a bit of a control freak, and I don't like surprises. I guess it's all a little breathtaking yet overwhelming." She raised both hands, palms facing forward.

22

Was that a jagged fingernail? Yes, that one fingernail was broken. The clasp on her purse did it every time. Thank goodness they had manicures booked tomorrow. If only her broken life could be as easily fixed...

"A control freak, huh?"

She took a deep breath. "I'm sure you know my story from last year. Nathan must have warned you about my plethora of issues."

Luke met her gaze and then melted her with those green eyes. "All I know is you were hurt and you found God. My brother isn't big on details. I'm a good listener, though, if you want to talk."

Madison sank back into the sofa and curled her feet under her.

Walls. I've got to break down these walls. He's virtually family, after all.

"It's kind of a long story, but I'll give you the basics. When Mom and Dad died in the plane crash, I was wrecked. I felt like the weight of the world was on my shoulders. Chloe was still in college and I wanted to take care of her. We've always been so close. I had finished my studies and was planning on going to Spain, but all that changed. No way was I leaving my sister on her own, and there was nobody to share the burden with. Sam worked for our father's company and came to my rescue. He swept me off my feet."

"You were vulnerable."

"I was naive and perfect prey. Sam told me what I wanted to hear, and before I knew it, we were engaged. He wanted to marry me straightaway, but I insisted on not rushing anything and waiting a year. For once, I think my caution served me well. When I think of what could have happened…" A shiver ran through her entire body.

"He wasn't who you thought he was?" Luke leaned forward and rested his elbows on his knees.

"No. He most definitely was not. He mentioned something regarding my bank account about a month before our wedding, and for some reason, it sent up red flags. I did some digging, and the truth began to unravel." Madison blinked back tears and focused on Luke's face. "He intended to marry me and then take off with my inheritance. It was a master plan, and he was willing to spend over a year waiting and scheming. Love wasn't even on his radar; it was one hundred percent for financial gain. He had over ten million reasons to pretend to love me." She bit her lip. "I had enough proof that he couldn't even attempt to deny it."

Luke's eyes darkened. "Unbelievable. I'm so sorry. How did you get over it?"

She groaned. Would she ever get over it? "I'm still a work in progress, but I found a heavenly Father who loves me unconditionally, won't ever let me down, and He saved me. I wish Chloe would take me seriously when I share my faith with her. She knows me better than anyone else on the planet, but she doesn't seem to want to know the Lover of my soul."

"I can relate to that. I'm Nathan's brother, remember? Something we can both be praying about."

"True. And then there's my parents. I don't know what they believed. It was never a topic of conversation in our home growing up. I'll tell you about it sometime. I think I've overloaded you with enough for one evening, although you *are* a great listener. Sorry if I've overshared."

"Not at all. Trust me—I do a ton of listening down in Mexico. I'm the resident agony aunt for all the kids as well as the workers." A hint of pain flitted across his face and he shifted on the couch. "I believe God's called me to be single, which gives me time for everyone else's relationship issues."

"Really?" The word came out more like a squeak. A sudden flood of disappointment at the reason for his singleness washed over her. *Humor. Brush it off with humor.* "Hmm, maybe singleness is the way to go. Sure would keep life simpler."

Luke grew serious. "It's not for everyone. Some people think I'm crazy, but I want to be fully committed to mission work, and right now, it's easier on my own. I don't have all the answers, and my life is far from perfect." He sighed. "But I do promise to pray for my friends. And I'll pray for you, too, if you'd like."

He broke into a smile, and his dimples made him look young, almost shy.

"Sure. I'd like that."

"Hey, you guys." Chloe's excited voice interrupted the moment. "Are we intruding on anything?" She opened her eyes extra wide.

Madison had lost track of time and of their surroundings. So much for being vigilant. "We were talking about God." That would kill any meddling or interest on Chloe's part. Would she and Nathan ever see the need for God in their lives?

Chloe planted her hands on her hips and shook her head. "That's too bad. So, are you ready to head on up?"

"Absolutely. Let's get our beauty sleep." Madison stood just as a raucous peal of laughter erupted from their right. She spun around and caught the eye of someone. He didn't look familiar, but he was staring right at her from where he stood next to a huge marble pillar. Madison's body tensed. Their eyes locked and he raised his chin. What was with those eyes? A chill swept over her, and she glanced away. The next second, she felt compelled to look back. He was stocky, muscular. Could he be a bodyguard? His black dress shirt and pants were a stark contrast to his short, white-blond hair. Was she imagining this guy? No, he was there, all right—still staring, as stoic as the pillar he leaned against.

Madison took one step closer to Luke, her eyes fixed on the stranger. As she turned to ask Luke whether she was paranoid, her flip-flop caught on the underside of the sofa, causing her to lose all sense of balance. Madison collided with Luke's broad chest and gasped.

He held her steady with strong arms. "Are you okay? You're shaking like a leaf."

"I'm so sorry." Madison pulled away and straightened her dress. "I wasn't paying attention and I tripped…"

His warm hand touched her shoulder, and he dropped his voice to a whisper. "Hey, no harm done, but are you sure everything's all right? You look like you've seen a ghost."

She took a deep breath. "Yeah, yeah, I'm fine." She looked back to the pillar, but it was empty. Of course it was…

"Madi?" Chloe wrapped an arm around her waist. "You're pale. Something's wrong. What is it?"

Tears surfaced. "I thought someone was watching me. That's all."

"Where?" Nathan rotated and scanned the lobby.

"He's gone." Madison rubbed her arms. "I'm okay. It's my crazy imagination." But it wasn't. Not this time.

Chloe squeezed her in close. "Poor thing. You're having a tough night."

Luke stood right in front of her. "Can you tell us what he looked like? Maybe he's still around here somewhere."

"It was just for a few seconds, but I'm sure he was blond and stocky. He wore all black." She shuddered. "It was his eyes that freaked me out. They penetrated right across the room and I felt the look right in here." She pressed a hand against her stomach. "They were icy blue. I've never seen eyes like them."

"Icy?" Nathan's eyebrows rose.

"Creepy," Chloe whispered. "But he's gone now. He probably thought you were gorgeous. You get it all the time, sis. Try not to worry."

"I'm sorry, you guys." Madison shook her head. "I'm overreacting. I think I need a decent night's sleep. Sorry to freak you out."

"No problem." Luke touched her arm. "You get frightened, give us a call. Right, Nathan?"

Nathan still glared around the lobby.

"Hello?" Chloe caught his attention.

"Yeah. Sure." He grabbed her hand. "Let's get out of here. Right now."

Madison's shoulders slumped. *Great. My burly new brother-in-law is as paranoid as me. But why?*

27

CHAPTER THREE

LUKE SURVEYED THE LOBBY ONE more time in search of the stocky blond guy and then followed the others to the elevator. What was with Nathan? He was acting skittish, which was out of character. Mr. Cool was rarely bothered by anything and cruised through life on his own terms. What was with him scouring the room with a wild look in his eye, shaking like a leaf? *I'm going to grill him later about this.*

The elevator dinged and the doors swooshed open. "After you, ladies." Luke ensured the doors didn't close on them. Madison squared her shoulders. Something had spooked her earlier, but now the color had returned to her cheeks, and she didn't appear to be shaking. Brave girl. When she breezed past him, the scent of vanilla made him heady. It was fresh and warm and suited her perfectly. He inhaled. *What is the matter with me?*

He gave his head a subtle shake. He was here for a week, then in Seattle for a further six days before heading back to the orphanage in Mexico, where he would return to his regular single life. Unless he heard otherwise from God in the meantime. This could be a pivotal week, and he needed to focus on his future, not a pretty girl. His stint in the Mexican orphanage was coming to an end, and he had a huge decision to make: Should he renew his contract and stay two more years in Mexico, or was God calling him somewhere new? Or even back to Seattle?

As the doors closed, he was treated to another waft of vanilla. Madison. She wouldn't be interested in any romantic relationship after her experience last year anyway. Their earlier conversation about her ex-fiancé confirmed that fact. His heart ached. How could anyone deceive this beautiful woman?

While Nathan pushed the buttons for their respective floors, Luke chanced a sideways glance at her. Yes, he was single and intended to stay that way—but Madison was stunning. Not in a showy way, but she exuded class and gentleness and had a natural beauty about her.

Long chocolate-brown ringlets framed a flawless porcelain face. A smattering of light freckles on her nose gave a youthful appearance, even though she had to be in her mid-twenties. Twenty-five? That seemed about right. Her whole face lit up when she smiled, yet it sometimes hinted at a great deal of hurt still being worked through. That much was clear from their conversation. She was a long way from being ready to dive into another relationship. But those captivating dark eyes...

Had he really offered to help her overcome her fear of water this week? Since when did he have the gall to invite a gorgeous woman to spend time with him in paradise? Good grief. Madison should be like a sister. After all, she was a sister in Christ as well as a future sister-in-law. She was vulnerable and off limits, even if he were looking for someone special in his life. Which he wasn't. *Right, God?*

The ding and swish of the elevator doors stirred him from his musings. Chloe squealed. She was not about to let any creepy guy dampen her enthusiasm.

"This is our stop. My goodness, this is it. I'll see you at four tomorrow. Nathan?"

Luke glanced at his brother. He was staring straight through the open doors in some sort of daze. He snapped out of it in time and bent down to kiss Chloe's cheek.

"Sorry, honey. I guess I need some sleep." His voice was way too cheery. "You have a great day tomorrow, and I'll see you when you're dressed in white and ready to race down the aisle to me."

She shook her head. "You do need sleep. Luke, promise me you'll look after this guy and make sure he's not late to our wedding?"

Luke reached over and ruffled his brother's hair. "I take my responsibilities seriously—don't you worry. He'll be there." He looked at Madison. "Enjoy your day tomorrow."

She grinned. "We will. It's the last chance for me to have my sister all to myself."

Chloe pecked Nathan's cheek and linked arms with Madison as they exited the elevator.

As the doors slid together, giggles faded into the night. The guys traveled up two more floors in silence. Seconds later, the doors opened one last time, and Nathan stepped out, followed by Luke. The air smelled like jerk chicken as they made their way down the dimly lit corridor until they reached their room.

"I have my key here. Give me a minute." Luke managed to get the temperamental piece of plastic to work on his second attempt. He held the door open for his brother and flicked on the lights.

Nathan plodded over to the wide expanse of windows, where he stood with his hands in his pockets and gazed out over the ocean.

Something was bothering him, and since Nathan wasn't one to open up, this could make for an awkward conversation. Luke gave him a moment and then joined him at the window.

"So, you must be looking forward to having a couple of weeks off work?"

He nodded.

Luke shoved his hands in his pockets and stared at his brother's profile. "How are things going in the world of realtors these days? Business picking up yet?"

"It's not bad."

"Chloe must be thrilled about your new place. Mom emailed me some photos—it looks amazing. She's a talented designer."

"Yeah."

Luke raked his fingers through his thick hair and sighed. "Scintillating conversation. What's wrong with you? You're acting weird."

Nathan continued peering through the window. "Nothing. I'm good."

"No, you're not." Luke shook his head. How many scrapes had he rescued Nathan from over the years? Would he ever grow up? He was getting married tomorrow. *Lord, I need a good dose of patience and wisdom here.* "Something's upset you and I don't think we're talking pre-wedding jitters."

Nathan glared at him. "How would you know? I don't remember you ever getting married before."

31

"No, you don't. You can't fool me, brother. I've known you your whole life. I know how that brain of yours ticks, and something got under your skin down in the lobby." He put a hand on Nathan's shoulder. "Did you see Madison's mystery guy—the one with the ominous eyes? Because that's when you started acting all paranoid, and you're not one to get spooked by some random character."

Nathan shrugged away from Luke's hand and stomped over to the armchair next to the bed. He collapsed into it and folded his muscular arms. "No, I did *not* see Madison's guy, okay? I'll bet she imagined it anyway. Chloe says she's a bag of nerves."

Luke could take rejection from Nathan, but he wouldn't have him attacking Madison's character. "That's not fair. She's been through a lot. I heard some of her story tonight. And the way she trembled afterwards, I'm positive she didn't see the Invisible Man."

"Maybe it was a ghost. She's super spiritual, you know."

Luke clenched his jaw. Always the spiritual dig. "She's a Christian, like me."

"No duh." Nathan squinted and tapped his fingers on his chin. "Hmm, seems to me like you're being overly protective about someone you just met. Has the single guy been smitten with all this talk of weddings?" He waggled his eyebrows.

Luke blushed. Hopefully, his Mexican tan disguised it. "I know you're trying to deflect the attention here. And don't be crazy. I've known her for what—six hours?"

Nathan stood and unbuttoned his shirt. "Yeah, but she's your type."

"Which is?"

"In need of rescuing, a Bible basher, and beautiful. Your perfect combo."

Luke exhaled a bubble of laughter. "That's nonsense. You know I haven't any intentions of getting married, and as much as it irks you, that's how it is. I don't expect you to understand but I'm happy being single. It suits my life on the mission field." *At least that's what I thought until now... Perhaps it's just the wedding atmosphere messing with my head.*

"I respect you, man, but I sure don't understand you. All I remember of our childhood is you wanting to be a missionary."

"Yep. Since I went to Bible camp when I was eleven years old. Accepting the invitation to go with my buddy from school was the smartest thing I ever did. It changed my life. Mom and Dad had never even mentioned God to us up until then."

Nathan sighed. "I'm quite sure they didn't want to mention Him after that either. Work is Dad's jam and shopping is Mom's. They're happy enough, so why mess with it?"

"Because I love them and I want them to know Jesus like I do. They're not happy deep down. They don't have peace." Luke's heart ached. "Do you?"

"Dude, you're way too serious. Don't you ever wish you had a wife? I mean, doesn't it ever get lonely for you? You sure aren't getting any younger. Just saying."

Always the deflection. The conversation was going the same way it always did. Luke grabbed a throw pillow and hurled it at his brother. "Thirty is the new twenty. Look. I know it's different for everyone, but I think God used my lack of family responsibilities to make me available to work anywhere He led me—India, Africa, and, for the past five years, Mexico. Sure, I prayed about it quite a lot in my early twenties, but He gave me contentment in being single." *And that's where I'm staying until I hear otherwise. Loud and clear.*

"Weird."

"Maybe. But I don't know any different. You know I only ever had two girlfriends in my life, and that was in ninth grade."

Nathan jabbed his brother's chest on his way to the bathroom. "Hey, man, third time's a charm."

"I don't think so," Luke whispered into the empty room.

What would it be like to share his journey with someone special? These past months, he'd caught himself daydreaming in the long evenings, all alone. His thirtieth birthday was fast approaching, and with tomorrow's wedding on his mind, Luke couldn't keep his thoughts straight. Thirty. Where had the last decade gone? Perhaps he was going through some sort of early midlife crisis. He began pacing.

It's all in Your hands, God. My future, wherever that might be. Do You want me back with my family in Seattle? He was close with his parents and brother, and his home was always full of love and laughter, but none of them shared his faith. It was tough growing up as the only one with any beliefs. His parents and Nathan were supportive of his vocation, but it would mean so much more if they understood his passion for sharing God's love.

The shower blasted in the bathroom, and Luke stopped pacing to lean against the window. Nathan was always the clown in the family, and they were surprised when he announced his engagement to Chloe. How long had they been dating then? Three months? And then they wanted a short engagement with a simple wedding. Typical Nathan.

There's no denying the boy is in love. Luke had spoken several times with his brother by phone and was shocked to discover he had fallen head over heels. Chloe fit into the Alexander family seamlessly. Luke closed his eyes when he pictured his mother's smile on the screen as they had video chatted—she was overjoyed to have another female in the family at last.

He took a deep breath. His little brother was beginning a new life tomorrow. Chloe and Nathan were indeed a perfect match. Maybe one day they would both share a real faith to make their lives even richer. *Lord, help them to see their need for You. How much richer their relationship would be with You in the midst.*

Several minutes passed until Luke opened his eyes to the ocean view. Even at night, it was glorious, bathed in the glow of the moon. Maybe Nathan would come snorkeling with him in the morning. Share in the pure joy of being in the water. He could never get enough of the ocean—swimming, sailing, diving, whatever was available. How heartbreaking it must be for Madison with her fear of drowning.

I can't imagine anything worse. If only she could get past her fears and experience God's peace in her life. Then she might even take him up on his offer to help overcome her water woes this week. He bit the inside of his cheek. It could be uncomfortable for them both or it could be amazing. What if it were amazing? What if the attraction was one-sided? What if he quit overanalyzing? Fresh air was required.

Luke opened the French doors and stepped out onto the balcony. The night air was warm and humid, much like Mexico.

Something caught his eye farther down the beach.

"Strange."

Flashlights shone out from the end of the second dock, and several men waved their arms at one another with raised voices. One of the lights shone onto the side of a small vessel. Luke squinted. Painted in bold letters were three words: *Glass Bottom Boat*.

"Sweet. I've got to check that out this week."

The commotion intensified and a smack sounded from the dock. Luke spotted one guy lying sprawled out, clutching his nose. This was turning nasty. He saw enough violence overseas and was never one to sit by and ignore someone in distress.

They might not hear him, but he could hear their muffled cries, so it was worth a shot. "Hey, you guys. *Stop.* Or I'll call the police."

In a matter of seconds, the whole group dispersed and the area was deserted.

Nathan stepped onto the balcony, clad in a fluffy white towel. "Bro, who on earth are you hollering at? Do you know how late it is? You're not in Mexico now, you know."

Luke pointed to the second dock, which now held one boat and zero rowdy men. "Yeah, yeah, I know. But I saw some guy being beaten up down by that boat and I figured I could at least try to scare them off by shouting. I didn't exactly have time to catch the elevator."

"Want me to call security?"

"I don't think so. The excitement's over."

Nathan leaned over the railing and looked down toward the two docks and the stretch of beach to his left. "Where is he now? I don't see anything suspicious."

"That's because they all scattered when they heard me, even the guy on the floor. The second dock's empty, other than the boat. I guess he wasn't too injured. Better to be safe than sorry."

Nathan patted Luke's back. "Well done. A Good Samaritan off the mission field as well as on. I'm impressed."

"Yeah, well, I hope they didn't see which room I was yelling from. I have you as my beefy bodyguard for one more day; then I'm on my own." Luke elbowed his brother. "But I think I'll take a trip out in that little glass bottom boat this week..."

Nathan's mouth fell open. "What are you talking about? There's no glass bottom boat at this resort—we already asked and they said it was away getting repaired."

Luke pointed back at the dock where all the action occurred. "Either they fixed it or there's a little miracle out there bobbing in the ocean."

Nathan stared bug-eyed at the boat as his voice dropped to a whisper. "You have to be kidding me."

CHAPTER FOUR

"MORNING, BEAUTIFUL BRIDE." MADISON SWISHED the voluminous curtain aside and allowed the bright Jamaican sunshine to pour over her sister, still burrowed under the rumpled bedding. "And this, my dear, is why you didn't get married in Seattle." *I could get used to waking up to glorious sunshine every day. I wonder if Luke takes that for granted in Mexico.*

Chloe rolled onto her back and pulled a pillow over her face. "What?"

"No chance of rain today. It's perfect. It's seven o'clock already, so do you want to laze around in here for a bit while I shower? Or you can shower first, bride's prerogative. Or I could go for a run." A run would be good. In spite of a fitful night's sleep, Madison was determined to make the most of every moment of this special day and put yesterday's scare behind her. Mornings were so full of promise—wasn't there a Bible verse about God's mercies each morning? She twirled around the room while waiting for a response.

Chloe's face emerged from beneath the pillow. "You're chipper this morning. Anyone would think it was *your* wedding day."

Madison stopped twirling. A year ago, it should have been hers. Would she ever experience a beautiful wedding day? "I wish..."

Chloe sat bolt upright in her queen bed. "I'm so sorry. That was horrible. Me and my big mouth. Why am I such a grump in the morning?" She ran fingers through her long hair, catching a few knots in the process, then rubbed her face until it turned pink.

Madison perched on the edge of Chloe's bed. "Don't be silly. Although I think I should warn Nathan to give you a wide berth first thing. You've never been a morning person."

"Yeah, unlike you. I hope Nathan is okay. He seemed preoccupied last night after you mentioned your stalker, don't you think?"

The guy with the piercing eyes had invaded Madison's dreams last night. Her stomach turned. But no, today was all about Chloe, and nothing was going to ruin the wedding. "Nathan was being protective. That's all. And he wasn't a stalker. My nerves were giving me the jitters. I don't want you giving it another thought." *That's my responsibility—I'll worry so you don't have to.* "This is your one precious wedding day and I intend for it to be perfect. Okay?" She took Chloe's hand and gave it a reassuring squeeze.

"You're right. Only isn't it supposed to be me with the jittery nerves? I'm the one committing to a lifelong relationship. It *is* rather daunting." She gazed through the window to the sublime ocean view. "I believe Nathan is the one for me, but how does anyone ever know for sure?"

Madison took a moment before answering. She thought she knew Sam and that he was the one, but she wouldn't be fooled again. That was before she knew God. Everything was different now. "I think for me, next time, if there ever is a next time, I'm going to be confident because I'll pray through every step of the relationship."

Chloe wrinkled her nose. "What if the guy isn't religious?"

"Then it won't work. He'll have to share my faith, Chloe. I don't trust my own judgment much anymore, but I do trust God's."

"I suppose that makes sense." Chloe smirked. "So, what you're saying is Luke *would* be an ideal husband for you."

Madison grabbed a pillow and whacked her sister around the head. "Enough. Would you please quit with the matchmaking?"

"But don't you think it would be perfect? You're the only religious fanatics in our respective families. Plus, he's smokin' hot. I know it's weird that the first time we get to meet him is right here at my wedding, but it's obvious he's an amazing guy. Nathan talks about him all the time. You two would make the most adorable babies with your chocolate-brown ringlets, his green eyes..."

Madison gasped at her sister's audacity. "Are you contemplating our babies? My walls are officially up, remember? You can forget your quest to find me love anytime soon. Even with the hunky missionary."

"So, you *do* think he's hot, then. Interesting."

Incorrigible. Madison grabbed the pillow and clouted her sister over and over, until Chloe picked up another and gave Madison a good thump in return. Madison burst into laughter and Chloe collapsed on top of her on the disheveled bed.

They caught their breath and Madison sighed. "I'm going to miss you so much, little sister. More than you can ever know." Their enormous, five-bedroom house was way too big for one person. "Home won't be the same without you."

"It's okay for you to sell the house, you know." Chloe plucked an elastic from her wrist and pulled her hair into a bun as she spoke. "You don't need to stay there all by yourself. I know we wanted to live there after Mom and Dad died to keep their memory alive, but now that I'm moving in with Nathan, it might be good for you to move on."

Madison blinked back tears. "I know. Half of me wants to start afresh and get my own place, but I love our family home. We grew up there, and I can't imagine someone else living in it. But you're right. I guess it's time for me to move on—with my whole life." She glanced up through moist lashes. "Promise me you'll be my interior designer if I ever get my own place?"

"I should hope so."

"Good. But don't worry; I have no intention of rushing into any major decisions anytime soon. And today, I'm so happy for you, I could burst." Why did this have to be so bittersweet? She would savor every last moment of it being just the two of them and lock them in her heart to hold on to always.

Chloe kissed her cheek. "You've been a rock to me. And before you say it, I know you'll tell me it's because of your faith and all that, but I think it's because of *you*. You're stronger than you think."

"I'm not strong." Madison took a deep breath. "Really, I'm not. I still have my stupid fear of drowning, I still miss Mom and Dad every single day, and now I have crazy trust issues when it comes to men. Any strength I have comes from God, and He's still got a truckload of work to do with me. If I hadn't made the decision to step inside a church last year after I broke up with Sam, I dread to think what would have become of me."

Chloe gave her a big hug. "Will you be praying for me and Nathan?"

Looking through a blur of tears, Madison clung even tighter. Would Chloe ever embrace a faith of her own and share in the joy of knowing that a heavenly Father loved her? "Of course I will. Every single day."

*****

While Chloe claimed the shower, Madison changed into running clothes and pulled her hair into a ponytail. She slid a pair of sunglasses on top of her head, grabbed her iPod, and left her sister to enjoy some alone time in preparation for the biggest day of her life.

She descended the empty elevator and breezed through the lobby. Engrossed in selecting her iPod music, she barreled right into someone.

"I'm so sorry." She scrambled to hold on to her iPod while her sunglasses fell to the tiled floor. "I'm such a klutz." She looked up, ready to apologize further.

"No problem." Amused deep green eyes met hers, and she burst into laughter.

"Luke? Of course, it had to be you." Madison slipped the iPod into her armband while he bent down to retrieve her glasses.

"Here you go. One pair of sparkly, pink shades. I hope this doesn't mess with Chloe's tradition—the maid of honor seeing the best man before the wedding and all."

"No, I think we're safe, although I shouldn't mention this encounter. She's feeling nervous already."

Luke tilted his head. "Yeah, Nathan isn't himself either. But that's nothing for you to worry about. You look after the bride and I'll do my best with the groom. I guess she's not joining you for a run?"

Madison chuckled. "Not her thing, especially this early. What are you doing up and about?"

"I couldn't sleep." He rubbed his eyes and squinted. "I had a lot on my mind. So, I came down for a morning read by the pool before the crowds claim the loungers. I should get up to the room and wake that brother of mine."

Madison slid her sunglasses back on top of her head. "Thanks, and sorry about my clumsiness. We'll see you later."

Luke winked. "Absolutely. Have a great day."

"You too." Her heart skipped a beat. *Get a grip, girl.*

As soon as she reached the sand, Madison inserted her earbuds and started running. Perhaps the music would drown out the pounding of her giddy heart and ridiculous thoughts. No, he wasn't even on the market, and she wasn't ready to open her heart up to anyone. Was that why she felt so comfortable around him? It sure didn't explain the butterflies in her stomach.

Focus. I don't want to ram into anyone else today. She looked along the stretch of deserted beach. Hardly anyone else was around at this time, which made it even more special. Special yet unnerving. She would have to be vigilant, even at this hour.

Running on sand required extra effort, and Madison's thighs burned in protest. Slowing her pace, she pulled out her earbuds and savored the sounds of the island instead. She

43

inhaled and looked out at the shimmering ocean. Gentle waves lapped the shore alongside her, the water as clear as a sheet of glass. Birds swooped and cawed overhead, while palm fronds rustled in the breeze.

"Mmm. Paradise."

Paradise complete with a hotel security guard, who patrolled the entire stretch of beach, keeping unwelcome vendors and locals at bay. The image of the creepy guy from last night popped into her head. Thank goodness for hotel security...

Madison scanned the shoreline and noticed a couple walking hand in hand up ahead, and an older man snorkeled in the shallow water. She stopped to stretch out, bent over, and glimpsed someone lingering in the shade of a palm tree. A man she was sure hadn't been there a minute before. *Weird.*

He leaned against the tree and stared right at her. Instant goose bumps. Average height, stocky, spiky light blond hair, black shorts, black T-shirt, dark shades. Could it be the same guy as last night in the lobby? Hard to tell without seeing his eyes.

As she turned away to stretch again and calm her breathing, her mind went to Sam. Crazy, as her ex-fiancé loved his business suits and hated the beach. Plus, he had dark hair. Nothing like this guy. She shuddered when she remembered Sam's parting words: "You've made a big mistake, Madison." The biggest mistake she ever made was putting her trust in him in the first place.

She glanced up to see the man still under the tree. What was he doing? And why did the constant stress and paranoia from her overactive imagination make her suspicious of everyone? She shook her head and exhaled.

Natural—she had to look natural. She popped her earbuds back in, turned around, and broke into a jog back to the resort. Her heart pounded with every labored breath, but she managed to keep a steady pace. She slowed when a group of strolling seniors crossed her path. After waving to them, Madison allowed herself a quick peek behind. Nobody. The guy had disappeared. The lone security guard now stood in the distance at the edge of the hotel property.

She rolled her shoulders and took several deep breaths. Why did her body react with such intense fear to some unassuming stranger leaned against a palm tree? She continued on and grabbed a water bottle as she walked past the breakfast buffet. If only she had been able to see the color of the stranger's eyes.

CHAPTER FIVE

MADISON REACHED FOR HER GLASS and took a sip of pineapple juice. Her stomach churned. She had to put the earlier incident out of her mind and concentrate on Chloe, but why couldn't she shake the memories of Sam's deception? Brunch was over, and now she had to have this awkward conversation. She turned her head to gaze at Chloe relaxing beside the pool. She adjusted her lounger so she was sitting up and took a deep breath. "You know I want this to be a joyful day, but I do have to ask you something."

"Ask what? That doesn't sound good."

"I know Dad would have given you a grilling long before now."

"A grilling? About what? Nathan?"

Madison cleared her throat. "I know you're in love—and I like him, too—but are you quite sure money is not a factor in you guys getting married?"

"Really?" Chloe sat up and swung her legs to the ground. "I can't believe you're asking me this hours before my wedding. Just because Sam was a deceptive money grabber, it doesn't mean Nathan is, too." She yanked off her sunglasses and looked into Madison's eyes. "We fell head over heels in love before he knew anything about my bank balance or my address. He's not wealthy, but he's not exactly dirt poor.

They're a wonderful family. His brother's a missionary, for goodness' sake."

"I know. I know. And I like Nathan a lot, but I needed to ask, and you've answered, so we're good. I'm sorry." Madison exhaled. *Dad, that one was for you. You're welcome.*

"Do you ever hear from him?" Chloe wound a strand of damp hair around her finger.

Madison's eyes shot open. "Dad?"

"No—Sam. I know you don't like talking about him, but seeing as how we're doing the awkward-question thing, I had to ask."

"Sam? No, I haven't heard a word from him in almost a year, thank goodness." Madison shuddered at the thought of her narrow escape.

"Doesn't anyone know where he went? It's kind of strange."

Madison shrugged. "He had to stop working for Dad's company and I dropped all our mutual friends."

"I don't blame you. At least the jerk didn't get his filthy hands on your inheritance."

"Do you think that even matters to me? I don't care about the money. He stole my heart." *And my dream of a man loving me unconditionally.* Madison sighed. "But no more talk of Sam—it gives me the shivers. This is your day. Let's talk about you." She reached across and held Chloe's hand. "Do you know how proud I am of you, little sis? You graduated, got an awesome job, and now you're getting married. Wow. You're going to be the top interior designer in Seattle before long—I know it."

"Thanks." Chloe bit her lip. "For everything. It's going to be weird being apart, isn't it?"

"Yes. It's a new chapter. For both of us." *What will that bring for me?*

Chloe put her sunglasses on. "For the record, you deserve your Prince Charming, too, sis."

"Maybe one day. But right now, we should go indulge in some retail therapy in that gorgeous resort boutique. What do you think?"

"I'm all for shopping. I've had my eye on a dress in the window since I arrived. Lead the way."

*****

Madison leaned back in the recliner and allowed the spa staff to work their magic on her feet. She looked down at her arms. "That canary-yellow dress is going to pop against my tan, don't you think? Maybe I'll wear it tomorrow."

"No kidding." Chloe inspected her own skin color. "I could never wear yellow. I'm pleased with our purchases, though. I love my dress so much."

"It was a beautiful store. And now all you have to do for the next hour or two is relax."

"We should do this more often."

"I agree. You've been working so hard with that client, I feel like I've hardly seen you the past couple of months."

"I know. But I had to get everything organized so we could take some time off. I always thought being an interior designer would be so glamorous and that I could make my own hours."

"Remember when you used to renovate our big old dollhouse when we were kids?"

48

"Ah yes. That's when it all began. I was way too creative for my own good."

"And I was the neat freak who cleaned up all your messes."

"Good times?"

"The best."

Madison relaxed into the comfortable chair beside Chloe. Her feet soaked in some deliciously scented warm water while a manicurist made preparations to perform a color transformation on her toenails.

Soft reggae music played from nearby speakers and lulled her into a complete state of tranquility while she observed her surroundings. The spa was situated right on the beachfront with an unobstructed view of the inviting turquoise ocean. The area was given privacy by a row of palm trees and foliage separating it from the resort pools.

Even though they were in the shade, Madison kept her sunglasses on so she could enjoy gazing out at the glaring white sands beyond. It also aided in her vigilance. She was still in protective mode over her little sister.

"Chloe, I have to confess, I was a bit worried when you suggested having such a small wedding here."

"How come?"

Madison angled her head to face her sister. "I don't know. I guess I didn't want you to ever regret not doing the massive white wedding in a church packed with distant relatives."

"Hardly. Do you think I would rather be running around after a dozen bridesmaids, checking on the weather every five minutes, and worrying about what embarrassing comment Great-Aunt Gladys might make during the ceremony? I don't think so."

Madison grimaced as she recalled those exact concerns when she was planning her own wedding last year. "Yeah, you're right. This is the perfect way to go into a marriage—relaxed and happy." *Lord, if I ever get my Prince Charming, would you remind me of this wisdom?* "You're a smart girl."

Chloe grinned. "I am, aren't I?"

Madison chuckled and they fell into a comfortable silence. Peace and contentment were luxuries she hadn't experienced in a long time. It felt good. While Chloe dozed in the next chair, Madison prayed for her little sister. Today her friends at church in Seattle would be praying for sure, and she felt the bond of her spiritual family even across the miles. *Across the miles.* She arched her back in the chair. Would she ever live in another country? Now that Chloe was moving on with her life, would Madison's dream to live in Spain ever become a reality? Maybe. Maybe not. God was in control now. *And I'm fine with that. Right now, this is perfection.*

She opened her eyes to take another peek of paradise from behind her sunglasses, and her breath caught in her throat. She probably looked like she was napping beside her sister but her eyes fixed on something in front of her. Someone.

The same blond guy from her run this morning. Still dressed in black and wearing shades...and still staring at her from beside a palm tree. Unbelievable. How dare he watch her from less than fifty feet away?

Should she jump up and scream or play possum while studying the man for any distinguishing marks. That would be useful. Yes, she spotted some kind of tattoo on his left forearm. Ugh. A snake or a dragon or something gross.

What was he doing now? He slid a phone from his pocket and had the audacity to snap a photo of her. Enraged,

Madison sat bolt upright, and the next second, he vanished behind a palm tree.

"Miss, is everything okay?" The manicurist stopped painting a toenail midstroke.

Madison remembered to breathe out and reclined back into the chair. "Yes, I'm sorry about that. Something made me jump. That's all." She forced a smile.

"Madi?" Chloe stirred in the chair next to her. "What's up?"

"Oh, nothing. I jumped in my sleep. You know how I am." Unshed tears burned her eyes.

"Yeah, I do. This day is so perfect, though, isn't it?"

"Absolutely." Madison straightened her sunglasses. Chloe couldn't see the tears of fear and look of panic on her face.

Her pulse returned to normal and her hands stopped shaking. Thank goodness the manicurist was busy massaging her calves and wasn't trying to wrestle with her fingers yet. *Calm down, girl. Hold it together.*

She focused on the fuchsia nail polish. That guy could be the same one from last night. If only she had seen the eyes hiding behind those shades. On second thought, those icy blue eyes were the last things she wanted to see. *Who on earth is he? And what does he want?*

Nothing was going to get in the way of Chloe and Nathan celebrating the most important day of their lives. There must be some logical explanation anyway. Maybe he was taking a photo of the spa for his wife. *Yeah, right.* With a shudder, Madison realized she would be on her own after this evening.

So would Luke. *Luke.* He had a quiet, solid strength and a genuine heart. He would know what to do and she would feel a lot better telling someone about it. Maybe tonight after the wedding dinner? Yes, they would chat together then. She let out the breath she had been holding. He succeeded in calming her down without even knowing what she needed.

As much as she didn't want to admit it, the missionary occupied her mind an awful lot, and she feared her obsession might spread to her heart.

Madison bit her lip. The last romantic experience left her shattered and hollowed out, and she could not allow that to happen ever again. It would be her undoing.

CHAPTER SIX

LUKE STOOD IN THE SHALLOW water and secured his snorkeling mask. He turned to Nathan, who lazed on a beach lounger as he worked on his already-perfect tan.

"You sure you don't want to come? The water's awesome."

"Nope. I earned the right to relax by beating you mercilessly on the golf course, dude."

"Whatever. It's your loss."

"No, I think you're the one doing all the losing so far today." Nathan laughed at his own joke and lay down.

He was missing out for sure. There was something soothing about the ocean, and Luke could always rely on a good float, swim, or snorkel to melt his worries away. For a time, at least. Stress shouldn't be on the agenda right now — the lull of the Caribbean was supposed to be the idyllic break he needed. But Nathan worried him. All day he'd been acting out of character, and it had caused some funky friction between them. Okay, so some of it could be wedding nerves. It was a huge commitment, after all. But no, there was something else.

Luke watched his brother fidget, twisting around as if looking for someone. But whom? After last night's lecture, he knew Chloe wouldn't dare risk breaking with tradition and venture near her groom-to-be. Was he trying to attract the attention of a bar server for a cool drink?

Nathan, you're a basket case. I thought you wanted to relax. Now you're making me antsy, too.

Luke turned to the horizon and trudged into the warm water as he thought back to last night when it had all started. When Nathan had wandered onto the balcony and seen the glass bottom boat, something dislodged. It was as if he'd seen a ghost. He had snapped out of it but refused to discuss it further, insisting it was nothing and using the 'pre-wedding nerves' excuse. Luke wasn't buying it. He craned his neck to check whether anything was happening over at the two docks on his left. No boats at the main dock, but on a Saturday afternoon, that was not unusual. They would all be in use. And by the looks of it, down at the second dock that glass bottom boat was still moored but out of action for some reason.

Nathan was hiding something. He couldn't keep it from his perceptive brother forever. Luke snorted. He would give him the benefit of the doubt today. It was his wedding, after all. *Make the most of it, buddy. When we get back to Seattle, I'm going to find out what's eating you.* Nathan was the beefcake and capable of holding his own, but Luke was still his older sibling and would protect him no matter what.

Luke slid beneath the water and allowed the ocean to envelop him. He instantly unwound. Listening to his own breathing sounds magnified through the snorkel, he prayed for Nathan. How many hours had he spent praying for his brother? For him to find God, to get out of the bad crowd he ran with after high school, for a career to get his teeth into, and for a good wife to settle down with. Three out of four wasn't bad, and God hadn't finished with him yet.

After surfacing to gain his bearings, Luke glanced back at the white beach and panned across to survey the spa area. *I wonder what Madison's doing now. I hope she recovered after that scare last night with the guy in the lobby. She seemed happy enough this morning.*

Luke took off his mask and gave his head a good shake to clear his thoughts.

Quit thinking about her, single guy. Maybe pray for her instead.

He adjusted his mask and dove down deeper than before. He spotted some interesting coral reefs farther out. Now, this was more like it. In the mysterious underwater world, he was surrounded by a colorful array of parrotfish, clownfish, and angelfish all going about their business and ignoring his human presence. It would be so special to share this magical moment with someone.

Madison.

Except she'd never agree to see this beauty. Not with her unresolved fear. His heart dropped. He could tell she longed to regain her confidence in the water, but it could be a slow process. One he was prepared to help with even if it would take a great deal of convincing to rebuild her trust.

Thank You, God, for saving her from so much. You saved her from the ocean years ago and from the ex-boyfriend who deceived her and from a life of hopelessness when she found You. She's been through so much. Help me to be a good friend.

Friend. Such a disappointing and pathetic word. Maybe he should go back to the beach and focus on looking after his brother instead. Just a few more minutes. He needed more prayer time to settle his soul.

*****

"Hey, man. See any decent ocean life out there?" Nathan took a swig from a water bottle and threw a full one to Luke. "I thought you were never coming out."

"It was fantastic. Sure you don't want to have a quick dip before we go get ready? It's baking hot out here." Luke shook his sopping-wet hair and showered Nathan with the spray.

"Nope. Seems I'm quite cool now." He twisted around to peer at the pool area.

Luke toweled off. "You want to talk about it?"

"About cooling off?" Nathan squinted up at Luke backlit by the blazing sun.

"No. I mean the reason why you've been acting so skittish all day. I hoped the fact that you hammered me at golf this morning would calm you down a bit."

Nathan picked at a thread on his beach towel. "I am calm. I don't know what you're talking about."

"You're usually the coolest dude in the room, but I can assure you, you're not today. And you weren't last night either. It's not wedding nerves. I know you too well." He squatted down in front of his brother and lowered his voice. "It's like you're watching for someone, although I can't imagine who you might know in Jamaica. Why can't you tell me what's up? You know I'm a good listener. Please, let me help you out here?"

"It's nothing." Nathan closed his eyes and lay back on the lounger.

"Was it the guys on that dock last night? You're not worried they're going to come and beat me up or something, are you? I'll bet they didn't even see which room I was shouting from, so you don't need to be stressed."

"It's not that."

"Then it *is* something?"

Several seconds of silence passed and Luke felt sure his brother would open up. But instead, Nathan swung his legs around and stood. He grabbed his towel and the water bottle fell in the sand.

"Enough of this touchy-feely pouring out of the heart. I've got to focus on Chloe and the wedding today. We need to get back to our room. It's not going to take me long to make myself even more dashing, but we've got some serious work to do on you." He flashed a superwhite smile that didn't quite reach his eyes.

"Fine. You know I'm here when you need me." Luke shrugged. Nothing was going to be resolved today. He gave his brother a rapid flick with his towel. "Let's get going, groom."

*****

An hour later, a suitably primped Luke stood with Nathan and the photographer at the wedding arbor on the beach, while the wedding planner flitted between the aisle and the hotel lobby, where the girls would soon emerge.

"How's this?" Nathan put an arm around Luke's shoulders and they both grinned like Cheshire cats.

The photographer nodded his approval and took several candid shots while the brothers adjusted each other's bow ties.

"So, how's the bride holding up?" Nathan looked at the photographer. "I guess you've already been up there taking some pics?" He took a handkerchief from his pocket and dabbed his glowing brow.

The Jamaican grinned. "Mon, she's doing fine, and she is one beautiful bride. You're a lucky guy. I wish you every happiness."

Nathan ducked his head. "Yeah, I am lucky. Although right now, I wish we'd vetoed the tux idea and gone for T-shirt and shorts. I think I may melt before she arrives."

Luke gazed past his brother and saw a suited man with two women approaching, one of them dressed in white. He poked him in the ribs. "Don't look now, but your bride is here."

Nathan nearly choked. "Do you mean I do look or don't look? I've forgotten everything she told me. I can't mess this up."

Luke put a hand on his brother's shoulder. "Relax. The pastor's going to tell us when we should turn around, but let's look ahead at the ocean and let the ladies get themselves organized, okay? Deep breaths with me? Come on. In and out..."

Nathan copied his breathing. He used the handkerchief again on his sweating neck. "You do have the rings, don't you?"

Luke raised a brow and patted his pocket. "Do you think I might have thrown them away since you asked me three minutes ago? Yes, I have them both safely tucked away. It's going to be perfect, so quit worrying and enjoy your wedding, okay?" *Wow. Seems like getting married is beyond stressful. May have dodged a bullet.*

Nathan nodded. "Yeah, you're right. I need to chill. This is the most important day of my life."

The photographer disappeared and was replaced by a jovial Jamaican pastor who joined the men at the arbor.

"How you doin', mon?" He shook Nathan's hand.

"Fine. I think." He attempted to turn around.

The pastor put a hand out to stop him. "Wait, mon. Just give the ladies some time. The bride is savoring this magical moment with her sister."

"Right." Nathan leaned over to Luke and whispered. "Do you think I should have asked Mom and Dad to come? I feel bad they're missing this now. I mean, if you're doing the single thing for the rest of your life, this is their only chance to see a family wedding."

Luke jolted at the thought.

Am I breaking my parents' hearts by honoring what I think God wants from me? His mom never complained about his singleness, not in so many words. She acted worried sometimes, as if he were missing out on something by not having a wife, but she never pressed the issue. On the other hand, she never understood Luke's devotion to God, and his dad often joked Luke was a religious fanatic, so perhaps they both thought he was some kind of monk. Good grief. If only they knew the struggles he faced before coming to the decision of remaining single. It was the hardest decision of his life. The wedding stuff was messing with his head. *I know marriage isn't for me. It's as simple as that.*

"Luke?"

"Hmm?"

"Mom and Dad? Should I have invited them today?" Nathan bit his lower lip.

"No, man, I think you made a good decision. Not to mention, it's kind of late in the game to be having such thoughts. Of course, it would be different if Chloe's parents were alive, but I think you might have acted with uncharacteristic sensitivity for once in your life."

That earned him a thump on the arm.

"Luke, thanks."

"For what—insulting you?"

"No, for being here for me. It means a lot."

Luke looked into his brother's eyes and a lump caught in his throat. "Anytime, little brother. I wouldn't have missed it for the world."

The pastor coughed. "Gentlemen, I think we're ready to begin." He nodded at the wedding planner, and the air was filled with classical music played through speakers. "You can turn around," the pastor whispered. "You won't want to miss a single second."

Luke had butterflies in the pit of his stomach. Whether for his brother or himself, he wasn't quite sure, but nothing could have prepared him for the vision before him.

Madison almost floated down the petal-strewn aisle, gracefully walking in time with the music. *She's a goddess.* Luke remembered to breathe. She wore a full-length, straight orange dress and clutched a huge bouquet of some sort of tropical flowers in an abundance of color, and one of the flowers was set in her long brown hair.

Luke's world tilted on its axis and his mouth went dry. How on earth was Nathan going to react when he saw his bride? Madison's eyes roamed the arbor as she moved closer until they met Luke's. He knew he grinned like an idiot because she hid a giggle. Her beautiful face lit up the whole enchanted vista.

"Hi, gentlemen," she whispered and then took her place to one side.

Nathan caught his breath and Luke followed his gaze down the aisle. Chloe looked stunning. Luke didn't know much about weddings or dresses, but this lady got it right. She was an angel in white and was smiling from behind her short veil. Her bouquet was an even bigger version of Madison's, and some of her blonde hair was piled up on top, making her look sophisticated and flirtatious at the same time.

Luke's heart sank—Chloe was walking down the aisle by herself. Why hadn't he thought about this before? She must be missing her father dreadfully at this moment. This would have been his special, bittersweet daddy-daughter experience as he gave her away. No wonder the girls had needed a moment before the ceremony began. They must be feeling the massive loss of their parents, today of all days. *Lord, help them.*

When Chloe approached the arbor, Nathan seemed to tense every muscle in his body. Luke could feel it from where he stood at his brother's side and patted his back in a gesture of reassurance. Nathan beamed and nodded as he faced his bride. He was going to be fine.

Luke chanced a subtle peek at Madison. Her smile was genuine, but her hands trembled beneath the bouquet. Poor girl, this was such an emotional day for her. She was dealing with her parents' absence and her sister's marriage—and then thoughts of her own canceled wedding must be at the forefront of her mind, too.

He caught her gaze and mouthed, "You okay?"

Madison nodded, but her dark eyes pooled.

If only he could take her in his arms and offer comfort.

CHAPTER SEVEN

MADISON STEADIED HERSELF, WISHING SHE'D picked flats instead of heels, but this was a wedding, and she was the maid of honor, so comfort took second place to fabulousness. If only she could stop her hands from shaking.

The whole experience was surreal. Here she stood, in Jamaica with the turquoise Caribbean Sea for a backdrop, watching her little sister get married. Chloe looked breathtaking.

She was head-to-toe perfection from the bejeweled tiny tiara to the sparkly strappy sandals hidden beneath her hem. The ladies at the salon had styled her hair, pinning most of it up and curling the wispy blonde strands around her face. The strapless white wedding dress was full length and softly pleated, much like the style Madison was wearing, complemented by a diamond-encrusted belt to showcase Chloe's tiny waist. The subtle veil shimmered in the gentle breeze. A fairy-tale princess.

The music stopped, and the pastor began with "We are gathered here today..." Poor Nathan already had beads of sweat forming on his forehead. Guys always got the short straw at weddings, having to wear tuxes or being stuffed into suits. But the Alexander brothers did look exceptionally handsome today. She stole another quick look at Luke's profile.

They both wore black tuxedos and bow ties, on Chloe's insistence. Luke's wavy dark hair was expertly groomed this afternoon, and his tan popped against the white collar of his shirt. Broad shoulders filled his jacket with just the right amount of muscle—yes, he was perfectly proportioned and made for his tux. Unlike his brother, whose biceps looked ready to burst right out of his sleeves. Luke's strong chin and straight nose looked good in profile, and when he glanced in her direction, dimples appeared in his cheeks, making him look ten years younger. She whipped her head back to the pastor.

"Who gives this woman away?" The pastor looked at Madison.

She inched closer to Chloe and put a hand under her elbow. "I do," she said, "for our mother and father." She kissed Chloe's cheek and they shared a sad smile. As she took the bouquet from her, the afternoon sun caught the diamond in Chloe's necklace.

Chloe had been so excited with her special wedding-day gift. Madison spared no expense and bought her a necklace from Tiffany, which she'd presented to her earlier this afternoon while they were dressing. The simple silver chain held a diamond solitaire set in a locket. Inside the locket were two tiny photographs, one of their mom and one of their dad. "So, they could be part of your wedding day," Madison explained before they both dissolved into tears and were forced to redo their makeup.

She stepped back and placed Chloe's bouquet on an ornate side table. Thoughts of their parents swirled in Madison's head while the pastor continued with the rest of the formalities. They would have loved this day. Dad would have been proud to walk Chloe down the aisle, and Mom would have bawled like a baby. Madison felt her chin quiver and dabbed the corners of her eyes with a tissue tucked under her bouquet.

"If anyone has any objections to this man and woman getting married, let them speak now or forever hold your peace." The pastor paused and Madison half expected her stalker to appear. Crazy. She peeked over her shoulder at the beach, just to be sure.

The rest of the ceremony went smoothly, and by the time Chloe and Nathan both said the romantic vows they had written to each other, everyone was in tears. She even spotted Luke wiping his eyes with a handkerchief. Before she could blink, the couple were pronounced man and wife and shared a kiss as the photographer snapped away.

"Congratulations, little sister." Madison set down her bouquet and pulled Chloe into a huge hug. "I'm so proud of you. Everything was exquisite."

Chloe threw back her head and laughed. "We did it." She clutched her locket. "Thank you for sharing all this with me."

Nathan joined them and kissed Madison's cheek. "I guess we're family now."

"Welcome." Madison gave him a squeeze. "You two make the most adorable bride and groom I've ever seen."

"They certainly do." Luke joined them for a group hug.

Right away, the wedding planner, pastor, and resort manager all offered their congratulations, armed with flutes of champagne for the wedding party. As Madison sipped her drink, she saw several fascinated vacationers photographing the festivities, and the excitement in the air intensified when the reggae band started playing outside the resort restaurant.

After a few moments, the wedding planner clapped to gain everyone's attention. "And I think our photographer wants the bride and groom now for some romantic shots on the shoreline."

Chloe picked up her bouquet from the table and squealed as she led her new husband by the hand back up the aisle and toward a private section of beach, leaving Madison and Luke at the altar.

"That was so beautiful. But maybe we could find some shade for a few minutes?" A trickle of sweat meandered down Madison's back. "I'm sweltering, so you must be roasting in your suit."

Luke fanned himself with both hands. "I'm about to pass out. We can watch them from under the gazebo on the beach if you'd like?"

They walked down the aisle and were halfway to the gazebo when Madison realized something was missing. "I'm sorry. I left my bouquet on the table back there. You go ahead and grab us a couple of seats, and I'll follow in a second."

"You want me to go fetch your bouquet for you?" Luke glanced between the shady gazebo and the arbor.

Madison giggled. "As much as I'd love to see you prancing down the aisle with a fistful of gorgeous flowers, I think I'll let you find us somewhere to sit instead before you faint in this heat."

"That sounds great. Thank you." Luke hurried off to the shade.

While she strolled back up the aisle, Madison's heart was heavy with unfulfilled dreams. *This could have been me last year, the blushing bride.* She could be blissfully married if Sam hadn't turned out to be such a cold-hearted fraud. Not for the first time, she sent up a prayer of thanksgiving that she found out the truth *before* they were married.

She collected the bouquet, swung around, and started back toward the beach again. As she walked, a chill passed over her. Almost like someone was watching again. Out of the corner of her eye to the right of the aisle, she noticed a black-clad man standing alone on the beach, just staring at her. The other clusters of gawkers had already dispersed. Madison refused to even peek in his direction; she picked up her pace and found Luke seated at a small table next to a bush with tropical foliage. She hadn't realized her breathing was so rapid and shallow until she sat down and Luke put a hand over hers.

"Madison? What is it?"

He was so in tune with her emotions.

"Nothing. I think I'm getting overheated. That's all." She tried to sound nonchalant and calm. Chloe could see them from where they were posing for photographs on the beach, and there was no way she wanted to project any alarm.

His eyebrows met in the middle and his green eyes filled with concern. "I'm serious. Something's wrong and I know it. Between you and Nathan, I don't know what's normal anymore." He followed her gaze to the newlyweds and lowered his voice to a whisper. "Please tell me. I want to help."

Madison sighed and stared at her shaking hands clutching the bouquet. She willed them to stop. "I think someone's watching me again, but please don't make a fuss. This is Chloe and Nathan's special day, and I don't want anything to ruin it. Promise me?" She looked up into his eyes.

"Fine, but on one condition. We're going to talk about this later. After Mr. and Mrs. Alexander decide to ditch us for the honeymoon suite, you and I are going to try to get to the bottom of this. Okay?" He rested his hand on her arm and gave it a gentle squeeze.

"Sure." *And maybe I'll stay holed up in my room all week just to be on the safe side.*

"Where do you think this guy is right now? Is it the same one as last night?"

Madison twisted around as if stretching her back as she searched the pool area and the beach. The whole resort was humming with people sunbathing and swimming, making the most of the last couple of hours before sunset. "I don't even know. It was a split second, a guy on his own. Wearing black. Maybe he wasn't even watching me and I'm losing it. Let's blame the heat." *Am I going to be scared of every blond guy I see wearing black from now on? This is crazy.*

"Hey, you guys." Chloe called from the beach. "Can we have you for some more photos? You might want to take those heels off, Madi. I totally sank in the sand."

Madison forced a laugh. "We're coming." She gave Luke one more pleading look.

"Later." He squeezed her hand.

Her secret was safe. She squared her shoulders and resumed her maid-of-honor frame of mind. Time enough to worry about her stalker later. At a resort full of people, how much danger could she be in?

CHAPTER EIGHT

THE SUNSET WORE A STUNNING splash of gold, deep purple, and vibrant orange, which streaked across the enormous sky. Madison leaned back in her chair in the elegant beachfront restaurant and appreciated yet another beautiful image from the day. She offered a heartfelt prayer of thanks. Nothing catastrophic occurred, Chloe and Nathan enjoyed every single minute, and the newlyweds were now cheek to cheek on the dance floor as husband and wife.

"How are you holding up?"

Madison glanced at Luke and shrugged. "Pretty well, I think. I'm guessing our duties are almost over for the day." She nodded toward the happy couple. "They're in paradise, and that's all that matters."

Luke pursed his lips. "Talking of duties, I have something to confess. I feel kind of awkward about it, so I'm just going to come out and say it."

Madison's heart raced, and she leaned closer over the table, sensing he was somewhat embarrassed. "What is it?" she whispered. "You can tell me anything."

Luke ducked his head. "I can't dance."

Madison's mouth twitched. "You what? I couldn't quite hear." She kept a straight face. Was this strong, confident man admitting his inept dancing abilities? It was so sweet.

"I said I can't dance, and I would ask you to, if I had the slightest idea which foot to place where, but I think I would smash those sparkly sandals of yours to dust. I'm so sorry."

He looked up with puppy-dog eyes, and Madison burst out laughing.

He blushed and looked uncomfortable, but for some reason it was amusing to her. After all the insecurities and fears she had racing through her head, he was concerned that he couldn't take her dancing. Really?

"I apologize." She regained a measure of control. "I'm not laughing at your two left feet. I promise. You looked so worried, I thought it was some deep, dark secret I was going to be privy to."

Luke ran his fingers through his hair and sighed. "Sorry it was such a boring confession."

"No, I love boring—trust me. I need more drama in my life like a hole in the head right now. And I don't think I have the energy to dance tonight anyway. It's been such a long day." Her feet throbbed, even after she shed her shoes under the table.

Luke turned to watch Chloe and Nathan. "Yeah, a long day but a good day. I'm happy for them."

"Me too." Madison sighed. Their decorated table for four was set in its own little candlelit area, swathed in billowing white silk, with flower petals strewn on the floor around them. The dinner had been divine and now she felt full and exhausted. But there was still something they needed to discuss.

"Luke, I don't want to put a damper on the evening, but I know you wanted me to tell you about what happened earlier.

I think it would make me feel better to unload, if you don't mind."

Luke shifted his chair closer to hers, where they enjoyed a good view of the dance floor in case Chloe or Nathan came back to the table. They waved and smiled when a new dance began. "Of course. Tell me what you remember. Anything at all about this guy."

Madison shivered. "Well, like I said, I didn't get a decent look after the wedding ceremony. I could sense someone there watching me." She wound a ringlet around her finger while she spoke. "But there was more, earlier today—"

"Seriously?" Luke's jaw dropped.

"You know when I went out running this morning?"

"Of course. You almost mowed me down. Was there someone in the lobby again?" He gritted his teeth.

Madison shook her head. "No, it was when I was right at the end of the beach. I stopped to stretch, and there was a guy." *My own personal creepy dude.* "He stood there staring right at me, so I pretended not to be freaked out and ran back."

"Was it the same guy? The one with the icy blue eyes?"

"I don't know. He wore shades, so I have no clue about his eye color." She bit her lip. "But that's not all."

Luke glanced over at the dance floor. "Tell me, please?"

"Okay. After lunch, when Chloe and I were at the spa, he was there again. But this time he was closer, and he probably thought I was sleeping because I had my sunglasses on, but I managed to see a tattoo on his left forearm. A snake or a dragon or something gross."

He frowned. "What did he say?"

"Nothing. He took a photo and then disappeared. Still wore the shades." Her voice cracked.

Luke poured Madison a glass of sparkling water from the decanter and put it in front of her. "He took a photo? What nerve. Did Chloe see anything? Was she there with you?"

She picked up the glass and took a sip. "Chloe was napping, thank goodness. I didn't want to alarm her. Not today."

"Right." He shook his head. "Maybe we should mention it to the hotel security so they can be extra vigilant. Let's go to the front desk and speak with someone when we're finished here, okay?"

Madison shrugged. "Sure. But it sounds so lame. A guy with blond hair in dark clothes is watching me. They'll think I'm crazy."

"It's what their security guys are here for. They may have received other complaints—you never know. And we should tell them about the distinct eye color and tattoo." He drummed his fingers on the table for a moment. "Were you having any trouble like this back in Seattle before you left to come here?"

Madison looked out over the ocean and thought before answering. She didn't want to sound unbalanced, but she had to be honest. No use in keeping up the walls if he wanted to help her.

"Not recently." She tucked a few strands of hair behind her ear. "After the breakup with Sam about a year ago, I got a few phone calls where nobody would speak when I picked up. You know, the cliché heavy-breathing thing. It did scare me, but the calls stopped after a few weeks. It got my nerves on edge, though, because I kept thinking I was being followed in my car."

"Did you report any of it? Did you tell anyone, even your sister?"

She groaned. "No. Chloe didn't know about it, and I convinced myself I was reacting badly to the thing with Sam. I became engrossed in my teaching and offered extra classes whenever I could to keep myself occupied. Then Chloe and I spent Christmas in Hawaii, and after we came back home, everything settled down. There's been nothing major for the past six months. On the odd occasion, I still felt like someone was following me, but I daresay that was me being paranoid. I wanted to move on and leave those fears behind."

"Do you think it was your ex-fiancé?"

Madison shook her head. "No way. When I first uncovered his elaborate plan to marry me, take my money, and run, he was quite threatening at first and insisted I made a huge mistake." She rubbed her arms as a chill swept through her. "But when he saw I had proof and was serious about him leaving for good, he begged me to keep it quiet and said he would leave the area and never contact me again."

"And you believed him?" Luke raised a brow.

She shrugged. "Yes. I had to, for my own sanity and to move on. I know I should have reported him to the police, but I was more concerned with my broken heart. And I haven't seen or heard from him or any of his friends since. That's almost a year now."

"Hmm. That must have hurt his pride, though."

"I'm sure. But our breakup was not the first time I've been stalked. After my parents' death, word leaked out about the inheritance and the size of our estate since Dad was well known in the business world. I had all sorts of crazies trying to meet with me to discuss finances, and then your average creeper sending love letters and marriage proposals to the new heiress. I got followed home from work a few times." She shivered at the memory. "But that's in the past. Chloe and I refused to move from the home we grew up in. We changed our phone numbers, installed extra security systems, stuff like that. Once all the legal proceedings were over, we were left alone. Unless you count Sam swooping in to take advantage of my weakness."

Luke sat back in his chair. "You've dealt with a lot. I had no idea. I think you're a lot stronger than you give yourself credit for."

"Hmm, I'm not so sure." A peal of familiar laughter caught Madison's attention, and she waved at her sister. "But this is still the happy wedding day, and we should change the subject."

"Okay. But I think we should make a stop at the front desk when we head inside. And I'd feel happier if you had my number on speed dial." He reached down and pulled his phone from the pocket of his jacket draped behind him on the chair. "Can you put your number in for me?"

"Sure. I left my phone in my room." She took his phone and punched in her number while suppressing a chuckle. That was quite the pickup line, if he was in the market for a date. Which he wasn't.

"And please tell me even when you think something remotely suspicious is going down. Deal?"

Madison handed him the phone. "Deal."

He checked the screen and hit reply. "Now you have me at your beck and call."

"Safe and sound. Thanks." Her shoulders relaxed. She looked around at the flower-laden dance floor, where couples swayed to the lilt of the music and no doubt also whispered sweet nothings. It was romantic but so quiet... "This resort is serene and stunning. But something's missing." She glanced at Luke. "Know what I mean?"

Luke tapped his chin and surveyed the beach, restaurant, and dancing area. "It's too tranquil from what I'm used to. I know what I'm missing most of all."

He was on the same wavelength as her. She knew it. "Kids?"

"Got it in one. I love the peaceful ambience—don't get me wrong—but it's strange not having the excited yells and bubbles of laughter all over the place. Were you thinking the same?"

Madison nodded. "Yes. I know I have my fair share of teenagers five days a week, but it seems odd to be at a beach with no squeals and crying babies. I've never been at an adults-only resort before."

"You long for the sound of crying babies?" He raised his eyebrows.

Madison laughed. "I wouldn't put it quite like that, but can I tell you a secret?"

"I'm the world's best secret keeper." He folded his arms on the table and lowered his voice. "Fire away."

"I love babies so much, I signed up to do nursery duty in church every week. Like every single week. I know it's excessive, but we have two services back to back, so I still get to hear the message and everything. I love being around the little ones. They're so...nonjudgmental and trusting. With them, life is simple and the little things are special. And they smell so good." She clasped her hands and sniffed the air.

Luke was quiet for several moments.

"Uh-oh. Now you must think I'm a crazy woman."

"No, I happen to think it's awesome. I'm a bit of a baby whisperer myself."

"No way." Was this guy for real? Could he check any more boxes in the "perfect husband material" questionnaire?

"Way. Babies intrigue me. I sometimes think I may have been a pediatrician if I hadn't gone the missionary route. At the moment, we have a six-month-old baby at the orphanage—she's an absolute darling." His eyes lit up as he spoke. "Sophia has the biggest brown eyes you could imagine and I'm the only one who can make her smile." He shrugged. "What can I say?"

"I thought you would enjoy kids because of what you do. But babies, eh? Interesting." *And also somewhat attractive in a man.*

Luke focused on the lit candle between them. "One of the tougher things about being single and one of my major struggles, if I'm going to be honest. I love kids, and sometimes I wonder what it would be like to have my own flesh and blood running around." He looked up at her. "Do you know what I mean?"

Madison nodded. A lump caught in her throat. If she couldn't get past her fears, would there even be children in her future?

"And you're going to think I'm being geeky here, but I even enjoy reading parenting books..."

Madison tapped her chin. "Let me guess—with the pretense it would help your work in the orphanage?"

"Hmm, I think you know me well already. In reality, I'm curious and want to know as much as possible about rearing children. I know how to make a macho impression, don't I?" He grimaced.

"I think it's sweet." She pointed over to Chloe and Nathan. "We'd better start praying for a little niece or nephew, then, don't you think?"

"Ah yes. The only problem will be when we fight over said baby." Luke held up his fists and then dropped them. "I don't think we'll have to worry about that for a while."

"True. Too bad, though." How long would her sister wait to start a family? Their kids would most likely be blond and beautiful... "You know, Chloe thinks you and I would make the most amazing babies."

"Say what?"

Her face heated. Had she said that out loud? "Umm, forget I said anything. She was busy matchmaking—I don't think she realizes you are strictly single. For the record, she thinks our offspring would be gorgeous with your green eyes and my chocolate-brown ringlets." *Stop talking, Madison.* "Hysterical, right?"

Luke took a long swig of water. And swallowed hard.

CHAPTER NINE

BE COOL, MAN. DON'T CHOKE on your water.

Madison touched his arm. "I'm sorry. I didn't mean to embarrass you with all the talk about babies." She pulled back her hand and set it in her lap. "Chloe was joking around. I have to admit, I thought it was quite amusing."

He managed a grin. *Let's keep this light.* "It's all good. I don't embarrass easily. And yeah, that *is* funny."

Luke set his drink on the table and tried to focus on the dance floor rather than the captivating woman next to him. Who had just casually mentioned what their babies might look like.

Women didn't affect him like this. He swallowed. What was he thinking, pouring out his heart to Madison and divulging details about his desire to be a father? Talk about mixed signals. She must be beyond confused. Here he was, claiming his calling to be single, and then he gets all mushy and talks about babies. What an idiot. *Although why would God plant such a strong desire for fatherhood in my heart if I'm supposed to stay single? Maybe so I can be a better father figure at the orphanage?*

Madison laughed, and he looked over to see Nathan's sad attempt at dipping Chloe at the end of the song. Chloe may have been joking, but Madison would make a wonderful mother. She had a caring nature; he could tell by the way she protected Chloe. But that was as far as he dared daydream. Being an aunt and uncle someday would have to suffice. So, why did a boulder the size of Texas settle in the pit of his stomach?

God could use him far more effectively on the mission field as a single guy. He'd believed it for years already. No family responsibilities, no ties. Falling in love was his greatest fear and the furthest thing from his mind. He'd seen how disruptive it could be and the heartache it could cause when two of his own friends had left the mission in the name of love, only to have it implode. It had been awful watching his best buddy, Steve, get his heart broken and life derailed. *No, thank you.* He didn't need complicated right now. *I can do this. Platonic.* He caught a waft of Madison's vanilla scent as it drifted on the tropical air between them.

Oh, mercy.

*****

"Morning." Sunshine filled the breakfast buffet area as Madison waved from a table in the corner. She looked gorgeous in a large straw hat and a white sundress. "Is this spot okay for you?"

Despite his early-morning Bible reading on the balcony, Luke was no closer to guarding his heart while standing guard for her. *Lord, please let me come off as a friend and not a lovestruck teenager. A nice missionary guy with a listening ear. Nothing more...*

Luke stuffed his hands in the pockets of his board shorts as he walked toward her. "This is great. I'm famished. Are you ready to grab some food?"

"I've been starving since I woke up. Let's go."

His annoying alarm had allowed him time to feed on the Word already, but his stomach was growling for physical sustenance. They loaded their plates with a selection from the elaborate array of breakfast fare and returned to their table, which was set with a silver coffeepot for them to share.

"If there's one thing I miss about Seattle, it's—"

"Good coffee?" Madison raised a brow.

"How did you guess?" He poured them both a cup. "It's not that bad in Mexico, but I think I've been spoiled for life being raised in the Coffee Capital of the States."

"Me too." She took a sip from her cup. "Although this stuff is delicious."

Luke glanced from his own plate to Madison's and cringed. "Is that all you're having?"

Her plate held fruit, yogurt, and a croissant. Lady food. His was laden with bacon, eggs, sausages, hash browns, and some Jamaican dish he was unfamiliar with. His definition of *starving* was quite different from hers.

She stabbed a strawberry with her fork. "This is plenty for me. Don't worry. I'm not starving myself here—it feels like we are constantly eating at this resort. But you go ahead and stockpile—I'm sure you'll burn it all off with your water sports."

"Maybe I'll tempt you to join me?" That sounded a bit too forward. *Keep it platonic.*

She shrugged. "We'll see."

Okay, moving on. "So, no problems during the night? I hoped you would take me up on my offer to call me if you were worried. I presumed no news was good news and that you managed to get some sleep?"

"I slept like a baby. Thanks so much for looking out for me—your number is now on speed dial. I promise. But I want to apologize. I didn't mean to ruin yesterday with my woes, and I don't want to encroach on your vacation time, especially with all my issues." Her cheeks turned pink. It was pretty on her.

"I told you I'm here for you, and I meant it." *Cool. Keep it cool.* "We're family now. Think of me as your big brother."

"Yes, yes, we are." Madison bit her lip and lowered her eyes.

They ate in silence for a while, and Luke enjoyed the aroma of fresh-brewed coffee before taking a swig. "You were right. This is the best coffee I've had in a long time." He looked at Madison over the top of his cup. "What do you want to do this week? Any big plans?"

"No plans. Except, as you know, Chloe booked an excursion for us all to climb those giant waterfalls, which freaks me out no end with my huge affection for water." She grimaced.

Luke laughed at the face she made. "I think you'll be okay. I read up on it. The water's knee deep at the worst and even children climb it with ease. It'll be like taking a shower and scrambling up a steep hill at the same time. Should be fun."

"I know. I can do this. I'm not as wimpy as I might appear."

"I have no doubt. Any woman who can hold their own teaching a room full of high-school teens has my utmost respect."

Madison beamed. "Teaching has its challenges for sure. But I'll be missing it by the end of summer break." She sipped her orange juice and patted the corners of her mouth with the blue cotton napkin.

"Do you want to look around the town sometime? It's safe, from what I hear, and I always love mingling with the locals a bit when I travel. It gives a more authentic sense of the culture. I think they even do some organized excursions with the resort staff." Luke scooped up the last of his scrambled eggs.

"Sounds fun. But today, I think I'd like to hang out around here. Yesterday was wonderful but draining, and the idea of lying in the sun doing nothing is appealing to me."

"You think I might persuade you to come swimming?" Baby steps, but they had only five days left for her to learn to love the ocean again.

Madison cringed. "In the pool?"

Nice try. "I was thinking the ocean. I told you I'd help you rekindle your sea legs if I could. We can take it really slowly."

"Really, *really* slowly?" She pointed over at the two docks. "As long as we don't have to go out on a boat. Especially the one with the glass bottom?"

"I promise." He placed a hand over his heart.

She folded her napkin and looked straight into his eyes. "Okay."

"Awesome." Luke grinned. "If you're not fed up with my company yet, why don't we go and change once we're done with our coffee and then meet out on the beach? Bring a book and sunscreen. Let's get you reacquainted with the ocean, even if it's wading up to your knees."

"Sounds great, as long as you don't feel like you have to babysit me."

"Trust me—this is no hardship." *So much for staying cool.*

Madison blushed, and Luke had to force himself not to reach out and touch her glowing cheek. *Where is this coming from?* So much for trying to keep his feelings big brotherly— with Madison Grey, it was easier said than done.

*****

As the sun climbed higher into the cloudless sky, Luke grinned at Madison across the giant floating ring. They were perched either side of its five-foot diameter like a pair of bookends bobbing on the water. "This isn't so bad, now, is it? You're right in the ocean and you don't look petrified anymore."

Madison giggled. It had taken a full hour to persuade her to come out as far as her thighs. "I know it's not deep, but it's a start. I have to admit, this is relaxing." She turned her face up to the sun and soaked in the rays.

The sunshine caught golden highlights in her hair as it cascaded over her shoulders. Her soft ringlets looked so silky, so touchable... *Whoa. Don't go there, dude.*

This was going to be more of a challenge than Luke expected. His heart flip-flopped. Think about mundane things: Soccer. The orphanage. Mom and Dad. No, that didn't work. She was too much of a distraction. He had to stick to his convictions, right? *God, how can I help her get over her fear without getting in over my head?*

Madison closed her eyes. The silence between them was comfortable, as if they each knew the other had a great deal to contemplate.

"It's where I do my best thinking, in the ocean." He looked down at the crystal-clear water and sprinkled a few drops in front of him.

Madison stirred. "Are you close to the ocean where you live in Mexico? I'd love to hear all about it. You know a lot more about me than I do about you, missionary boy."

Luke shifted on his side of the ring. "Yeah, at the orphanage I'm right next to a small beach. We spend a good deal of time there playing on the sand with the kids. It's a basic village and poor in some areas, but the people are fantastic. I fell in love with the culture straightaway. I guess that's why I stayed after my initial yearlong contract."

She cocked her head. "Do you speak in Spanish all the time there?"

"*Sí, señorita.* At least, most of the time. Although, we teach the kids English because it helps them when it's time to leave school and get a job. Our church is Spanish speaking, which took a bit of getting used to, but it's so lively and genuine. I love it."

Madison nodded and swished her feet in the water. "Sounds wonderful."

Some guy yelled from the shore, and Madison spun around to see what was going on. She almost lost her balance on the ring and let out a yelp as she grabbed the floatie with both hands.

Luke looked beyond her and saw there was nothing to worry about. "Hey, we're okay. He's just trying to get someone's attention for a soccer game, by the looks of it." With that frown, she might take some convincing. "Need me to pull you closer to the beach?"

Madison exhaled and met his gaze. "No, I'm fine. He made me jump, and then I thought I was going to fall in. Just when I was starting to relax." She slowly turned back to check the shoreline.

"I understand if you want to go in for a while. You've done great so far." Except now her face looked a few shades paler.

She lifted her chin. "I'm fine. Really. What were you saying about life at the orphanage?"

A distraction. Yes. "Let's see. No two days are ever the same—that's for sure. My three coworkers and I do whatever's needed. I'm house papa, caretaker, nurse, chauffeur, teacher, cook, and pastor."

"Sounds fascinating. How many kids?"

"We try to keep it to a dozen max, although we'll have an occasional emergency we have to take short term. There are some tragic cases, and my heart gets trampled every now and then, but the four of us on staff support each other and we get by okay."

"I can't even imagine. It makes my job sound thoroughly mundane."

She was loosening the death grip on the ring. Good. "Somehow, I can't imagine your job is a walk in the park. What made you decide on teaching?"

Madison looked down into the clear water between them. "It seemed like the logical thing for me to do. I love kids and always admired my own teachers. I've been doing it full time for a year, and it's great. Of course, my original dream was to go to Spain—I'm still not sure what I would have done there, but I always loved the language and the culture and was obsessed with the idea of moving to that country and finding my way into an ideal occupation. Outlandish for the control freak that I am now, but everything changed after my parents' accident."

"That must have been a tough decision for you to give up your dream."

"I don't think so. There was no way I could leave Chloe all on her own, so I grew up overnight and took responsibility for my little sister. She was just nineteen and still in college and needed me to be in Seattle. I already had my degree so just had to get my teaching credentials while she finished up her interior-design course. Then, when a local position was posted teaching Spanish, I jumped all over it."

"And Chloe is moving on and you're still there." His heart lurched when she wiped a tear from her eye.

"Yes. But it's not so bad. I'll sell the family home when I'm ready and find a smaller place nearby. Plus, Chloe's only going to be an hour away on the other side of the city, so I'm sure we'll still see a lot of each other. And I truly do enjoy teaching."

Luke doused his overheated shoulders with cool water. "You know, Miss Grey, you mustn't think your life has to stay the same for the sake of it." He chanced a look into her eyes. "Pray about it. Maybe God has something exciting planned for you which you know nothing about yet." Perhaps even in Mexico…

She shrugged. "Perhaps. But I feel like I'm your teacher when you call me Miss Grey."

You don't look a thing like any of the teachers I remember.
"Okay, so tell me this—would you still be open to moving to Spain?"

"I don't know. I was so adventurous with my big dreams before all the bad stuff happened. I think it knocked the stuffing out of me." She glanced up through long dark lashes. "But I have to admit, listening to you talking about life in Mexico stirs something in my heart."

It stirs something in my heart, too.

After several seconds of silence, Luke cleared his throat. *Church—bring the conversation back to churchy things. Way safer.*

"So, how *did* you end up at a church in Seattle—if you don't mind me prying? I guess you're not from a churchgoing family."

Madison didn't answer at first. She faced the beach now and something drew her attention. He swiveled on the ring and knew right away whom she was watching. A blond guy with black swim shorts and shades stood looking out in their direction. Luke looked back at her. "Madison?"

"No. That's not him. Too tall and skinny." She shook her head. "What's the matter with me? I'm sorry. You were asking about my church experience."

So much for a relaxing day at the beach. This girl was living in constant fear. "No worries. You sure you're comfortable staying out here?"

"I'm fine. And I like that you want to know about my faith. People don't tend to ask. It's true; I never considered God as important or even relevant to me until about a year ago. I'm so thankful I ducked into a little church one rainy Sunday night. I thought I was finding shelter from the rainstorm, but it turns out I found a Refuge who transformed my whole life, and now church is my second family."

"You're among the rare few who thank the Lord for rain in Seattle..."

"Right? I was on a destructive path—inconsolable, hurt, and untrusting of anybody after my breakup with Sam. Poor Chloe was scared for me. But that night I met Jesus for the first time and He gave me a peace I had never experienced before. I've always been a worrier—and a complete stress ball since my parents' accident. I spoke with the pastor's wife after the service, and she prayed with me." Madison grinned. "I was changed."

Luke leaned back. "I love how God works. I wish you hadn't been through all the heartbreak, but it led you to Him, and that's fantastic."

"Yeah, it is. I've still got stuff to work through. My nerves are on edge most of the time, but I'll get my life together eventually."

She dipped one hand in the water and poured out a stream in front of her. "Perhaps God can use me for something worthwhile one day."

"What do you mean? Of course God can use you. He *is* using you. Don't ever think you are not good enough or brave enough or ready enough. He doesn't ask for perfection—just a willing heart." His own heart raced at the opportunity to encourage her in her new faith.

"Even mine?"

"Especially yours."

The air between them was thick with something almost tangible—trust, truth, and hope. Luke pinched his thigh to come back down to earth and then looked over at her.

"Maybe in time you could rekindle your dreams and go overseas to see if He has something for you there?" Somewhere like Mexico...

Madison rolled her shoulders. "Ugh, I don't know. I have so much to work on first. My biggest dream, to be loved unconditionally, has been met by God, but maybe one day I can trust enough to see if it can come true with a man, too." She slapped a hand over her mouth and cringed. "My, I think I opened up too much there again. Last night with the baby talk was bad enough. I'm so sorry."

"Don't be sorry. I hope that dream becomes a reality for you." *Hold it together, Luke. Hold it together.*

"Maybe. 'One day at a time' is my mantra." Madison smirked. "And I think I'm doing great with this ocean challenge of yours." She wiggled her eyebrows. "I believe it's time to lighten things up a bit."

Thank goodness.

She reached down and scooped handfuls of water before soaking Luke.

Luke caught his breath. She needed a taste of her own medicine, so a raging splashing battle ensued, with no winner in the end. And still she looked stunning.

They slid from the floating ring and sloshed through the water back to the beach.

"Here you go." Luke handed her a fluffy blue-and-white-striped towel.

"Thanks. I can't even remember the last water fight I had. Is it all part of your therapy to win me over to the ocean again?"

Luke held his palm up to her. "You started it. But I think it might have helped, don't you?"

"Definitely." Madison slid on her pink sunglasses and brushed the sand from her feet before collapsing onto the lounger. "Thanks for this. And thanks for our chat. It's exactly what I needed today. I'm glad you're here."

"I'm glad I'm here, too." *Even though I'm more confused than ever.*

Lord, what's going on in my heart?

CHAPTER TEN

"WHEN DID YOU KNOW YOU wanted to stay single?" Madison took a bite of seafood salad as they sat at a dinner table for two beneath the strand of twinkle lights on the outdoor patio.

Luke stabbed a potato with his fork and prayed for wisdom. They had already discussed her life in great depth, so she had every right to dig into his. But this was going to be tricky. Particularly if he wanted to protect his heart...and her feelings.

He glanced down at the vase of tropical flowers between them. "There wasn't a lightning bolt with a note attached or anything. I must have been twenty-four or twenty-five, when I was in India. I'd been praying on and off for a couple of years about whether I should get married—you know, settle down and even head back to the States."

Madison nodded for him to go on.

"I had a couple of good friends on the mission field when I was in Africa, and they were both in serious relationships. One was even engaged to a girl back in New York. He deliberated for weeks whether he should return to the States or not. The poor guy was a mess while he tried to figure out what God's will was for his life."

"What did he decide?" She set down her fork, her eyes wide.

"He said goodbye to Africa and set an official wedding date with his girl. The following year, we heard they broke the engagement when she found someone more stable."

"After he left the mission field for her?" Madison's jaw dropped.

"Yeah. He never got over it. I stayed in contact with him for a few years while he figured out what to do with his life. As far as I know, he's still hopping from one dead-end job to another. And then my best buddy, Steve, fell head over heels with one of our colleagues serving alongside us in Africa."

"That's so romantic. Falling in love on the mission field of Africa. Please tell me they lived happily ever after?"

"I would love to, but they didn't."

"No." She covered her mouth with her hand.

"They were engaged for about six months or so, but malaria put a stop to them serving in Africa anymore. Steve got sick, and they decided to both return to the UK with the dream of coming back one day."

"But they didn't?"

"No. He never fully recovered from malaria and his faith took a real beating. Last I heard, the girl married someone else and went into nursing."

"So, you were jaded?"

Luke thought for a moment. "Not jaded so much as concerned. I knew I was supposed to be a missionary wherever God led me and I didn't want anything to sway me from that purpose. I watched what happened to my friends and I think it freaked me out." He set his fork on the plate. "I was starting to get close to one of our other coworkers at the time, but she knew I had reservations, and in the end, our mutual decision to stay platonic prevailed. So, when my stint in Africa was up, I prayed about what I should do with my future, and the desire I once had to be part of a couple kind of evaporated. I can't explain it, but it's as if God filled that need and gave me a different perspective."

"There's been nobody since? No señoritas quickened your heart?"

"Honestly, no. I guess my life goes at an insane pace most of the time. I can't believe I'm turning thirty. You know the whole thing about Mexico being slow living and relaxed with siestas?"

"Uh-huh." She pursed her lips.

"Siestas don't often happen in an orphanage. But I'm not complaining—I love every minute of the busy chaos."

"But it leaves no time for romance." She nodded. "I can see that."

"No desire either. Do I sound weird?"

Madison tilted her head. Amber highlights shone through her hair in the soft glow of candlelight. Beautiful. And it dawned on him that she hadn't scanned the resort for stalkers all evening. This was a good sign. He tried to focus as she spoke.

"No, you don't sound weird at all. But do you think it will ever change? That God might say it's time to marry?" She shrugged and then gave him a coy smile. "You mustn't think your life has to stay the same for the sake of it. Pray about it. Maybe God has something exciting planned for you which you know nothing about yet."

Luke laughed out loud. The exact words he used on her this afternoon when they were floating in the ocean. "Touché."

He'd enjoyed their conversation. Her faith was vibrant and fresh, and he had no doubt she would be a wonderful woman to journey through life with...

Is God using my own advice to Madison to speak back to me? The topic was dangerous. Luke needed time alone to ponder and pray and think it all through. But he didn't want the evening to end. Not yet. For now, a change of subject was in order.

"You did well in the ocean this afternoon."

She wrinkled her nose. "I went out as far as my waist—that's not particularly impressive." She looked toward the water. "I've got a long way to go in facing my fears, haven't I?"

"One step at a time. I think you're doing great. Imagine what you can achieve by the end of the week." *I wonder if I'll find answers to my questions about the future by then.* He took the napkin from his lap and wiped his mouth. "If you're finished eating, do you want to take a walk down the promenade? The resort has some of the local crafts and jewelry and things on display. Plus, I should walk off this steak."

Madison placed her napkin on the table and picked up her clutch bag. "This resort is huge. I wondered what they were setting up earlier. Sure, let's do it. Sounds like fun."

She looked a vision tonight, wearing a bright yellow dress with a matching flower in her hair. Did this woman ever look anything but stunning? It made it difficult to remain neutral. The jovial lilt of steel-drum music played on the beach, and the air was perfumed with something intoxicatingly floral. The night was perfect.

They wandered for several minutes and then stopped in front of a silver jewelry display, where a woman sat on a stool, polishing her jewelry with a soft cloth. Madison picked up a silver bracelet and held it up. "This is so pretty. Did you make it?"

As the women chatted, Luke noticed the price tag. He cringed when he calculated how many meals that equated to back at the orphanage. Madison inspected the tag and didn't flinch. Their financial situations were worlds apart—could that be an issue? He was deep in thought when Madison screamed.

Luke's heart stopped as he spun and clutched her arm. Behind her were Chloe and Nathan. "Couldn't you guys just come and say a simple 'Hi' like normal people?"

Chloe giggled while Nathan wrapped his arms around her waist.

Madison growled. "You frightened the life out of me, Chloe." Then she managed a smile and gave her sister a big hug.

"What has you so jumpy?" Chloe asked. "I only touched your shoulder."

"Nothing much. I wasn't expecting to see you. That's all."

When Madison glanced at Luke, he caught the pleading look in her eyes. As if he would let on about her stalker—her secret was safe with him. He gave a slight nod, and she turned back to her sister.

"You look beautiful, by the way. Marriage agrees with you. But I thought you guys were heading out to some romantic restaurant tonight?"

"We're on our way. I spotted your yellow dress from where we were waiting and I had to come see you. Is Luke keeping you company?" Chloe's attempt at wide-eyed innocence fell short. Madison was right—the woman had matchmaking on the brain.

"Yes, he's putting up with me." Madison blushed.

"It's my pleasure." Luke received a nudge in the ribs from his grinning brother. Great. Chloe had a partner in crime.

"It's so weird being in the same resort but not hanging out together, don't you think?" Chloe flicked her long blonde hair behind her. "Anyway, now that we know you're both surviving without us, we should go. We have reservations, husband dearest."

"Bye, Mr. and Mrs. Alexander. Enjoy your dinner." Luke waved.

"You two behave yourselves." Nathan looked over his shoulder and winked while being dragged off toward the lobby.

Luke turned to Madison. "Sorry about that brother of mine. He doesn't give up. Let's carry on, shall we? Then maybe we can relax in the piano bar if you like?"

Madison scrutinized him for a moment. "Be honest. Do you really want to go to that swanky place, or would you rather hunker down by a bonfire on the beach and listen to the crash of waves?"

How could she have figured him out already? Beautiful *and* perceptive. He shrugged. "I want to do whichever you are most comfortable with."

"You've done a wonderful job catering to my every whim, but I promise you, I'm totally at ease now. No stalkers or creepers today. So, as long as you swear you won't take me out on a boat, I'm happy for you to make the decision."

As she went to tuck her hair behind one ear, her hand brushed his, sending a shot of electricity through him. Dangerous. Was it sensible to take her to the bonfire? He glanced over and saw there were others sitting around on blankets and loungers. At least they wouldn't be alone.

"Okay." He realized the woman selling jewelry was eavesdropping on their conversation. "After we finish looking at the jewelry, which I know you want to do for sure, let's grab some dessert and take it down to the beach bonfire."

"It sounds like the perfect end to a perfect day."

It did his heart good to see her this happy. *Makes we wonder what it would be like to spend every day with her...*

CHAPTER ELEVEN

MADISON SIPPED ON HER COFFEE with her feet propped up on the balcony table, appreciating the tranquil Caribbean Sea stretching out majestically before her. Now *this* was the way to start a Monday morning. The familiar rich aroma stirred her senses. She took another sip and set the cup on a patio table. She closed the Bible in her lap, then picked up her journal and pen.

The corners of her mouth lifted. Yes, three days into her stay in paradise, and she already had so much to write about. Nibbling on the end of her pen, she paused for a moment and then poured her heart out onto paper.

MONDAY, JUNE 24th:

Yesterday was one of the happiest days I can remember. Ever. I felt carefree and young and courageous for the first time in years. I'm so relieved everything went as planned for Chloe at the wedding on Saturday—my little sis is a married woman now. Who'd have thought it? I'm beyond thrilled for her and Nathan. Of course, it broke my heart not having Mom and Dad here to see their youngest daughter looking so gorgeous and happy, but I'm grateful I got to witness such a magical occasion. I wouldn't have missed it for anything. I think they're going to be good for each other, which brings me to my other new family member...

Luke Alexander. What an amazing guy. He loves God so much, which makes sense for a missionary, but he's real and honest in the way he talks about his relationship with God. I like that. And he thinks the world of his family—I can see from the way he looks out for his little brother and how he describes his sweet parents. He loves babies—which I cannot believe. How many guys admit to that? Of course, looking after kids is part of his job, but he takes it to another level. He's a world traveler—he's been to a bunch of countries on his mission trips and adventuring... Boring he is not. I love that he's such a gentleman—always holds doors open for me and makes sure I'm comfortable. That says a lot about his upbringing. And then there's the added bonus that he is drop-dead gorgeous. Tall, dark, and handsome with those emerald eyes that make me giddy just thinking about. BUT...he wants to stay SINGLE forever.

What? Maybe that's why I feel so at ease around him, knowing he's not going to go down the romantic road. He even told me to think of him as a big brother. Easier said than done. Not that I'm looking for a relationship anytime soon. I'm still getting over Sam and my questionable judgment... Will I ever find the courage to trust a man again? But if I ever WAS ready to look for someone to share my life with, he would be like...

Luke.

What am I thinking? He believes God can use him more effectively single than married. Who am I to question that? But I'm not convinced. I know there's stuff in the Bible from the apostle Paul about singleness being cool, but couldn't a wife be good for Luke? Aren't two heads better than one or something?

Madison paused to take a sip of coffee. Almost cold, but still delicious. She lifted her eyes to the ocean and felt a bubble of hope form within. Yesterday, Luke helped her take the first step in facing her fear of drowning. Yes, it was a baby step, but she was going in the right direction. *Thank You, Lord, for giving me a glimmer of hope.* She looked down at her journal and continued writing.

I'm so grateful to have time this week to process everything. Move on from grieving. Move on from Sam. I want to embrace life and see what God has in store for me. I feel a new chapter is about to open up.

But I'm almost afraid to hope, with thoughts of that creepy stalker guy hanging over me. Was he really some random dude? I hated that he snapped a photo of me. Who does that? It must be the same man, the one from Friday night. I'll never forget those icy blue eyes as long as I live. He wore shades on Saturday, but I have a sinking feeling it was him again. Why do I attract the weirdos? Or am I being paranoid?

No, I will not allow him to ruin my precious time in Jamaica. I will NOT hide in my room and let fear prevail. Luke and I have another fun day planned today. He said he would be sleeping in this morning—although I can't imagine not getting up early to make the most of another day in paradise. The curse of being a morning person. Perhaps he hasn't been sleeping well—I should ask him. Or maybe he's using the early mornings to pray over all his decisions. Anyway, we'll meet for brunch at eleven. I told him I might even work myself up to some shallow snorkeling later on, although my stomach has butterflies thinking about it. But I trust him to keep me safe, and I never thought I would trust another man as long as I lived.

I better go and run off the chocolate cake we shared by the bonfire last night. My, that sounds romantic for a platonic relationship. Here's to another wonderful day in paradise...

Madison slurped the rest of her coffee, brushed her teeth, and laced her running shoes. After a few good stretches, she grabbed her iPod and made her way down to the lobby. She was ready to run in the fresh air before the humidity made it uncomfortable.

A few older people congregated at the coffee bar, and the servers were still setting the breakfast tables with white tablecloths and fresh tropical flowers. As much as she missed the presence of babies, an adult-only resort exuded a relaxed, sophisticated ambience, which was rather appealing. Especially first thing in the morning. Madison smiled when she remembered her confession to Luke. At least she could get her baby fix when she returned to the nursery at church next week.

A line formed in the lobby as several tanned vacationers checked out of the resort, presumably catching early flights. The soft hum of hushed chatter filled the air as Madison wove her way around guests and staff. She loved Seattle, yet there was something to be said for continual sunshine and running on the beach. *I wonder if Luke runs on his beach in Mexico?*

Once outside, she scanned the area for any suspicious-looking characters. Satisfied she was not being watched, she plugged in her earbuds and set off for the beach at a gentle jogging pace. A perfect breeze blew in from the water, and the sun blazed even at seven in the morning. A glorious start to the day.

Waving at other early risers along the shore, Madison soon got into her stride and found her happy place. No matter what stress she endured—emotional, physical, or spiritual—running was her therapy, and it helped release her pent-up anxiety. She discovered it after her parents' death, when she needed a form of release and a way to flee without actually running away from everything.

Since then, running was her way of starting every morning. Rain or shine—usually rain. If it was shaping up to be a crazy full day with emotional teenagers who had little or no interest in learning Spanish or if she was preparing to spend a Saturday alone, pining for what could have been, running kept her sane, whether at the gym or on her usual lakeside route. Plus, this week it meant she didn't have to worry about all the delicious food she inhaled at the resort.

Like the decadent chocolate cake. She salivated at the thought of last night's shared dessert. She should run an extra ten minutes to make up for that indulgence. Maybe it wasn't the cake that was so memorable. The whole experience was almost magical. Magical moments were rare in recent years, so she would keep the dessert by the bonfire, the intimate conversation, and the gentle ocean breeze all treasured up for a rainy Seattle afternoon when she was home alone.

The farther Madison ran, the fewer people were around. Not good. A third dock was up ahead, so guests must come this far. She was fine. *Calm down.* The irrational paranoia seemed to follow her like an unshakable shadow, but she tried to slow her erratic breathing. Should she turn back now? No. Security patrolled all the way to the patch of palm trees up ahead, so she should be fine to go that far.

To take her mind off her fears, Madison prayed while she ran, remembering her pupils back at school, Chloe and Nathan and their new life, her church friends and the meetings going on back in Seattle this week, and Luke. *I don't know why I'm praying for Luke, Lord. He seems to have everything figured out. But thank You for his friendship this week. And, well…if it's meant to go any deeper, I guess You'll have to make it obvious to us both. I pray for his precious little orphan children back in Mexico…*

A quick movement in her peripheral vision caught Madison's attention, and she turned her head toward the third dock. It was right in front of her now. Something moved, but there was nobody there. Just the glass bottom boat. Weird. All weekend, the boat had been tied to the second dock, a jetty closer to the resort buildings. They must have moved it. But why farther from the resort? Perhaps there was some private party using it.

She looked along the stretch of beach ahead—it was deserted. Wasn't the security guy supposed to be around? Of course, he couldn't be everywhere at the same time, but Madison's skin prickled. Another movement, and she whipped her head back to the dock. Maybe it was a bird. Or maybe she was going crazy.

She slowed her steps. Time to turn back. *For the thousandth time, I wish I could be courageous.*

She caught her breath and took one more look around in case the security guard appeared. Maybe that would help her heart rate return to normal. Jogging in place, she faced the ocean, shielded her eyes, and tried to make out whether there was anyone or anything at the end of the dock. Only the one boat was moored, but it didn't look like anybody was out there. Unless someone was inside the boat, of course. It was difficult to tell. She removed one earbud in case there were voices…

A heavy hand on her bare shoulder spun her around. Madison gasped. She was face to face with him. In her next breath, the man held her in a rough embrace.

"What's going on?" Her voice was shrill, fearful. "Who are you and what do you want?"

Where had he come from? The palm trees? Madison tried to wriggle out of his strong arms as panic pulsated in her chest.

"I want you." The stranger growled and turned her toward the ocean.

It was him, the blond man who had followed her the past weekend. Same black clothing, shock of blond hair, shades. And he was pure muscle. She struggled again to get free, ripping the remaining earbud from her ear. He pressed her hands alongside her body and tipped her off balance, and she watched her silver iPod and her sunglasses hit the sand.

An ugly tattoo of a dragon danced before her eyes, writhing while the man's arm flexed around her waist. Madison screamed, but his meaty hand stifled it. In one fluid motion, her legs went from under her, and she was being carried to the dock. In a mad scramble, she flailed her legs and twisted her head around to slam it into the guy's face. He grunted when his mirrored shades flew off. Icy blue eyes stared back at her, haunting and evil.

No.

He studied her intently for a heartbeat, their noses almost touching. The strong scent of expensive cologne stung her nostrils and he squeezed her even tighter. Blue Eyes marched on, and through her tears, she saw their destination and somehow found the energy to thrash in his arms one more time.

Where was everyone? Why couldn't anybody see what was happening? Was she being kidnapped?

She glanced back in the direction of the deserted beach. Not a soul walked along this stretch. Why had she chanced running this morning? And why hadn't she turned back when she first felt anxious? Was that God nudging her? Foolish girl.

Madison bared her teeth and bit into the fleshy part of Blue Eyes's palm. He didn't even flinch but clamped his hand even tighter. She fought the growing nausea in the pit of her stomach. Another man wearing sunglasses and a hoodie appeared as they neared the end of the dock. Two against one would be no match. Madison used every last ounce of energy she could muster to kick and elbow her kidnapper. But he was too strong, and he leered as she fought back. It was hopeless. The other man took something from his hoodie pocket. With a flourish, he brandished a yellow cloth, and as Blue Eyes pulled his hand away, the cloth was pressed across her nose and mouth.

"*No*." She screamed into the fabric. The suffocating smell of antiseptic and alcohol consumed her senses. Thoughts of Chloe in her wedding dress, her parents in their backyard, her students at school, and then Luke by the bonfire swirled lazily in the corners of her mind. *Focus, Madison. Focus.* She tried to turn her face away from the cloth, but the other man's firm hands grasped the back of her head in a vise grip. She could see a blurring image of hoodie guy as he stood over her and watched for several seconds, his head cocked like he was memorizing her.

And the last thing she spotted before the haziness turned black was the glass bottom boat.

CHAPTER TWELVE

SINCE WHEN DID HE SIT around with a big grin on his face?

Luke glanced around the open-air restaurant to see whether anyone had noticed, but truthfully, he didn't care. Something about Madison Grey fascinated him and he looked forward to spending another day getting to know her better. He checked his watch. Past eleven o'clock. She would be here any minute. His heart skipped a beat. When was the last time he had such feelings of vulnerability in the relationship department? He shook his head. Many, many years ago, if at all.

There hadn't been anyone serious since high school, and even then, it was far from true love. He flexed his fingers around the sweating glass of iced tea. The nearest he had been to a romantic relationship since then was with his coworker in Africa. *Jennifer. Haven't thought of her in a long time.* They were close and even prayed about the potential relationship developing, but they both came to the conclusion it was not God's will. Couldn't argue with that. She married someone else the following year. And he accepted life as a bachelor.

He picked up the brunch menu and scanned it for the third time. This morning served as a good opportunity to think about his life, pray for guidance, and request a huge dose of wisdom. He loved being a missionary and was willing to stay in Mexico forever, if that was what God wanted him to do. But something inside shifted. Nothing definite, but a nudge of some sort, almost daring him to open up to Madison. Was it his imagination? Was something blossoming? Maybe he should nip it in the bud before either one of them got hurt.

Luke pulled his shades from his face and rubbed his eyes. He had spent hours awake last night, praying. That magical bonfire had ignited feelings he didn't even realize were lying dormant. He couldn't be sure yet, but he had a sense that she was developing feelings for him, too. Of course, there was the real possibility he was so out of touch with romance that he was misguided. Maybe all she wanted was a friend for the week or a shoulder to cry on and another Christian to talk to.

No. It's more than that. The way those chocolate-brown eyes spoke to him last night at the bonfire was not his imagination. Madison wasn't good at hiding her emotions, and there was no disguising the transformation over the past three days. Could the wary, untrusting young woman he first met be the open, hopeful girl he saw at twilight yesterday?

Luke gave his head a shake and slid his sunglasses back on. He checked his watch yet again. Twenty minutes late for brunch. Where could she be? He already picked up the fact that Madison was punctual to a fault and the most organized person he had ever met. So far, she had been early to each meal or activity, and he noticed she had lists for everything. He could go up to her room to check on her, but it may be inappropriate. She might have taken a nap after her run, or she could have lost track of time. Surely, she hadn't blown him off? A fleeting thought of her stalker crossed his mind, but she would have contacted him at the first sign of trouble. She had his phone number, after all.

Luke poured himself another tea and decided to give her ten more minutes in case they had their wires crossed. Perhaps she thought brunch was at eleven thirty instead of eleven. What if she did decide to cool things down and not see him again? His heart sank and that's when he knew it for sure. He was falling.

An hour later, he had fallen into a pit of despondency, as nothing about the day was going as planned. Luke ate brunch alone and with little appetite. He tried multiple times to contact Madison by phone—but her voice mail picked up each one. After leaving a message with the concierge for her to call him if she came by, he now sat alongside the pool, still waiting. Like a dumb puppy dog waiting for a treat.

Lord, is this a sign for me to back off? Is this the "No" I asked about? It didn't seem right to give up. Not after the promising signs of yesterday. Perhaps he would wait a few minutes longer.

His neck ached from craning every time a brunette walked by in case it was Madison. People were going to get the wrong idea about him soon. Should he try to get ahold of Chloe? Umm, no—his brother would never let him hear the last of it if he interrupted their honeymoon.

He finished his mystery novel. Time for a trip up to his room. A replacement book would at least relieve the boredom of waiting. Maybe he would check again with the concierge on his way back down or even knock on her door. He got up from the lounger, threw on a T-shirt, slid into his flip-flops, and grabbed his novel. Scanning the crowd, he sauntered through the lobby and caught the elevator.

Luke slowed his steps in the corridor when he noticed the door to his room was wide open. Curious. Housekeeping could be in there, although they usually left their cart outside. His heart rate sped up as he reached the room. Could the guys fighting at the second dock on Friday night have discovered his room number? Or was Nathan in some other kind of trouble? Tentatively, he poked his head around the doorframe.

"Luke, I was about to call you on your cell." Nathan paced by the French doors.

Luke exhaled. "Hey, I guess you still have your key. What's up? Did you forget something?"

"I just received this." Chloe sat in the armchair to his right. She burst into tears.

Luke rushed to her side. "Chloe, what is it? Are you okay?" His first thought was of Madison. Where was she?

Nathan pointed to the piece of paper in Chloe's trembling hand. "No, she's not okay, man. Read it."

Luke looked from Nathan to Chloe. Had Madison checked out and gone back to Seattle? He forced himself to focus on the letter. It was typed on generic printer paper, stark and bold. He read aloud:

CHLOE GREY-
WE HAVE MADISON. SHE IS ALIVE...FOR NOW.
IF YOU WANT TO SEE HER AGAIN, DO NOT CONTACT THE POLICE.
YOU HAVE 24 HOURS TO GET 2 MILLION DOLLARS CASH TOGETHER.
WE KNOW THIS SHOULD NOT BE A PROBLEM.
HAVE IT READY BY MIDDAY TOMORROW AND AWAIT FURTHER INSTRUCTIONS.

EXPECT A CALL TO YOUR ROOM AT 2 P.M. TODAY TO
PROVE WE HAVE YOUR SISTER.

Luke's hand shook.

His ears whooshed and his heart thumped. He had the
numb feeling one had when floating between a dream and
reality. Maybe it was a sick hoax, or maybe he was still asleep
by the pool, having a surreal nightmare…

"Luke?" Nathan shattered the dream illusion.

"Where did you get this?" Luke handed the note back to
Chloe.

She wiped her eyes with a tissue. "They phoned our room
from the front desk and said there was an urgent message, so
we went down to check. I thought maybe one of you was sick
or something. Anyway, the receptionist handed us this piece
of paper in a sealed envelope."

"Did she say who delivered it?" Luke raked his fingers
through his hair. Could it be her blond stalker? Maybe security
cameras would have caught something.

Nathan huffed. "No. She said it was left sitting on her
computer keyboard so she couldn't miss it. But nobody saw
the person who put it there."

"This is insane. Who would do a thing like this?" Luke
collapsed onto his bed, feeling a hundred years old. "I should
go down and question the staff in the lobby again. Maybe
someone else saw something." He tried to recall whether
anyone fitting Blue Eyes's description had been hanging
around when he was there earlier leaving a message for
Madison. No. He had eyes only for a certain brunette this
morning.

Chloe stood. "Please don't. We have to be careful not to attract too much attention. No police, remember?"

Nathan joined his wife and settled her back into the chair. "We'll be careful—don't worry. No police."

"I'd prefer to have the police on our side. We know nothing about this island. But I agree." Luke crouched in front of Chloe. "Do you still have the key to Madison's room?"

She nodded. "We checked to make sure she wasn't there. I was hoping it was some hoax. But the room is empty and there was no sign of a struggle."

"Okay. The last time I saw her was last night at around midnight. We ate dessert down by the bonfire after we ran into you guys. And then we were supposed to meet at eleven for brunch. I know she was going for her usual run on the beach first thing. Who would have taken her in broad daylight?" Yet, that was her fear, wasn't it? On Saturday when she suspected she was being watched—should he have insisted on security looking into it more thoroughly? And this morning, there he was, sipping his iced tea and eating brunch while Madison was being kidnapped...

Nathan shrugged. "But how many people are up and about super early on a resort like this?"

"Good point. But wouldn't someone have noticed? Where was that security guy? He's always on patrol." And the resort manager promised to be extra vigilant after their report on Saturday night. "Was she whisked away in a car? Or maybe someone tricked her into going somewhere with them. I can't believe this. Poor Madison." Luke's heart rate quickened as he pictured her chocolate-brown eyes so full of fear.

Chloe looked up. "My sister is the most cautious person in the world. She would never accept a ride with a stranger. She's

110

THE GLASS BOTTOM BOAT

not into wild adventures and she's scared stiff of the ocean. She was taken. They kidnapped her for sure. I hope they haven't hurt her."

Luke stared at the wall. They had just begun to conquer that fear of the ocean. *God, please let her be safe.* "When she didn't show up for brunch, I thought she forgot or maybe changed her mind or got distracted..."

"Madi doesn't get distracted," Chloe whispered. "They must have taken her earlier this morning."

"I should have offered to go running with her, and then we might not even be in this mess." *Why didn't I think of that? She shouldn't have been alone.*

"Don't beat yourself up." Chloe curled up in the chair. "It's my fault she's even on this island in the first place."

Nathan leaned over and hugged her. "Hey, I asked you to marry me, so we could keep playing the blame game all day. We need to focus."

Luke stood. Nathan was pretty cool about all this. Was he being brave for his wife, or was he still hiding something? No, if Madison's life was at stake and Nathan knew something about it, he wouldn't keep it a secret. "Okay, let's try and think this through. Chloe, can you think of anyone who might do something like this? Has anyone threatened you or mentioned wanting money from you recently? Other than the Sam situation, I mean?"

"No, I've been racking my brain, trying to think of anyone who would do a thing like this. At first, I thought maybe it was some sort of prank, but it's not, is it?"

Nathan stroked her wavy blonde hair. "I don't think anyone would try to pull a stunt like this, honey. It would be sick and wrong. I hate to say it, but we have to believe these people are serious."

"How can this be happening?" Chloe wept into Nathan's side.

Luke felt sick to his stomach, but someone had to keep them focused on sorting out this mess.

"Chloe, these guys seem to presume you can come up with this much cash overnight, so I'm wondering if your money has been in the news lately for any reason? I'm a bit out of the loop in Seattle these days." *And out of my league talking about millions of dollars.*

"No, nothing. Madi and I had our fair share of weird phone calls and stuff straight after our parents' accident was in the news, but that's going back a while now. Daddy was well known in the business world, and you wouldn't have to be a genius to work out we inherited a sizable chunk. We never flaunted it, though. Madi protected me—I know that much. She had a lot more of the pressure being the eldest."

Luke chewed his lip. "Hmm, if it was a couple of years ago, your money's not breaking news, then. What about this Sam guy, Madison's ex-fiancé? Would he stoop to something like this? From what I've heard about him, he sounds like a nasty piece of work." Luke clenched and unclenched his fist as he recalled Madison's faltering voice when she mentioned Sam's final threatening words.

Nathan shrugged. "I never met him. He was out of the picture before I came along."

"Yeah." Chloe screwed up her nose. "I can't imagine Sam still hanging around Madison after a whole year. She told me he'd been out of her life since they broke off the engagement. He was a prize jerk and was ticked off when she discovered he was only after her money, but neither of us heard from him since then. I think he was relieved to get away without Madison pressing charges. He'd be a fool to try anything else."

"Sounds like a real gem." Luke reached out a hand. "May I?" He took the letter back from Chloe and studied it, looking for inspiration, a clue, anything. "Madison mentioned to me she was worried about someone following her for a while after the breakup with this Sam. Do you know anything about that?"

"She was so upset and nervous after Sam ruined everything, it doesn't surprise me one bit. Look how jumpy she was when we saw you guys last night. She tried not to get me involved, but it was easy to see how freaked out and nervous she was all the time. But as the weeks went on, she became less agitated, so I presumed everything was okay. She started going to church, and from that time on, faith played a major role in her life—you get that. As far as I know, she hasn't had any weird stuff going on for months. I'm sure she would have told me otherwise, although I know she always likes to protect me." Her eyes pooled. "But she doesn't have anyone to protect her now, does she?"

Luke's heart leaped at the thought of being her protector. It felt right. He was in deep. "Okay. We need to have a plan here, guys." He paced back and forth from the bed to the windows. "As much as I'd like to go straight to the police, I think we need to believe they are serious about their threats, so we have to rule out that option for now."

"So, where does it leave us?" Nathan leaned down and kissed the top of his wife's head.

"I'm not sure, but we can't put Madison's life in danger, no matter what. Do you agree, Chloe?" Luke stopped. "I can't even imagine how hard this is for you. I'm so sorry."

Chloe sniffled. "Madi is the only family I have left." She looked at her husband. "I know I have you now, but you know what I mean. We have to play this by their rules if I want my sister back safe and sound. I can't bear the thought of anything happening to her."

Nathan held her in his strong arms. "It'll be okay, honey. We'll figure this out. Right, Luke?"

Luke nodded, deep in thought. "Listen. I think we need to take a breather here for a moment. There's too much at stake and a lot to consider. Chloe, try to clear your head for a while. We've got about thirty minutes before they call. Think about anyone from your past or your family's past who might go to this kind of extreme to get to your money. Go as far back as you need to."

"You're right. We have to be smart. Like the police on those TV shows."

Nathan shook his head. "But, dude, shouldn't we get out there right away and start looking for her? She's already been gone for several hours. Time is of the essence."

"I know what you mean." Luke stared at the ceiling. "It's beyond frustrating, but where would we even start looking? They could be on the other side of the island in a getaway car by now."

"So, what should we do?" A vein in Nathan's neck pulsated.

"First things first. I need you to make some calls. See how feasible it is for you guys to get the money wired out here from the States. We have to be prepared to hand over what they want if we have a hope of getting Madison back safely. I have no idea how the money transaction works, but I'll bet our kidnappers have already looked into it and know if it's doable. Otherwise, they wouldn't have asked."

"Sure." Nathan nodded and squeezed Chloe's shoulder. "Sounds good. I'll get right on it. I may need you to be close by, honey, for verification and stuff." He turned to Luke. "What are you going to do, bro?"

Luke looked at the newlywed couple. Their new life had plummeted from ecstatic to traumatic in the space of hours, and his heart lurched. He walked over to the room safe and grabbed his wallet. "I'm going to be ready to leave the resort if necessary. I think we should all head up to your room in about ten minutes in case they phone early and sit tight to wait for the call. It may give us some kind of clue to go on. I know you guys aren't big on faith and hope, but I am. I feel out of my depth here, so I'm going onto the balcony to spend a few minutes doing something vital for Madison. I'm going to pray."

CHAPTER THIRTEEN

MADISON CRACKED ONE EYE OPEN and then the other. *Where am I?*

Some sort of hut. Stuffy and hot. Sunlight poured in through a single window as she pulled herself up to a sitting position. Nice...and...slow.

Nausea swept over her like a tidal wave and she forced herself to hold still until it passed. She leaned back against a plank wall and exhaled. What happened? She looked down at her running shorts, shoes, and tank top. Yes, she was out for a morning run. And then someone attacked her out of nowhere and another guy had a yellow cloth...

Her head pounded. Most likely from dehydration, not to mention the aftereffects of being unconscious. She stretched out her limbs and probed for wounds. Nothing, other than a bump on the side of her head. Several bruises were developing on her arms, which felt sore to the touch, but no bones were broken, and she didn't seem to be drugged. At least, not anymore.

She fixed her ponytail and noticed her clothes were damp and smudged with dirt. The glass bottom boat. The last memory before blacking out resurfaced and Madison clapped her hand over her mouth. *Thank the Lord I was unconscious.* Had she been out on the ocean with the creepy guy? Wait. There were two of them. What had they done to her and where was she now? Madison's head spun, and she hugged her knees to her chest. Had they bundled her into a corner or hung her over the edge? Judging from the smudges on her tank top, wherever she had been, it was filthy. Just as well she had no recollection.

Oriented, she surveyed the room. An ancient surfboard leaned against one wall, and snorkeling gear was heaped in a pile in the corner by the door. One small wooden table sat below the window, and a plastic folding chair was pushed underneath. No expense spared here. No food or water or bathroom—was this a temporary holding place? What did these animals want with her?

Madison stood on shaky legs and walked three steps to the wooden door. She turned the metal knob. Careful. Best not to attract any unwanted attention. The lock caught. There was no getting out of here the easy way. The window? She stumbled over and inspected it—there was no way to open it at all. She peered through the grubby glass and saw another shack beside hers, small and basic. They were right on the beachfront, the ocean lapping the shore in front of them. Horribly close, in fact. Twenty feet or so? She pressed her ear to the glass. No voices. Just the gentle rustle of palm fronds and the rhythmic crash of waves pounding the sand. Where were her captors?

She stretched her arms above her head, grateful she was not bound or tied up, and attempted to right the crick in her sore neck. Wishing for a watch, she guessed it must be close to midafternoon, judging by the angle of sun and intensity of heat. The air in here was heavy and humid and smelled of stale sweat and salt. Jamaican heat was wonderful when air-conditioning or a cool swimming pool were available. Like at the resort.

Is anyone missing me yet? Luke would be. She was supposed to meet him at eleven, so he would be worried. Had he waited for her? Had he given up, thinking she didn't care? No, he would be concerned—maybe he contacted security or even the police. But Chloe wouldn't have a clue. She was enjoying her honeymoon in paradise, unaware her sister was being held in some shack, goodness knows where.

Madison forced herself to breathe in through her nose and out through her mouth. She was in danger of hyperventilating if she considered the possible outcomes of her predicament. There must be a simple explanation. Could it be some prank? Really *not* funny. Was someone after her money perhaps? But who? Who would do something so reckless? And why not kidnap her in Seattle? She didn't know a soul in Jamaica.

Her thoughts shifted to Sam, the most calculating individual she'd ever encountered. He was vindictive and cruel, but he'd been out of the picture for a year, and kidnapping was not his style. He was far too sophisticated for something so base. Unless he hired those thugs. Perhaps it was a complete stranger who plucked her at random from the beach. There was a good chance anyone from their luxurious resort would have money.

Then she remembered the guy with the icy blue eyes. Yes, he was the one who kidnapped her, and it was no chance encounter. He followed her all weekend, biding his time and waiting for an opportune moment to strike. He was bad news. *Why did I chance going for a run on my own this morning?* Tears surfaced. Yesterday was so wonderful, she let her guard down. And now here she was. Not just followed, but kidnapped.

Madison shuddered. What would he do to her? Hopefully, he wanted only her money. She gulped. What if he planned to take her away somewhere? Marry her off or keep her prisoner forever? Rape, maim, or even murder her? Then there was the other man on the dock to consider, the one with the cloth. What was his part in this plan? Several nasty scenarios ran through her mind and she started to pace the room. With four steps in each direction, she felt like a caged lion.

Something outside slammed shut—a door perhaps? A key turned in the lock of Madison's door and she froze in place. The door burst open, bringing with it a brief, refreshing gust of cooler air—and the hulking figure of Blue Eyes.

He marched in and thumped a bottle of water onto the table and then approached Madison, his piercing stare the most menacing she'd ever encountered.

"You're trembling, princess."

Madison took a deep breath and jutted her chin.

"Nice sleep, sweetheart?" He grinned and trailed one finger down the side of her face.

Madison flinched and backed up against the wall. "Who are you? What do you want?"

He let out a cold laugh and wiggled his bushy blond eyebrows. "You'll have to be patient, beautiful. You might want to make yourself comfortable here. It's going to be a long, long night."

He stood close enough for Madison's senses to be overpowered by the stench of aftershave, cigarette smoke, and beer. No chance trying to defend herself against his bodybuilder physique.

"Get away from me."

"For now…" He smirked and then turned and stormed back out through the door, locking it in his wake.

Madison sank down the wall and collapsed onto the slatted wooden floor. She might have been able to remain composed in front of Blue Eyes, but now she dissolved into tears.

All her previous fears and insecurities paled in comparison with what she was feeling right now. Helpless and hopeless.

Wait. No. I'm not helpless or hopeless. That was the old me. I have God with me now. He's my help and my hope. Father, forgive me for forgetting You are in control here, not some bully. Please give me the courage I need to get through this. I can't do it on my own. I can't.

Her sobbing subsided and an inner strength took over. Madison stood and stumbled back over to the table. She twisted off the bottle cap and gulped a swig of water. It was far from cool and refreshing, but it would keep her from dehydrating. She needed to keep her strength up and stay strong and alert. There had to be a way out of here.

She sorted through the junk in the room, hoping to find something to use as a weapon or at least in defense. There was nothing sharp or heavy, other than the chair. She picked it up and lifted it above her head to see whether it might work as a battering ram of some sort.

Madison was so out of her comfort zone. Should have taken those self-defense classes with Chloe years ago. She unleashed her inner tigress, growled, and raised the chair again, ready to take aim at her captor. A movement at the window caught her attention, and she spun around to look. She dropped the chair and screamed.

There was Blue Eyes, his face squished up against the glass in a horrific leer. Her skin crawled.

Why hadn't she checked the window for spectators before acting like a gladiator? Madison threw back her shoulders and retreated from the window to the sound of her kidnapper cackling outside. She could also hear the other guy's muffled voice. Two against one. Two men against one woman. She bit her lip and forced herself to breathe.

God, I know You're bigger than all this. Please help me not to fall apart here...

The door swung open again, and Blue Eyes swaggered to the table, a cell phone in his hand.

"Okay, Miss Grey. We have a little phone call to make."

"You know my name?" Her stomach lurched. This was personal.

"I know everything about you, beautiful. I know you're a rich young lady, thanks to the hefty inheritance that dropped into your lap. Bad luck for your parents, good luck for you, and better luck for me."

Madison clenched her fist by her side. Best not to slap his smug bronzed face. "Are you from Seattle? You sound like you're from farther south, but you seem to know plenty about my family. How long have you been following me?" Her voice sounded tinny and hollow in her ears. *Keep him talking. Find out anything that might give a clue.*

He held up one hand. "Enough. I'm the one who gets to ask questions here. And I'm about to question how much your little sister loves you."

Madison gasped. "My sister? Leave Chloe out of this. She's on her honeymoon, for goodness' sake."

"You'd better hope she put her honeymoon on hold for you, sweetheart, because she's your only chance. If she refuses to cooperate, I'm not sure what will become of you. But you can kiss your old life goodbye. That's for certain."

"What do you mean?" Her heart raced and her mouth went dry. What did they have in mind for her? Breathe. Pray. *Lord, help me.*

"The boss has too much invested in this. There's no going back, and only your little sister can make it happen."

"And who *is* your boss?"

"He'll reveal his identity when he's good and ready. Don't you worry your pretty little head about that. In the meantime, let's have a nice chat with your newlywed sister, shall we? Unless you would prefer her to be a widow by the end of the week. Or for that husband of hers to be a widower..."

"Don't you lay a finger on my little sister." Madison's breath came hard and fast.

"Yeah, she's not having a good day today. She'll be bawling her eyes out after reading that sweet note I left for her this morning. But don't panic. If we're going to lay a finger on anyone, it'll be on you."

Madison wiped clammy palms on her shorts. "What do you want? Money? Is that what it's all about? You don't have to hurt my sister or me. We'll give you your stupid money."

"Let's hope so, for your sake. You had better behave yourself and play nice, okay? I can't promise to keep my hands to myself if you misbehave."

He looked her up and down, leaned a hip against the rickety table, and dialed a number into his phone.

Repulsed, Madison glanced away at the chair. If only she had the strength to pick it up and smash it over his head. But even if she did, what about the other guy outside? She steeled herself, ready to run or shout a message to Chloe. Something. This could be her one chance to give her sister a clue. But what would she say? "I'm in a little hut on a beach somewhere"? No help whatsoever. *God, any wisdom would be great about now.* Blue Eyes stared directly at Madison and she knew what clue she could give.

"Yes, room 400, please." He raised a brow and sneered.

Madison inched closer to the table, hoping to hear Chloe's voice, even if it meant getting closer to the stinking hulk.

"Hello?" Chloe's voice was shrill. "Who is this?"

Madison closed her eyes, thankful her sister was safe and hadn't tried anything foolish.

"I'm glad you received our message, Miss Grey. Or should I say 'Mrs. Alexander'? I'm the one who has your sister." Blue Eyes winked at Madison.

"What do you want with her? How do I know she's all right?" Chloe's voice cracked. "I need to speak with her."

"First things first. I need to make sure we will have our money at noon tomorrow. I hope you'll be waiting for our call. I'll give you details of the drop-off location then. And remember, no police. And that includes hotel security. We will know if you break that rule—and you'll all be sorry. So, will we have our money?"

"Yes, yes. We're working on it right now. But I have to know Madison is safe."

"She's safe. Shaking like a leaf, but if you do your part and we get our money, you can have a sweet family reunion." He chuckled at his own humor.

"I'll get the money. I don't care about that. But please, don't hurt her. Can I speak with her now? Your note said you'd give me proof she is alive."

He moved the phone toward Madison. "Blue Eyes has me." Madison screamed the words to be sure her sister would hear. *Please let Chloe or Luke know who I'm talking about.*

"Silly girl." Blue Eyes slapped Madison's cheek so hard, she staggered back across the room and landed in a heap by the snorkeling equipment.

"We mean business." He yelled into his phone and then snapped it shut.

Madison flinched when he strode past her, but he didn't even look down to acknowledge she was there. He slammed the door behind him and locked it from outside.

Tears flowed down her burning cheek, and she curled herself into a ball, closing her eyes. They must have heard her. If so, it was worth the slap. If it were a nightmare, maybe she would wake up soon—she would quit feeling more alone than ever before, and this fear of her unknown future would evaporate. With no idea where she was, who her captors were, or whether she would even get out of the sickening situation alive, she cried until sleep finally claimed her.

CHAPTER FOURTEEN

LUKE HEARD EVERY WORD AND watched Chloe's face crumple. She took a shaky breath and flung the hotel phone onto the table as if it burned her.

"Why are they doing this?" She plucked a pillow from the bed and hugged it before collapsing onto the armchair. "Blue eyes?" Sobs racked her petite frame while Nathan stroked her hair.

Luke met his brother's gaze. Nathan opened his mouth as if to speak and then bit his lower lip and looked away.

"Blue Eyes," Luke whispered. He was close enough to hear Madison scream those two words, and it broke his heart when he heard the slap. "She was giving us a clue. You know that's the guy who's been following her this weekend. At least I think it was the same guy as Friday night in the lobby. Remember when she freaked out because someone was watching her? We were hoping he was a random—"

"Wait. You two were discussing it?" Chloe stopped crying and stared at Luke. "What was there to discuss? I thought that was a one-time incident. Did she see him again after Friday night?"

Luke winced and perched on the end of the bed. "You have to understand Madison didn't want to worry you. It was your wedding day, after all."

"What?" Chloe swiped the tears from her cheeks. "How could she keep something like this from me? Nathan, did you know about this?"

"No clue. I'll get you some water." He plodded over to the suite's bar area.

Chloe blew out a long breath and pulled her hair into a ponytail. For a second Luke saw the resemblance to her sister, and it felt like a punch in the gut.

"Tell me everything. And don't candy-coat it. I don't deserve to be kept in the dark when my sister's life is on the line."

Luke went into as much detail as he could recall. He explained how the man appeared and stared at Madison on her run, followed by the unnerving spa incident with the camera and then her suspicion of being watched straight after the wedding ceremony.

Chloe accepted the glass of water from Nathan and guzzled half of it down. "I can't believe I was oblivious to it all. So, this creep was watching us both at the spa? I was right there next to Madison and didn't have a clue. Why am I so self-absorbed? This is awful." Her face paled.

Nathan leaned against her chair. "Sweetheart, it was your wedding day. Don't blame yourself. It's the one day in your life you're allowed to think about yourself first. And you can't blame Madison. If it were the other way around, wouldn't you do everything possible to give her a perfect day and protect her from anything spoiling it?"

"Of course I would. But I still feel guilty. She was kind of jumpy, but I guess I've gotten used to it. She was trying so hard to protect me."

And Madison needed someone to protect *her*—so far Luke had failed dismally. But he could change that. Starting now. *Think.* "She said she knew the guy was watching her rather than you. He made it obvious he was photographing her, even though you were close by. Madison knew you weren't in danger, Chloe."

"But didn't she want to report him? There must have been something she could have done to stop him."

Nathan squeezed her shoulder. "It's no use worrying about that now."

Luke cleared his throat. "Actually, we reported it all to the resort security late Saturday night. Not that they could do much with what we told them. It's not like they could harass someone for having icy blue eyes and a camera." *And we can't even check with security now anyway.*

"Icy eyes." Nathan shook his head.

"Yeah." Luke glared at his brother. What was bothering him? "The guy that freaked you out so much on Friday night."

"I should never have left her alone." Chloe hugged herself. "She's been through too much already this past year. Did you hear him on the phone call? Luke, that thug hit her. I can't bear the thought of anyone laying a hand on my sister."

Luke's nostrils flared. They better not lay another finger on her. "She's stronger than you think." He clenched his jaw as he pictured her with Blue Eyes. "She refused to let this guy scare her enough to keep her locked away in her room all week. He didn't appear anywhere yesterday, and by last night, it didn't seem to be on her mind at all. She was relaxed and happy. She wouldn't have gone out running this morning if she harbored any fears about him still stalking her."

Chloe sniffled. He had to be calm for her, even with his heart beating out of his chest.

"I don't need to tell you that your sister has a solid faith in God. She knows she's not alone wherever she is, and I guarantee she'll be praying her way through this. It'll keep her strong." *God, please be with her right now.*

Luke observed Nathan. He stood and shifted his weight from foot to foot and raked his hands through his blond hair. Something was wrong. Something other than concern for his sister-in-law. Luke knew Nathan almost as well as he knew himself, and he was usually a tower of strength.

"What is it?" Luke slid off the bed and stood toe to toe with his brother. "Come on. I know something's off with you. You're cool in a crisis, but right now, you look like you want to flee any second."

"Nathan?" Chloe pulled herself up from the chair and touched his arm. "Are you okay? You look awful."

"Blue Eyes." His voice was monotone as he stared at the far wall. "Madison said the dude had the most piercing icy blue eyes she had ever seen. Right?"

"Yeah. They freaked her out." Luke folded his arms across his chest. "Listen. I know the whole incident in the lobby on Friday made you skittish. Is there something you're not telling us?"

"Nathan?" Chloe raised her voice and broke his trance.

He came to life and started pacing, avoiding eye contact with either of them for several seconds. "You have to hear me out before you start grilling me, okay?"

"Sure." *Perhaps we'll get to the bottom of this at last.* Luke held his breath.

"What is it?" Chloe rubbed her arms. "You're scaring me."

"Let me start way back, about three months ago. Chloe, when we announced our engagement, I was approached by a bunch of wedding planners and stuff. Remember?"

She nodded. "That newspaper announcement stating our intentions to have a destination wedding? The worst idea ever. We were inundated with wedding planners. It was a nightmare."

"Exactly. I met with some of the planners. I wanted to have this resort arranged to perfection for you. One meeting was kind of creepy, and I never told you about it because you had enough to think about getting your business off the ground. There were these two guys, photographers specializing in destination weddings. They came to my realty office in the city and gave me the hard sell—you know, tried to persuade me they were giving me the deal of the century, blah blah blah."

"Okay." Chloe squinted. "What about them?"

"The one guy gave me a bad vibe. They seemed legit with their portfolio and stuff, but they were super pushy. Wanted to know every detail about the wedding. This bad-vibe guy even said Madison's name, guessing she would be a bridesmaid before I even mentioned her..."

"What?" Luke frowned. "How would he even know about Madison?"

"Who knows? Their dad was well respected and his death was all over the news when it happened. It wouldn't be hard to deduce Madison would be in the wedding party. Plus, I think these dudes did their homework online about the family before pitching their services."

"All right, but what makes you think they would have anything to do with this kidnapping thing? It's a bit far-fetched, don't you think?" *And why on earth didn't you mention any of this before?*

"Bro, that's it. One of them—the bad-vibe guy—had the freakiest eyes I'd ever seen. They sort of looked straight into you. Made me uncomfortable to be in my own skin."

Chloe gulped. "Freaky eyes? Like how?"

"Real light blue. And cold. Icy. I think it could be Madison's stalker." He stopped pacing. "And before you ask, I deleted them from my phone contacts—out of sight, out of mind."

That would have been helpful. "And you don't have any emails or anything from them?"

"No. None. It was a couple of meetings in person and maybe three calls."

Luke stared out the window at the ocean. He bit his tongue. Why hadn't Nathan offered this information on Friday night rather than keeping it to himself? It was obviously preying on his mind. He gnawed on his lip. This kidnapping was well thought out and planned. Whoever held Madison hostage was serious about getting his money. The whole scheme had been in the works for months.

"I'm so sorry, honey." Nathan pulled Chloe close and held her. "I should have said something on Friday. I hoped it was a weird coincidence. That's all. I wanted our wedding to be perfect. I hadn't thought about those guys in months. They weren't even on my radar. Heck, if I knew he was following her on Saturday, I would have found him myself. I feel such a fool. I only hope she's okay."

Luke tapped his chin with his fingers. Something wasn't quite adding up. "What I don't get is why you didn't mention this to *me* on Friday night. I understand you not wanting to upset Chloe the night before your wedding, but something hit a chord with you. You should have shared the burden, man." He shook his head. "No wonder you were so edgy. Hey, these guys never hounded you again, right?" He shot him a big-brother stare.

Nathan's shoulders slumped. "That's not quite the whole story." He held Chloe at arm's length and looked straight into her eyes. "I never spoke to the dude with the blue eyes after the one meeting, but the other guy was more persuasive. He was the one who suggested we come to this resort, and he even pulled a few strings for me to get a good deal, even though I didn't hire them as the photographers. Said he had connections. You know I can't resist a good deal, honey, don't you?"

Chloe's eyes filled.

"I got suspicious when he started asking details about Madison being your bridesmaid, and then he got pushy about arranging one of those glass bottom boats for the wedding party."

Luke's mouth fell open. The glass bottom boat was involved? No wonder Nathan looked sick at the sight of it when the fight happened on that dock on Friday night.

"The guy thought it would be a cool idea, but I said I'd have to run it by you and Madison, and he didn't like that. He wanted it to be a surprise for you. He got kind of mad and frustrated, but I put my foot down. Why would we want to go on a stupid boat on our wedding day? There was nothing more to arrange, so after the meeting, I stopped having any contact with him. That was months ago. I swear I haven't heard from him since."

Chloe shook loose from his grip and collapsed back into the chair. "Wait. A glass bottom boat? Madison got super upset on Friday night when we went for our walk and she thought she saw someone watching us from one of those kinds of boats. It was hitched to the secondary dock." She pressed a hand to her stomach. "I was about to go charging over there to prove she was imagining things until she made me stop."

Nathan knelt by her chair. "I'm sorry. For all this mess."

"What was the second guy's name?" Luke rubbed his chin. "Presuming it was his real name he gave you."

"Jacobs. Steve Jacobs. He seemed like a good guy, as long as he wasn't with Blue Eyes. He was kind of pushy about the boat idea but a solid businessman type. Smart, smooth, eloquent…"

"What did he look like?" Chloe's eyes were wide. "This Jacobs guy. Can you describe him?"

Nathan squinted and pursed his lips. "He was a bit taller than me, maybe six foot two, skinny, tanned, great hair. Jet black and wavy—you know, kind of movie-star hair. Always wore a suit. He drove a black Beemer, I think. Older model."

Chloe gasped. "No. It can't be."

"What's wrong?" Luke's stomach tightened. "Do you know who it is?" There was only one man he was aware of who had threatened Madison.

Chloe grabbed her husband's arms. "Did he ever ask to meet with me? Did he even want to say hello?"

Nathan frowned. "No. We met a couple of times, and I suggested we invite you, but he thought you would prefer to think I planned everything on my own. Like a gift to you. I said it was cool. That's why I never mentioned it. Why?"

Tears streamed down Chloe's face while she looked from Luke to Nathan. "Because this man, this partner of Blue Eyes, sounds just like Madison's lowlife ex-fiancé. He's behind all this. He knows Madi is petrified of drowning and has this crazy fear of glass bottom boats. He would only suggest it in order to get back at her for canceling their wedding before he could steal her money." She buried her face in her hands.

Luke's mouth went bone dry. "Sam kidnapped Madison."

CHAPTER FIFTEEN

LUKE TOOK A DEEP BREATH and exhaled. Could this situation get any worse? Chloe sobbed and Nathan apologized over and over.

"Look. This isn't your fault, man." Luke put a hand on his brother's shoulder. "There's no way you could have known these guys were on some kind of con scheme, for goodness' sake. Especially as you'd never met Sam before."

Nathan stood up straight, a weight lifted. "The girls didn't have a photo of him or anything lying around their place. I had no idea what Sam looked like. I swear. I never even thought about the connection with the boat."

Chloe slid an arm around her husband's waist. "It's okay. I know it seems weird and obsessive, but Madi wanted to remove anything that reminded her of Sam. Photos, gifts he bought her, everything to do with her wedding. I don't blame her, either. She was so jumpy for months after they split up. She thought someone was following her, and in hindsight, maybe she was right. He must have been scheming all along. I should never have doubted her."

Luke stuffed his hands in his pockets. "I don't want to be insensitive, but do you know if Sam was ever violent with Madison? Did he ever threaten her physically or anything?"

"No, I don't think so. I thought he was kind of wimpy. He never gave off any violent vibes and he's super skinny. Tall, dark, and handsome, I suppose, but not much meat on his bones. Madi never mentioned anything about him being physically abusive—even when she was super mad with him at the end." She chewed on her thumbnail. "After she uncovered his plan, she was anxious, but I think it was more because she was wounded in her heart than anything else. When she falls for someone, she falls hard."

Luke met Chloe's gaze for a beat too long. This was awkward. Could she see how much he cared for her sister? Was he getting in too deep without knowing for sure how Madison felt?

"Okay." He cleared his throat. "So, we can assume all he wants here is the money."

Chloe shrugged. "He might not be violent, but Sam kind of gave me the creeps sometimes. He worked for Dad for years and seemed to swoop in on Madison straight after our parents' accident. But he was so charming toward her, right up until she discovered the truth. I remember she told me it was like a mask fell from his face when she confronted him and he admitted he was purely in the relationship for her money. She said it was as if he transformed into something ugly. I guess he could only keep up the facade for so long."

"What are we going to do now?" Nathan wiped beads of sweat from his forehead. "We can't just sit here until noon tomorrow waiting for them to phone. I should go make another call to the bank. A guy I spoke with earlier was looking into the money wire for us. At least then we'll know what we need to do."

"I suppose so," Chloe whispered. "I think I should stay here. You never know—they might try to make contact again, and I don't want to miss them." She climbed onto the bed and curled up.

"I'll call for some room-service snacks to tide us over." Nathan picked up the menu from the bedside table. "Not that anyone feels like eating right now, but we may be grateful for it later." He looked up at Luke. "What about you?"

"I'm going to retrace Madison's steps from this morning. See if I can find anything at all that might give us some clue if there was a struggle." He checked his pocket for his phone. "I'll ask around, too. Maybe someone spotted her. We're presuming she wasn't taken last night. I saw her to her room and everything was fine. I think it must have happened on her run, but it would be good to get some confirmation."

Nathan nodded. "Be careful who you speak to. We shouldn't make it sound like an emergency, or the resort management might want to involve the police."

"True, especially after our chat with security on Saturday night. Don't worry. I'll be subtle. Hey, Chloe, I don't suppose you know what color running clothes Madison might have worn?"

Chloe turned onto her back. "Of course. Black shorts and black runners. She always wore her hair in a ponytail when she ran. And I'm sure she brought tank tops because we packed together. That's what she wore when she went running on Saturday morning, too." She sat up. "Wait. I know what color top she would have worn—hot pink. I remember giving her a hard time for bringing three identical tank tops with her. She said it was a triple pack and she didn't have the heart to separate them." Tears pooled in Chloe's eyes. "She's such a softie."

Luke attempted a smile. "Try to get some rest, okay? The phone is right next to you so you won't sleep through it. But it could be a long night for us all. I'll be back soon."

"Luke?" Chloe swallowed. "Please find my big sister. I don't know what I'll do without her."

He nodded and left the room before his emotions got the better of him.

*****

For the next fifteen minutes, Luke spoke to several people in the lobby and down on the beach. He avoided the management staff and questioned a few servers handing out cocktails around the pool and bar areas. No luck. He even shared a photograph from his phone of Madison on Sunday evening at the bonfire. It didn't jog anyone's memory.

He gave the ruse that she was running late for an appointment, hoping his casual nonchalance would override his desperate panic. One elderly lady with a British accent swore she saw Madison at the poolside bar an hour before. Luke caught his breath until the daughter apologized and explained her mother had a vivid imagination and suffered from dementia. This was proving to be impossible.

Luke sighed. Nobody had seen her. Not one lead. It was about seven hours since her run, maybe even more. She could be anywhere by now.

Lord, I know You're with Madison wherever she is. Please keep her calm and safe. Help me to know what to do here. I don't want to get her into any further trouble, but I'm anxious to do something instead of sitting around waiting. I could do with a double shot of wisdom about now.

He took another peek at the photo on his phone. Her smile lit up her face, and the wind caught her long dark ringlets bouncing around her tanned shoulders. *I have to find her somehow.*

Luke slid the phone into his pocket and put on his shades. He needed to retrace her jogging route. Yes, that seemed logical. He walked down the beach in the direction Madison must have run that morning. It was the longest stretch, and she had told him it was the best for running. The first dock had two speedboats moored and a couple of resort staff talking to guests. He surveyed the expanse of sand while he marched along, desperate to find something. *It's not like I'm going to find her running shoes with a note or anything...*

The beach wasn't crowded; it hadn't been all weekend. As he passed the second dock, he noticed it was empty. *No glass bottom boat here anymore. Interesting.* He continued on. Occasional palm trees dotted the area, and couples found shade beneath little tiki huts. It was almost unnatural. Luke was used to the shrill screams of children playing on the beach and splashing each other in the ocean. He sighed. The little ones at his Mexican orphanage had a piece of his heart, and it was hard to imagine not living in the place where chaos and calm collided daily. Life was never dull, yet there was a serenity that held it all together. Madison would love it there. *Madison.*

An abandoned black shirt lay in the sand farther along the shore, but someone ran up and claimed it before Luke even came close. The stretch of beach narrowed and a clump of palm trees gave the illusion of an oasis. This was such a gorgeous resort. He hadn't ventured this far along the shore up until now. What was that up ahead? Something shiny glinted in the sunlight. It was half-buried in the sand and could be nothing, but Luke wasn't leaving any stone unturned.

When he reached it, he crouched down and his heart almost stopped. He brushed away a section of sand and unearthed a pair of sparkly pink sunglasses. They were Madison's for sure. He'd held them a couple of days ago when she bumped into him in the lobby, and he noticed she had worn them again yesterday. They had to be hers. *Madison.*

A cluster of palm trees rose out of the sand about fifty feet away. Had someone surprised her from there? It was possible. He tenderly picked up the glasses, stood, and scanned the beach. No road came close enough to make a quick grab by car. He turned to the ocean. There was a third dock right in front of him, but nothing was tied there at the moment. Luke clutched the shades and gazed down the length of the beach back toward the resort. His stomach knotted.

The glass bottom boat.

It had been moored at the second dock all weekend—he was sure of it. He'd spotted it from his balcony on Friday night when the scuffle took place, and it was there again yesterday. Madison even pointed it out to him and made him promise not to take her out on it. Strange that nobody was using it. Why hadn't he been suspicious of that? It should be taking regular cruises throughout the day. And now—surprise, surprise—it was nowhere to be seen. Nathan said Sam made some sort of fuss about using one for the wedding ceremony. This had to be the connection.

Luke needed answers. He broke into a jog and headed back to the room to speak with his brother and to confirm with Chloe that he was holding her sister's glasses.

*****

"Goodness. Yes, yes, these are definitely Madi's." Chloe took the sunglasses from Luke and held them with care. "Wherever did you find them?"

Luke groaned. It was further confirmation of the kidnapping route, and it wasn't easy for any of them to digest. "They were lying in the sand, quite a way down the beach near a clump of palm trees."

Nathan set mugs of steaming coffee before each of them and they sat around the small table by the French doors. "Caffeine to keep us going. Any other clues? Any idea at all what might have happened, bro?"

Luke took a sip of hot coffee. "It might be nothing, but I want to get everything clear in my head. What's the deal with this glass bottom boat thing, Chloe? Madison mentioned how much she disliked them and even begged me not to ask her to go out on one, but I didn't push for why."

Chloe pursed her lips. "I think glass bottom boats are her idea of the worst possible scenario. Imagine you are petrified of the ocean—wouldn't it be awful to be able to see right down deep? After that incident when we were kids and she almost drowned, she started having dreams. They were horrid nightmares. I don't think she's ever been on a real glass bottom boat, but the thought of it used to freak her out. It grew into a bit of an obsession when she was young, and I guess it left a mark. She mentioned the other day that our parents' accident dredged up all her bad memories with the ocean. I should have let her unload. She's always the one who listens."

"Hey." Nathan grabbed her hand. "Stop beating yourself up, sweetheart. You two are incredibly close, and I'm sure she would have told you anything important. She knew you had a wedding to plan so must have kept her worries to herself."

"Yeah, Madi would totally do that. You're right." Chloe bit back a sob.

"So, Sam knew for sure about this fear of glass bottom boats?" Luke guessed the answer but had to ask.

"Yes, he knew, all right." Chloe's eyes flashed. "They were planning on spending the rest of their lives together, so they shared their fears, hopes, dreams, and everything."

Luke grimaced. Madison opened her heart fully to a man who wanted to use her. No wonder she was so devastated.

"Sam fed her a load of baloney, of course. But she told him all about her past and the family. He was well aware she's petrified of deep water, too."

Luke inhaled. "Nathan, you said Sam suggested using the boat at the wedding, right?"

"Yeah. I thought it was bizarre at the time. In hindsight, he must have known Madison would have taken one look at it and refused to go on board. It doesn't make sense why he would even go there. Was he planning on taking off with Madison and dumping the rest of the wedding party or something?"

Chloe blew on her coffee. "Did he give a suggestion where it might have fit into the whole wedding package? Was he thinking after the ceremony for a sunset cruise or something? I don't get it."

"I can't remember his exact words. I kiboshed the whole idea because it wasn't something we intended to include. Plus, you'd already filled me in on Madison's fear of water. I didn't want to hear any more about it, and that's when he started getting all pushy about the boat."

"I'm sure you loved that." Luke shot him a look. Nathan did not enjoy being backed into a corner by anyone.

"Right. By that point, the resort was arranged, so I thanked him for getting me set up and said I wouldn't need his services for anything else. Chloe already decided to go with the resort photographer, so I didn't hear from Sam again."

"But why the boat?" Chloe asked. "I still don't understand the relevance."

Luke stood and started pacing. "I don't think he ever intended to use it for the ceremony, guys. I think he planned all along to wait until Madison was alone after the wedding. He would have assumed she was going to have a lot of alone time, right? He knew her well enough to guess she would be taking her morning runs or reading somewhere or walking by herself. My guess is he was biding his time, getting Blue Eyes to watch her routine until the moment was right."

Nathan nodded. "But the boat?"

"It was on standby. I'm sure it hasn't been going out on any organized cruises. I haven't seen it move once from that second dock."

"Remember when we arrived at the resort?" Chloe clutched Nathan's arm. "They gave us that orientation and said the resort glass bottom boat was out of action. Didn't it need some repairs or something?"

"Yeah, you're right. I know my ears pricked up because of Sam's request. I'd forgotten all about it up until then."

Chloe's forehead crinkled. "Madi and I saw it tied to the second dock the night before the wedding. Remember when we took a walk along the beach after dinner? I even commented on how strange it was to see one there. She was sure someone was on the boat, but I didn't believe her."

"Maybe they *were* watching her that night." Luke shrugged. "Blue Eyes could have gone from the boat to the lobby while we were at the piano bar. Or it could have been Sam in the boat."

"I should have listened to my poor sister. She was so upset about seeing some guy aboard, but I didn't get what the big deal was."

"There was no way you could have known anything was suspicious, honey." Nathan rubbed the stubble on his chin. "This is all beyond crazy."

"True." Luke's mind raced as he began piecing together the information. "But I guess it ties in with the scuffle I saw on that dock later the same night."

Chloe set her coffee down on the table. Hard. "What scuffle? More drama I'm not aware of?"

"It was nothing." Luke needed to defuse this one. "At least, we didn't think so at the time. While Nathan was showering, I noticed a bit of a fight break out on the second dock down at the beach. I couldn't see too well from the balcony, but I yelled, and it seemed to do the trick. The glass bottom boat was definitely moored there then, and a couple of guys were getting heated about something." If only he had been able to see them up close. Could it have been Sam?

"Yeah, it kind of spooked me for a minute there—hearing Madison talking about the blue eyes and then seeing the glass bottom boat—but I tried to forget about it. I had other things

143

on my mind." He rubbed his new wedding band and shared a look with Chloe.

"Like a wedding?"

"Something like that." Nathan pecked her cheek.

It was good to see him back to normal, and it looked as if they were going to work through this ordeal. As long as they found Madison.

Chloe's blue eyes widened. "Do you think it could have been Sam in the fight?"

"I was wondering the same thing. No way of knowing. It was too far away to see details." Luke drained the last of his coffee. "At least now I know what I'm going to do next."

"What, bro?"

"First I'm going to make some discreet inquiries with the front desk about the glass bottom boat. We need to know for sure if the one we all saw belongs to the resort or to a private company. And then I'm going to take out a speedboat of my own."

"Why? Where will you go?"

"That glass bottom boat's not at any of the docks anymore, which leads me to believe it's how Madison was transported. Her glasses were just feet away from a third dock down the beach—it's the one option that makes sense. They moved it along to a more remote location."

"My poor sister must have been petrified being grabbed. And then to be taken in a boat—I can't even imagine."

Madison's scream over the phone echoed in Luke's mind. "I know. But if that's the case, how many of those boats could be docked around an island this size?"

Nathan whistled. "Not too many. Do you want me to come with you? Two pairs of eyes will be better than one."

144

"I think I'll be able to spot a boat that size. You should stay with your new wife. But there's one thing you could do for me."

"Sure."

"Go online and check out all the glass bottom boats listed for Jamaica on this side of the island. Might save me some conversations."

"Sounds good. Keep your phone on you. Give me a call before you take off in the boat and I'll read you the list." Nathan handed Luke a pad of notepaper and a pen from the bedside table.

Chloe stood. "I need to do something, too. I think I'm going to pop down to Madi's room again. I still have the key and I might find something there to help us."

"I'll come with you. You shouldn't go alone." Nathan grabbed his room key from the table. "What do you think might be there?"

Chloe blinked back tears. "I don't know. But I can't sit here doing nothing. A clue of some kind? I might be able to tell if she left in a hurry this morning. I know she writes in her journal almost every day, and I hate to pry, but it might have some valuable information in there. And I can make sure her passport is still in the safe, as I have the combination—at least we can rule out her leaving Jamaica. Or I could even find a note. They may have contacted her, too."

"Good thinking. I should have thought of that earlier." Luke lifted a brow. What would Madison's journal reveal? Would he get a mention? "Give me a shout on my cell if there's anything there, and I'll let you know if I find something, too, okay? And if you feel like it, now might be a great time to start praying."

145

Chloe bit her lip. "It could be dangerous, you know. You don't have to do this…"

"Yeah, Chloe. Actually, I do."

CHAPTER SIXTEEN

"HI THERE, COULD YOU TELL me if you have any glass bottom boats available today, please?" Luke smiled at the receptionist behind the lobby counter. This would be the easiest way to determine whether the one they had seen was legitimate without raising suspicion.

He perched on a stool and leaned against the counter. Cool, calm, and collected. He realized his fingers were rapping on the desk like a woodpecker when the receptionist raised her perfectly groomed eyebrows. He stopped.

"I think our boat's out of action at the moment, sir, but let me check for you."

She typed on a keyboard for several seconds and adjusted her sleek glasses while she waited for some response. "I'm afraid I was correct. Our regular boat's being repaired, but it should be back with us on Wednesday." She smiled an apology. "Is there anything else I can help you with?"

Something was not adding up. "Too bad. We wanted to go out on it when we saw it tied up yesterday. It was on the second dock."

She pursed her bright red lips. "Sir, you must be mistaken. Our boat was taken away the middle of last week. The note here says we were supposed to have it back by Sunday, but there was an unforeseen problem with the motor, and they needed a couple more days."

"Really?" Luke frowned. "That's strange. Would anyone else have brought another glass bottom boat to any of your docks? Maybe from another company or something? I'm sure we spotted one." He shrugged. "Not a big deal, but now I'm curious."

The receptionist shifted in her swivel chair, causing her wrist full of bracelets to jangle. She leaned closer and dropped her voice. "It's possible. Sometimes other local water sports or boating companies try to entice our guests, but they are not officially allowed on our property. If we hear about it, they get into trouble. In saying that, some of the staff will turn a blind eye, if you know what I mean. "

"I see." Could be the reason for the Friday night scuffle. "Out of interest, are there many glass bottom boats nearby?"

"Some of the resorts along this part of the island have one. I don't know how many. Why do you ask, sir? I'm sure ours will be back in a couple of days."

Luke let out a casual laugh. "My girl took an interest, and I wanted to check it out. That's all." He stood to leave. "I guess we'll have to wait until Wednesday, then. Hey, one last thing. If I wanted to rent a speedboat for a few hours instead, do I go straight to the water-sports hut by the main dock?"

She smiled. He hit on a subject she could help him with. "Yes, they will be happy to assist you. Have a great day."

"Thanks. You've been helpful." *And now I know we're not looking at a boat owned by the resort.*

"No problem."

Luke picked up a map of the island on his way past the information booth and marched outside in the direction of the water-sports shack.

The heat hit him when he left the airy lobby and stepped onto the beach. It was a scorcher today. Was Madison suffering somewhere under the harsh sun? Thoughts of her tied up or hidden away were too much for him to process. *Don't go there, dude.*

Happy people surrounded him on the beach, all of them enjoying their relaxing vacation on this beautiful tropical island, without a care in the world. Ugly jealousy rose within. If only he could go back to yesterday—before this nightmare began. Swallowing the self-pity as quickly as possible, Luke hurried to the shack and focused on his mission. He had to find Madison, apologize for thinking she would stand him up, and explore the possibilities of a future together. Would Mexico be an option? Was she even that interested in him? Focus. First things first—he had find her. Fast.

A grinning face popped up from behind the water-sports counter.

"Hey, mon, what can I do for you today?"

The young guy had served Luke several times already the past weekend with snorkeling gear and the inflatable ring and was always more than helpful. His entire body moved rhythmically to the music blaring from his earbuds.

"Um, I was wondering if I could rent a speedboat." He pointed to the main dock. "Looks like you have a couple available."

The sports guy pulled one earbud loose. "Depends what you mean, mon. You want me to take you out for a cruise? We can do thirty minutes or an hour if you like."

Luke shook his head. "I want to take one out on my own. Can we work something out?"

"Sorry, mon. We can't do that for you. We can give you a private cruise, but we have to drive the boat ourselves. Insurance and everything. You understand?"

Luke's shoulders slumped. He hadn't anticipated an issue with the boat. "Are you sure? I've got tons of boating experience, and I can leave you with my credit card or whatever. It's important."

"I understand, but those are the rules for the resort. I'd get into major trouble, and I need this job."

Luke tapped his shorts pocket. He had some cash in his wallet, but bribing? No, that wasn't right. *God, what do I do here?*

The attendant leaned across the counter and looked straight into Luke's eyes. "Listen, mon. I'm not supposed to tell you this, but I know you are cool in the water. And I want to help you out here."

"Yes?" Luke tore off his shades and held his breath.

"My cousin, Jamal, he has a boat place five minutes from here. He will let you use one of his boats and he'll give you a fair price."

"Yeah? Do you think Jamal would let me use it for a few hours if necessary? I'm not sure how long I'm going to need it for. I'm good for it—I promise you. It's kind of urgent."

"He'll charge you more but he'll be cool with several hours. What's up, mon? You in some kind of trouble?"

"No, not me. I need to check on a friend. But I would appreciate your help here for sure. Could you write down the address of your cousin? I can get a cab right away."

"No problem. I'll phone and tell him to treat you well, okay?"

"Thanks so much." Luke exchanged a few dollar bills for a scribbled address from his new friend. The lead on a boat was worth every cent.

"Anytime, mon, anytime."

The guy removed the remaining earbud and picked up a cell phone to call his cousin. Luke looked down at the black iPod on the desk, and a thought hit him. The iPod. Surely Madison took hers on her run this morning? She was using it on Saturday when they collided in the lobby, because she was intently programming it instead of watching where she was walking. Could she have dropped it at some point during the kidnapping? It was worth checking into for sure. *Thanks, Lord.*

"Hey, excuse me. I don't mean to be a pain, but do I need to call a taxi from the lobby?"

"I can phone ahead for you and have one waiting at the entrance in five minutes. You want me to do that for you, mon?" He wrinkled his forehead.

Luke hesitated. Would five minutes give him time to check out the iPod situation? "Umm, sure. I have to check on something real quick, and then I'll run to the resort gate, okay?"

"No problem. You got five minutes."

"Thanks again." Luke waved and jogged across the section of beach.

He tucked the address in his pocket, raced back into the cool lobby, and found an available receptionist—the same young lady as before.

"Sir?"

"I'm sorry. It's me again." He gasped between breaths and collapsed onto the stool.

"Did you get your boat tour arranged?" Her warm smile and raised brow were bordering on flirty. No, thank you. Game face on.

"It's in process. But I have another quick question."

"Fire away." She huffed and picked up her pen in anticipation.

"Do you have a lost-and-found area anywhere? You know, for when people leave things on the beach, that sort of thing."

"Yes, we find all kinds of treasure, sir. What are you looking for?"

"An iPod."

"What color?" She tilted her head.

"Umm, I don't know."

"You don't know, sir? Is it yours?"

"No, it's my friend's. She may have lost it this morning on the beach. Do you need to know the color?" He glanced at his watch.

"Believe it or not, we have several iPods handed in. Most are collected, but some are never claimed. I can check to see if any came in already today if you like?"

"Yes. Yes, that would be fantastic. I'll quickly phone my friend and check the color."

The receptionist disappeared into a back office, and Luke dialed Nathan's phone.

"Luke?"

"Hey, yeah. Listen. Can you ask Chloe what color Madison's iPod is?"

"Her iPod? Sure, she's right here." He handed the phone over.

"Hi, Luke." Chloe's small voice came onto the line. "We're in her room right now. Did you find her iPod? It's silver."

"I don't know yet. I'm in the lobby getting them to check in case one was handed in today. I didn't think of it earlier, but she could have dropped it on the beach, right?"

"Of course, she always runs with it at home. Although with something like that, anyone may have found it and kept it for themselves. I think she listens to worship music and podcast sermons, so they'd be in for a possible conversion."

Luke grinned at the thought of Madison and her worship songs. Perhaps he could give Chloe something encouraging to listen to, to make her feel close to her sister and even to God. "Wait a moment. She has a couple to choose from here."

He nodded at the receptionist, and she placed four iPods with attached earbuds on the desk in front of her.

"Sir, we have two black, one pink, and one silver."

"Okay, great. One moment, please." He walked a few paces so he couldn't be overheard and then whispered into his phone. "Chloe, there's one silver iPod here. Are you able to come down and claim it? They might ask you what's on there or something to prove it's yours."

"Really? It could be Madi's? I'll come right down. We're finished in her room, and Nathan was about to head back up to ours to cover the phone. What made you think of looking for her iPod?"

"I don't know. For some reason, it seemed important at the time, but I know it's not going to help us find Madison. Maybe it'll help you feel closer to her."

Chloe sniffed. "Thanks. That's sweet. I think you're right. By the way, I found her journal. I'll let you know later if there's anything you need to know. Here's Nathan."

"Luke, did you find out about the glass bottom boat?"

"Did I ever. I'll explain everything later. Just so you know, the resort couldn't help me with renting a speedboat, but it's okay because I'm on my way to a guy's cousin's place."

Nathan groaned. "This does not sound cool. Please be careful, bro. "

"Always. I'll call you soon. Okay?"

"Sounds good. Bye."

Luke rushed back to the patient receptionist. "I'm so sorry to keep you waiting. My friend Chloe thinks the silver one could be the one she's looking for, so she's coming down right now because I have to catch a taxi. Is that okay?"

"No problem." She settled back onto her stool.

"I was hoping you would say that." He waved and sprinted away to the main entrance.

So far, so good, God. Would You pave the way for a speedboat and lead me where I need to go next? And please, please give Madison a sense of hope in all this.

CHAPTER SEVENTEEN

LUKE PULLED OUT HIS PHONE, and Nathan answered on the first ring.

"Hey, it's Luke. Sorry I couldn't explain things before, but I'm in a taxi right now." He gripped the car door handle as his driver sped with too much gusto around winding coastal roads.

"No worries. What's the latest with the boat?"

Luke tried to focus on the call as glimpses of ocean and palm trees whizzed by. "Yeah. The glass bottom boat we saw did *not* belong to the resort."

"No kidding? Makes sense, I guess. They told us that much when we arrived. So, Sam or whoever must have taken a chance and used their own."

"Looks that way, although how on earth did they get their filthy hands on one? They were lucky nobody found them out. Unless they paid one of the resort staff to keep quiet." He caught the eye of the driver in the rearview mirror. Had he overheard the conversation above the island music on the radio? Didn't bat an eyelid, so hopefully not. Luke's mouth went dry. Was he getting in over his head?

"Luke? You still there?"

The driver slowed and pulled to the side of the road in front of a boat-rental place. This was the destination.

"Yeah, can you hold on a sec? I think we've arrived." He leaned over and slapped some notes in the driver's open hand. "Thanks, man."

"No problem." The driver waited for Luke to climb from the taxi and tore away.

Luke exhaled and took in his new surroundings. "Sorry about that. I'm here now, and it looks like there are plenty of boats ready to be taken out. Let's hope this goes smoothly." Luke talked as he walked toward the jetty. Several boats were moored there, and a teenage boy manned a small kiosk. "I'm about to rent one from some guy called Jamal. He's a cousin of a friend at the water-sports desk."

"Is this safe? Sounds ominous."

"This was my best option. The resort wouldn't let me take a boat out by myself, so here I am. I think it's going to work out. Listen. The receptionist in the lobby told me there are a few other glass bottom boats nearby. Did you manage to pull anything from the internet?"

"Yeah, I have a list of the legit ones along the east coast of the island. If you need me to go any farther, let me know."

He pulled a map from his back pocket. "Okay, I've got a detailed map here, so my plan is to cruise along the beaches and match the boats I spot with the ones you have on the list. I'll call back and copy down the names once I'm in the boat. I think it's the best and quickest way until we find a rogue glass bottom boat with no official home. I'm expecting their boat to be tucked away somewhere rather than tied up at another resort, but who knows what their scam is."

Nathan let out a sigh. "Yeah, they've had months to plan this in detail, and we're going into it blind."

"We have faith, bro."

"You do, at least."

"You bet I do. It's going to be a long evening, but at least we're doing something to try to find Madison. If you have any other thoughts, let me know, but in the meantime I'm hot on their trail. At least, I hope I am." *Please let me know if I'm off base here, God. I don't have time to waste.*

"Thanks for doing this. I'm dying to get out there and do something practical myself, but poor Chloe's a mess here, and I can't leave her."

"Your wife needs you. I'll call you back in five for that list."

"Sounds good."

He strode up to the kiosk. *A reliable boat would be awesome, Lord.*

"Hi, you must be the American my uncle phoned about." The lanky teenage boy stuck out his hand, and Luke shook it. Jamaica was one friendly country.

"Yes, I'm Luke. You must be Jamal. But I thought he was your cousin."

"No, my father, Jamal, is his cousin, so I call him uncle. My father isn't here right now, but I can help you out. No problem." The boy came out from behind the kiosk and walked down the jetty with an air of authority.

"How long do you need the boat for?"

"That's the thing." Luke bit his lip. "I'm not sure. What are the rules?"

"You pay by the hour, mon. We know you're staying at the resort, so it's all cool. But if it gets dark, you're not supposed to be out there—you know what I'm saying?"

"I get it. I'll try my best to have it back by then, but I can't guarantee. I'm already starting off later than I'd hoped. I promise to get it back to you eventually, and I'll pay the hourly rate."

"Okay, then, let's get the paperwork figured out. I'll explain to my father when he arrives. He'll be cool."

"You sure?"

"Yeah, mon. It's Jamaica."

Luke laughed. "Of course."

After signing his life away along with a hefty deposit on his credit card, Luke was ready to go. He hurried to his allocated boat and performed all the necessary safety checks. At least this boat was a basic model with little to go wrong, and his extensive boating experience would serve him well. He checked the gauge—a full tank of gas would see him into the night. Plus, there was a jerrican with extra fuel, if needed. Water bottles, a couple of towels, and binoculars were stowed in a cubby. It all looked good.

He settled into the captain's chair and pulled out the map along with the pen and notepaper. A quick call to Nathan provided him with a list of authentic boat places. He sat back and groaned.

Okay, Lord, this is it. He surveyed the map. It was daunting. He closed his eyes. *I'm feeling overwhelmed and out of my depth on so many levels. Would You watch over Nathan and Chloe back at the resort? And for Madison...* She was in some strange place, afraid, alone. His stomach knotted. *She has to be safe, Lord. Protect her, please. Please...*

He took a deep breath and opened his eyes. Which way to go? It was anyone's guess, so he followed his gut. East looked less populated and commercial on the map. Sam would most likely take her somewhere secluded. He shuddered at that repulsive thought and started the boat. Head east.

The sun was less intense, and the wind whipped through Luke's hair as he coursed through the ocean. The beauty of this place wasn't lost on him, even during his rescue mission. Neither was his vulnerability on the vast ocean.

His confidence on the water was one thing, but what would happen once he located the first glass bottom boat? That part would take a lot of faith. Which meant his plan would be to play it by ear and exercise caution wherever necessary. If a vessel was being used and full of passengers, everything was operation normal and he could strike it from the list. But what if he saw a vacant boat moored? It would be awkward to make inquiries without sounding like an alarmist. Or having those boat owners call the police. *I can't risk alerting the authorities when Madison's well-being is in jeopardy.*

Luke settled into driving, and within thirty minutes, he spotted two glass bottom boats. Logos on the side of each vessel showed they belonged to the resorts along the coast, and they were in use, so he slowed down to cross their names off his list but didn't bother stopping. Two down, twenty to go...and five hours of daylight left, if he was lucky. This was going to be tedious and potentially unfruitful. Prayer. It was all he had right now. He would use his wits and implore God to keep Madison safe, believing he would find her. As long as he wasn't too late.

He sped along the coast, hunting for his proverbial needle in the haystack. There was the possibility the boat might not have been used at all, of course. Or it could have been a getaway vehicle for a short distance, and Madison could be held up in the mountains somewhere by now. Surely not. *My gut tells me the boat is key. And my heart tells me I won't stop looking for Madison until I find her. What does that mean for my future? No, I can't think further than the present.* It was shaping up to be a long night.

Most of the glass bottom boats like the one he was looking for had light-colored canopies, which made them easy to spot, and were labeled with resort logos. The next couple of resort areas didn't have any moored or out in the ocean nearby, so Luke pressed on. He rotated his shoulders and tipped his head from side to side. Keeping his eyes peeled for the boat and watching out for other ocean traffic were taking their toll. Catamarans, canoes, paddleboats, and the occasional sailboat dotted the turquoise water and kept him on his toes. Maybe Nathan's help would have been a good idea. But no, Chloe needed him this evening. Luke blew out a steady breath. Chloe must be beside herself with worry. She was counting on Luke to find her sister. He couldn't let her down.

An unexpected tear meandered down Luke's cheek. *Where did that come from?* He wasn't a crier, but the responsibility he carried tonight was getting to him. How could a woman he met three days ago have such a profound impact on his emotions? He brushed the tear away. Madison had already endured more than her fair share of tragedy and trials. How was she holding up this evening? *God, keep her safe.*

As he trawled past the next resort, Luke's heart quickened. Sure enough, a glass bottom boat was attached to a long dock, and it looked empty. This one had no logo and wasn't on their list, so it needed to be checked out. He slowed down and pulled into the next dock over. He waved at a couple of guys in red shorts who looked like they were in charge.

"I'm only going to be five minutes." He waved at Red Shorts. "Can I leave it here?"

"No problem, mon." It was the answer Luke had come to expect in Jamaica.

"Thanks."

He strolled along the shore and looked around for any signs of either Madison, suspicious-looking guys, or police. Should he ask Red Shorts about the boat or go and take a look for himself? He took a deep breath and decided on the latter.

A few people dotted the wide dock. A couple of shrieking children jumped off and dive-bombed into the ocean. Luke smiled. Just like his kids back at the orphanage. They would love it here. An older gentleman lay in a hammock, reading a book, and a besotted couple strolled hand in hand. The girl giggled when they passed by. She sounded similar to Madison. Luke bit his lip.

The boat was deserted. Nobody appeared to be in charge, and no customers waited for a cruise. Strange. He looked around and jumped on board. It was well maintained and could probably seat thirty passengers.

"Hey, mon, what's up?" Red Shorts appeared on the dock and pointed at Luke. "You want to go out or something?"

Luke remembered to breathe. "Um, maybe. I was wondering why it was so empty. No cruises today?" He jumped back off the boat and landed next to the guy.

"Yeah, they came back a few minutes ago. I'm not sure if they'll be taking it out again today—depends if there's the demand. It's getting late to set out."

Luke glanced out at the setting sun and sighed. "So, it's been busy all day, has it?"

Red Shorts shrugged. "On and off."

"Do you stop at any of the other resorts?"

"No. Most have their own boats, or they tell their guests to come here by taxi. You have a lot of questions. You want to go out on the next run or not?" He crossed his arms over his chest and glared at Luke.

"Whoa, I was curious. That's all." He held his hands up in surrender.

"You on your own, mon?"

Before Luke could answer, an even bigger pair of red shorts sauntered up the dock, and the burly guy stood right in Luke's face.

"We got a problem?" The newcomer's voice had an unbelievably low pitch.

"No, sir. No problem at all." The hairs on the back of Luke's neck stood to attention. "I was asking about the cruises on this boat."

"American?" He planted his massive hands on his hips.

Not keen on Americans, eh? "That's right. Although I live in Mexico. I'm a missionary there."

Both locals grinned, and the smaller of the two nodded. "Cool. We like missionaries. The thing is, we've had some trouble concerning this boat."

Luke's brows shot up along with his pulse. "With Americans?"

"Yeah, mon. A couple of meatheads wanted to use it and got uptight when we said no." He started laughing. "Like we can let anyone come and rent this baby. It belongs to the resort, for goodness' sake. They were crazy."

Bingo.

The big guy turned and wandered back to the beach, his bulging biceps quivering with every step. Luke needed to know details. *Do not appear desperate.* He leaned against a pole and brushed invisible lint from his shirt.

"These Americans, did they say why they wanted to use this awesome boat? Seems kind of strange."

"They were strange, all right. Arrogant, pushy, and I don't think they ever drove one like this before. That's the last we'll see of them, I can tell you. My brother wasn't friendly toward them. He got bad vibes, and that always sets him off."

"Oh dear." Luke watched the massive man move across the beach, grateful he hadn't set him off. "Was there a fight?"

"Almost. They left pretty quick and we never saw them again."

"When was this?"

Red Shorts slid his shades from his face. "Why are you asking all these questions, mon? You know these Americans? Do I need to get my brother back over here?"

Luke started backing away. "No, I don't know them at all. I'm only interested in the glass bottom boat. I guess I'll come back another day. You have yourself a great evening. Thank you."

Luke marched back to the beach and grabbed a sandwich on his way past a café hut. At least he could make his pit stop look intentional. Plus, his stomach demanded fuel. Before heading back on his own boat, he took the phone from his pocket and prayed for a good signal.

"Luke." Nathan's voice was tense. "We haven't heard from you in a while. How's it going?"

"Slow. Although, I'm certain our guys were trying to rent a glass bottom boat from the resort I'm at right now. The gentlemen here were none too impressed with them."

"No way. Did you find anything out?"

"Not really. I couldn't dig too much without looking suspicious. They were touchy about the whole thing. I don't think they're too fond of Americans in general anymore. I'm guessing if it was them, our Blue Eyes is lacking in social graces."

"I can vouch for that."

"How's Chloe holding up?"

"She's cried so much, I'm trying to keep her hydrated. But I managed to get the banking sorted out and can withdraw the cash tomorrow if we need it."

"Awesome." At least that base was covered. "How did you manage in a foreign country? I imagined a whole bunch of red tape."

"They were super helpful at the local bank. Plus, they get a decent bonus in the form of additional bank charges. It'll be there in the morning for us to collect."

Luke whistled. How would they go about picking it up? Would they need a suitcase? It was like something out of a movie. He was glad for Nathan's bodyguard physique. "Let's hope it doesn't come to that. I'm heading back to my boat, but you'll be the first to know if I find anything. Look after your new wife, okay? Make sure she eats something, too."

The jerk-chicken sandwich smelled amazing. He took a huge bite and chewed. Eating seemed wrong at a time like this, but he had to keep his strength up, too.

"Yeah, I'll try. And, Luke, thanks for going out of your way on all this. I don't want to put you in any danger."

Luke swallowed his mouthful. "It's my choice. I can't bear the thought of Madison being with those guys, and I want to show her not all men are going to let her down. It's not going to be easy, but she has to learn to trust again. I want to be there for her. Know what I mean?"

"Hey, wait—you're smitten, aren't you?"

"What?"

"My single brother is definitely smitten. Tell me I'm not right."

Several seconds of silence filled the air.

Luke gulped. "Maybe."

"Don't do anything foolish, missionary man."

"I've got God on my side. I'll be fine."

CHAPTER EIGHTEEN

MADISON'S EYES FLEW OPEN. WAS it a sound from outside? Had God woken her? She took in her surroundings and forced herself to breathe. The hut. She was still in the wretched hut. She raised herself up onto one elbow on the scratchy blanket and rubbed her sore head. It was early evening, judging by the light. How long had she been asleep? Her heart plummeted with the harsh reality of her predicament.

Everything was eerily quiet as she lay alone in her little prison, but at least the intense afternoon heat was less stifling now. Thanks to her aching head and frazzled nerves, exhaustion had claimed the past couple of hours. Now her stomach grumbled.

"What I wouldn't do for a glass of water and a chocolate bar." She usually ate breakfast *after* her morning run, so the last morsel of food she remembered was the divine chocolate cake last night. Not that her stomach could handle much at the moment. Her insides churned, but food would help clear her mind and keep her strong. Right now, however, water was a priority. Perhaps there would be a little swig left in the bottle from earlier.

She stretched out the kinks in her body, then pulled herself up and plodded over to the table. Yes, a mouthful of water beckoned her from the bottle. She drained the last drop and then inched toward the window, half expecting to see Blue Eyes's leer. The sun was starting its descent, casting a dreamy pink glow over the stretch of beach outside. If her situation weren't so dire, the moment would be breathtaking.

The truth hit her afresh—strangers kidnapped her, held her hostage in an unknown location, and the outcome was anyone's guess. Goose bumps rose in spite of the sticky heat, and she rubbed her arms. Her life could be over in a matter of hours, for all she knew. Her faith might be solid and her eternal destination secured, but that didn't make the present any less petrifying. *I'm not ready to die, not when it feels like I've started to live again.* Baby steps in fighting her fear of water—and opening her heart to Luke.

She squeezed the empty water bottle to her chest. What would life be like with someone like Luke? It was a harmless daydream with his intentions to stay single, right? She closed her eyes and allowed herself the indulgence.

"Luke and I would have a whirlwind romance, marry, and travel around the world to experience different cultures. He would show me all the places he worked as a missionary, and I would take him to Spain. We would settle down in Mexico and serve together at the orphanage before starting a family of our own. Nathan and Chloe would visit, and life would be perfect. He would love me unconditionally, I would trust him always, and every day would be a blessing." *Except he wants to stay single.*

Madison crushed the water bottle and dropped it to the floor. *In my dreams.*

Lord, will I ever be able to trust a man again? Everyone I love seems to leave me one way or another, except You. Even Chloe has a new life now, and while I'm glad for her, what about me? Is this how my life ends? In a kidnapping because of someone else's greed? How could she rely on the word of a blue-eyed monster?

She wiped her wet cheeks and opened her eyes. Through the window, she saw the other hut, but not a soul was in sight.

Maybe there's an outhouse?

Using a bathroom became an immediate necessity, and Madison stared at the closed door. If her creepy captor was out there, she would insist on finding some privacy, and if he wasn't around, maybe she could make a run for it instead.

Madison squared her shoulders and marched the three steps it took to reach the door. She twisted the metal knob. It was still locked from the outside. More tears pooled in her eyes while she rattled the doorknob.

The chances of anyone other than her captors hearing her were remote, but logic evaporated as panic set in. What if a local wandered along the beach or boaters pulled ashore? Someone might hear her and she had nothing to lose.

"Help!" Her throat was drier than she thought.

Nothing.

"Help!" She pounded her fists against the wooden door. She was about to take her aggression out on the window next when the key turned and the door flung open, pushing her deeper inside.

"Well, well, Sleeping Beauty is awake." Blue Eyes wore an amused grin. "Calm down, princess." He inspected the doorknob and followed her steps. "Looks like you've broken the lock. Feisty one, aren't you?"

Good. That could be my ticket out of here. Madison backed away until she was pinned against the wall.

"How long do you intend to hold me prisoner here?" She jutted her chin.

He shrugged. "Depends on your little sister. If all goes according to plan, you might be back at your posh resort in a day or so. But if she decides to get clever and involve the cops, we might have to keep you indefinitely. We could get to know each other better, Miss Grey. How would that be?"

"You have a high opinion of yourself, don't you?"

Blue Eyes laughed and flexed his huge biceps. "Who wouldn't want to get to know me better?"

Madison set her hands on her hips. " If you think I'm staying here all night, I'm going to need a bathroom. Now. Plus some more water. And some food." *Where was this courage coming from?*

"Hmm. Let me check with the boss. Hang tough. And don't go anywhere. We're watching your every move." He smirked and turned on his heel.

When the bulky guy disappeared outside, Madison breathed a sigh of relief. He was unpredictable and gave her the creeps, big time. She watched him through the window as he paced over to the beach hut to the left as she faced the ocean. She craned her neck and also spotted a red jeep parked close by, meaning the other hut must be their little headquarters. Interesting. There had to be keys.

Blue Eyes kept one eye on her door. An escape attempt would be futile.

Who is his boss? And how does he know Chloe and me?

Madison racked her brain, trying to come up with anyone who might go to this much trouble for money. Maybe someone their father had sour business dealings with? Or it could be anyone who followed the local news and liked the look of the Grey sisters and their financial gain. They probably appeared vulnerable and an easy target, and these days, the internet was able to spew out any information required. How much of a ransom had they asked for, and was it even feasible? Madison gulped. Chloe had to make some tough decisions, and Nathan and Luke were going to have to help her through this horrendous ordeal. Poor Chloe.

Blue Eyes turned from the entrance of the other hut and stalked back to hers. She held her breath and waited for the verdict. He swung the door open and poked his head inside.

"Okay, beautiful, you get a potty break, but make it quick. And don't even think of trying any funny business—you hear me?" He lifted his hand and she flinched. The earlier slap still stung her cheek and her pride.

Madison nodded and followed him outside. The ocean opened up wide before her as she stepped onto soft sand. She breathed the salty, warm air in through her nose and relished being outdoors. Even in the evening light, her eyes were sensitive after being in the dim hut for hours, and she squinted while glancing around for any clues as to her whereabouts. Not that she knew one beach from another in Jamaica, but there had to be a landmark of some sort—a road, another hut. Something.

"This way." He grabbed her upper arm and led her to the left of her hut.

Think, Madison. Think. Look around.

Only palm trees, beach, ocean, and now that she was outside, she spotted the awful glass bottom boat attached to a rickety dock. A chill grew up her spine. They hurried past the other shack, where "the boss" was residing, and arrived at a tiny outhouse. It was uninviting, to say the least.

"This is it?" She wrinkled her nose.

"You're being held for ransom, princess. Did you expect The Ritz? You got two minutes. I'll be right outside."

"Seriously?"

Madison plugged her nose and was in and out of the sorry excuse of a bathroom in seconds. Blue Eyes surprised her by thrusting a wet-wipe package into her hands. Must have had it stashed in his pocket. These brutes were concerned about hygiene? Fascinating. He grabbed her arm again and tugged her in the direction of her prison. He was strong. What if his boss was even more of a bully? Strange he hadn't shown his face yet. For the life of her, she couldn't recall much about him from her initial kidnapping. He had attempted to disguise himself with the hoodie and shades. Perhaps he was a local and couldn't risk being recognized.

She glanced at the boss's hut on their way past, but the door was shut, and the glass on the window was filthy. No clues there. The red jeep had no roof, and Madison's mind raced. She could run for it, jump in over the door, and be out of here in the perfect getaway vehicle. Blue Eyes could eat her sand. She peered closer to check for keys in the ignition, but Blue Eyes caught her gaze.

"Don't even think about it." He patted his shorts pocket. "That's my baby, and I keep the keys. How stupid do you think I am?"

Madison bit her tongue. So many answers came to mind.

Her steps slowed at the thought of being locked up again with nothing but stale air and cramped conditions.

"Can't I stay outside for a while?" She looked straight into those icy eyes and forced herself not to cower. "I can't exactly go anywhere without you seeing, and it's so stuffy in there."

171

He laughed in her face. "In your dreams. What makes you think I care about your comfort? I don't trust you for a minute after your little stunt on the phone. And don't worry. I'll be watching your door all night long now that your lock is useless."

Thanks for the reminder, goon. Madison's shoulders slumped when he steered her toward her door and pushed her through.

"Looks like the boss brought you some goodies. Only the best for you, eh? In you go. I'm watching, so don't get any wild ideas. Sleep tight."

Madison stared at the plate on the wooden table and didn't even turn around when Blue Eyes slammed the door behind him.

"What's all this? How strange. First the wet wipes and now a china plate?"

On a white china plate sat a pink cloth napkin, and on top of the napkin were two plump muffins.

Madison picked up a water bottle, grateful to see there were two more for later. So, they didn't intend for her to die of thirst or hunger. She drank deeply, hoping to clear her mind before looking back at the plate. No, she wasn't hallucinating. The muffins were still there.

No, wait. They couldn't be, could they? Her stomach recoiled and her hand shook when she lifted one of the muffins to her mouth. She sniffed and then took a bite. What on earth? Pumpkin and chocolate chip—her favorite.

One person other than her sister was aware of her obsession with pumpkin-chocolate-chip muffins.

"Sam?"

Madison's fingers trembled, and she dropped the muffin onto the plate.

That would explain the wet wipe. But why would he kidnap her? Surely he wasn't still after the money. Had it remained his obsession? How had his bitterness grown to this? Was his pride so damaged when the truth came out? Madison went out of her way to keep details of his planned fraud top secret, hoping he would be grateful, learn his lesson, and disappear. Only a select few individuals knew about his scheme to take her inheritance and run with it after they were married. Why hadn't she reported him?

She gasped. Of course, it was Sam she saw in the glass bottom boat the night before the wedding. There had been something familiar about his shadow even in that split second. That's why she turned back to take another look. She felt his presence in some strange way yet pushed it from the recesses of her mind in an attempt to protect her heart.

Madison slumped onto the hard chair and tried to steady her shaking hands. Her empty finger reminded her of the diamond solitaire engagement ring she wore a year ago.

Why couldn't her mom and dad be alive? They would have seen through his charm and deception in no time, and her father would have made sure Sam Kinkaid would never be in their lives again. Had she been naive to expect him to disappear without a trace? Yes, it appeared she was. Naive in every way. That much was obvious now.

"Daddy, you would have known he couldn't be trusted, wouldn't you?" Even as she spoke the words, she realized Sam worked for her father's company for a number of years and never was suspected of anything other than loyalty and dedication. No, he was a master fraud and had fooled everyone. "How can I ever rely on my own judgment again?"

Tears trickled down her face and splashed onto the ugly table. Sam was sitting yards away from her right now on this beach in the other hut. Laughing, no doubt. He was manipulating Chloe, robbing them of their inheritance, ruining the honeymoon, and shattering Madison's nerves for good.

She needed a plan. There was no way she would allow that lowlife to crush her twice. She wanted to smash the window and hurl the muffins into the sand but thought better of it. Sustenance was necessary and she needed to keep her cool. Sam must know by now that she had figured out his identity. No way was she going to cave to his power trip.

Madison the Nervous and Fearful stepped aside for Madison the Organized Planner. Praying the muffins weren't drugged or poisoned, she nibbled on one until it was gone and then washed it down with a swig of water. She hated how delicious it was. Yet sugar would give her the energy she needed and clarity of mind. Chew. Swallow.

Leaning her cheek against the window frame, she soaked in the final seconds of the most glorious sunset deepening over the ocean. She sighed. Her heavenly Father created every sunset and was ultimately in control—she knew it.

Give me wisdom and strength, God. Help me get out of here.

Madison finished the second muffin and drained another bottle of water while the evening grew darker. An escape plan percolated in her mind—she wasn't about to wait around to see what Sam and Blue Eyes would do if something went wrong with the money pickup. *I have to at least try.* What were the chances of them staying awake and watching her door all night long? She had detected beer on Blue Eyes's breath earlier and Sam was not a night owl. He needed his beauty sleep. They were bound to fall asleep at some point, and that would be the perfect opportunity to put her running training into action. It was worth taking the risk.

This could be life or death. I have to push my fears aside tonight...or die trying.

CHAPTER NINETEEN

THE TANGERINE SUN TOUCHED THE horizon and Luke's shoulders slumped.

Lord, I could do with some major assistance here. Nine glass bottom boats so far, and all of them in use and authentic. What do I do next?

He glanced down at the list of boats from Nathan and compared it to the map on the seat beside him. There were eleven still to check out.

He massaged the crook in his neck. "This is useless."

Most beaches were empty, and lights twinkled as guests sat down for their evening meals in oceanfront restaurants. Luke's energy and optimism were fading as fast as the remaining light. He reached over and checked the compartment next to the steering wheel. Yes, a flashlight. He would be needing that for sure.

Where on earth could Madison be? Was he wasting time cruising along the shoreline? The next beach came into sight. There didn't appear to be a resort here—just a few restaurants, private homes, and several boats anchored. A quick break sounded like a good idea, and it wouldn't hurt to check with any locals.

Luke pulled in, lassoed the boat's rope to the bollard on the dock, and secured it. He sank back onto the uncomfortable hard plastic seat and bowed his head.

"Lord, give me faith and patience and a whole bunch of energy. A guardian angel would be perfect, too."

Grateful for the stash of water bottles in his boat, he grabbed one and cut the engine. This day was proving to be emotionally and physically grueling, and it was far from over. Good thing he'd slept in this morning. No, scrap that—if he hadn't slept in, perhaps Madison wouldn't have been kidnapped and they wouldn't be in this nightmare. He twisted the bottle lid and took a swig. Did Madison have water wherever she was? He took another gulp. He would need a surge of energy when he found her. If he found her.

"Ahoy there."

Luke looked up and noticed a boat tied to the other side of the dock farther down. An older gentleman in a Yankees baseball cap waved to him...from a glass bottom boat. His heart skipped a beat. How had he missed that when he pulled in?

Waving back, Luke stood and picked up another water bottle to share before leaping onto the dock for a closer look.

No, this boat was not a contender. No way. He forced himself to keep his smile steady. He noted the logo to strike from his list. The ancient vessel was out of action for the foreseeable future. It was run down and in desperate need of a coat of paint. On deck, the shirtless man scrubbed at the bench seats.

"Hi there." Luke leaned against a wooden post on the dock. "Beautiful evening."

"Sure is. You American?"

"I am." Luke sipped the last of his water. "Seattle originally. I'm a missionary in Mexico now. I'm guessing you're New York?"

The man laughed. "The name's Joe. Been living here twenty years and still can't get rid of the accent."

"Luke Alexander. Pleased to meet you." Luke offered the water bottle. Joe caught it in his tanned, weathered hands and grinned. One gold tooth gleamed in the fading sunlight. It was like meeting a real-life cartoon character.

Joe twisted open the lid. "A missionary, you say? That's fantastic. I'm a churchgoing man myself. Got quite the lively little church in this village."

Another believer? Grateful for the momentary distraction, Luke collapsed onto the wooden dock and dangled his feet in the refreshing water. Heavenly. A two-minute break was just what he needed. "Awesome. What brought you to Jamaica to live? It's a big step."

"Fell in love with the place when I first visited years ago. The people, the natural beauty, the laid-back lifestyle—what's not to love? I owned a boat shop for years back in the US and decided to sell up and live out my days in a place where sunshine is like air. You on vacation?"

Luke felt a nudge in his spirit to share more than water with this man. "My brother's wedding. Listen. This is going to sound kind of strange, but I'm looking for a different glass bottom boat. It's a long story, but it's urgent. We're staying up at the Royal House Resort, and we believe the boat's been moored there for several days, but now it's disappeared. I have to find it and feel like I'm on a wild-goose chase. I don't suppose you've seen an unfamiliar vessel around here?"

178

Joe stroked his bristly beard. "I have a feeling I don't want to know why you're chasing a glass bottom boat, but I think I might know who it is you're looking for."

"Really?" Skin prickled on Luke's arms. "Tell me anything you think of. Any detail at all may be imperative."

Joe lunged from the old boat and perched on the dock alongside Luke. He wore the same cheap aftershave as Luke's dad. The familiarity was comforting.

"A couple of Americans were here a few weeks back asking about my boat. They wanted to fix it up and rent it for a week or two."

Luke sat up straight. "Go on."

"I explained it would take quite a lot of fixing. She's been out of action for a while and needed a sabbatical. They offered a lot of cash, and tempting as it was, this is my baby, you know? I enjoy working on her and puttering around. It's more a labor of love. I'm in no hurry. She goes with nobody else but me."

"Did they say where they would be taking it?" He held his breath.

Joe gulped back a drink of water and gazed across the darkening ocean.

"Hmm. Not that I remember. They were pushy. Made me real uncomfortable." He shuddered.

"Uncomfortable how, if you don't mind me asking?" Luke sat on his hands. Joe was taking his own sweet time compiling his recollections. Patience. Any hints could be vital at this point.

"It seems to me like there was one with the brains and one with the brawn, if you get my drift. Brains was a real charmer, although he was none too pleased when I turned him down.

There was something strange about Brawn, though." The elderly man removed his baseball cap and scratched his balding head. "That's it—his eyes. He took off those real dark sunglasses and he had the most menacing eyes I ever saw in my life. Gave me the willies, it did."

Luke nodded. "Icy blue kind of thing happening?"

"Yeah, icy, all right. I got the chills looking at him." He squeezed his water bottle.

"I've heard about those eyes. These are the men I'm looking for. Are you sure they didn't give you any hint as to where they would be staying or mooring the boat?"

"No, I'm sorry. Wish I could be more helpful."

Luke dragged his fingers through his hair. Really? Another dead end?

Joe slid his baseball cap back on and swigged more water. "But I guess they found their boat after all."

Luke's breath caught in his throat. "Why do you say that?"

"I recognized them sailing past here this morning."

"What?" Luke jumped up to his feet. "Do you remember what time?"

"I would say early." He squinted. "Maybe between eight and eight thirty, after my breakfast. I always treat myself to eggs and bacon on a Monday morning. Always have, always will. Afterwards, I came down here to work on this beauty, and there they were, sailing right past. I know every single glass bottom boat on this side of the island, and every owner, too. I have my binoculars right here, so I checked them out. These two bozos stood out like a sore thumb. They're not your typical locals, if you know what I mean."

Luke punched the air with his fist. *Thank You, God.* "Finally, something. I'm on the right track. You have been more than helpful. I guess they were heading east, then?"

"Sure were." He pointed to his right. "Thataway."

Luke shook his head. "This is amazing." But he needed as much information as possible. "Did you notice anyone else on the boat by any chance? A girl maybe?"

Joe waggled his eyebrows. "It's always about the girl, isn't it, young man?"

Luke shifted from one foot to the other. "It's not like that." He bit his lip.

"No, it never is. Sorry. I can't say I noticed a third person aboard. Anyway, I hope you find the boat, son. And your girl."

"Me too. She's not my girl." At least not yet. "But she's a special young lady and I'll go to the ends of the earth to find her." Luke's cheeks flamed as his spirit confirmed how revealing his words were.

"Why do you say she's not your girl?"

Luke cringed. *This guy is not shy, and I don't think he's going to let up.*

"The single life has served me well on the mission field. Helped me to focus on what God wants me to do without distractions."

"Up until now?" Joe's gold tooth flashed as he spoke. "Listen, son. I never thought I would marry. Not the marrying type. Had my faith, my boats, and my golden retriever. What else does a man need?"

Luke shrugged. *I'm starting to think there is something else. Someone else.*

"And then she walked into church one Sunday morning. She was new to town and fresh as a daisy. She turned my head, and then she turned my world upside down."

Luke was in a desperate hurry, but this guy knew how to tell a story. "Did you marry her?"

"Best twenty years a man could ask for. Went on home to glory way too soon, but I wouldn't swap my time as a husband for all the tea in China."

"She passed away? I'm so sorry, Joe. How long ago, if you don't mind me asking?"

"Twenty years, six months, and three days."

"And then you moved out here."

"You have to embrace whatever life throws at you, son. See the blessings as exactly that—blessings. Take them and enjoy them for as long as He sees fit."

Luke held out a hand, and the old man shook it with vigor.

"Find your girl, son." Joe's light gray eyes bored into Luke's.

"I intend to." Was that a solemn vow to find Madison? About his future?

"I'll say a prayer for her, particularly if she's with those guys. I'll be praying for you, too."

"Thanks so much." Luke jogged back to his speedboat. "I have a feeling I'm going to need it."

CHAPTER TWENTY

STARS APPEARED IN THE JET-BLACK sky, and Madison almost squealed when she saw a full moon. Light was essential. On unfamiliar terrain, she would need all the help she could get with navigation. She squinted through the window. During the evening, Blue Eyes came into her line of vision, popping in and out of the other hut. Low voices murmured. Sam. He had yet to show his face. Madison shuddered.

Now Blue Eyes slumped in a deck chair facing her hut. Several empty beer cans at his feet glistened in the moonlight. Maybe he was asleep at last. He hadn't moved in a while.

Madison paced and prayed while she waited to make her escape. What if she failed? There was a huge possibility she would enrage her captors and end up in an even worse predicament. But what else could she do? Sleep wasn't an option. Nobody would stumble across her on this little beach. It was almost pitch black in her hut, but the snorkel equipment mocked her in the corner. Had Sam placed it in here to prove a point? To torment her, knowing she would never have the courage to use it, even in escape?

No way would she flee via the ocean. She had to run. It was her only option. But when? Would her kidnappers presume she was sleeping by now? Blue Eyes called her

Sleeping Beauty. A precious princess. And Sam wouldn't expect her to make such a bold move. He knew her weaknesses all too well. Of course he did.

Her time with Sam was a period of her life she would rather forget. He came into the picture when she was already a fragile wreck, grieving for her beloved mom and dad. She touched the gold signet ring on her finger—a sweet sixteenth birthday gift from her parents. Their death had ended a part of her. Her personality was robbed of its spark, and she faded to a feeble, needy shell of her former vibrant self. It was weird how Sam was so attracted to her, and she often questioned him on why he chose to stay by her side. She should have known it was all too good to be true. Yet he claimed to love her and wanted to walk with her through the grief. He offered the bright future she craved. The scumball.

Madison rubbed her arms as goose bumps appeared with the memories. It was all a lie—the love, the safety, feeling cherished. Why had she not been suspicious of the unexplained absences? Silly girl. She presumed he was planning their wedding, when in reality he was planning his fraud.

Just as well he hadn't shown his face yet today. He must know what she thought of him and the reaction he was sure to get. Her Christian charity would be pushed to the absolute limit. Forgiveness was one of the hardest and most painful processes she experienced in her new faith. It was doable when she didn't have to look at him. She had pictured him scurrying off to the other side of the country like a wounded dog. She'd even pitied him at one point; how desperate must he have been to do such a callous thing? After this fiasco, there would be even more forgiveness to work through.

If I get out of this alive.

Madison closed her eyes and bit her trembling lip. Why the muffins? Why taunt and tease at this stage in the game? Why not keep his identity a secret?

Because he's heartless, cold, and calculating.

Before the betrayal, on Saturday mornings they had enjoyed a sweet little ritual. Madison always baked the pumpkin-chocolate-chip muffins after her run; then Sam arrived and they would enjoy breakfast together before heading to downtown Seattle for a wander around Pike Place Market or a shopping trip. Sometimes they took in a ball game and then a romantic dinner out somewhere special.

We must have looked so in love. What a sham.

This evening, the muffins were a real stab in the heart for Madison. Sam played the game for so long and so well, she struggled for months afterward to distinguish truth from lies, real life from imagination. She even went down the "maybe it was my fault" route for a while, thinking somehow she deserved it. He overpowered her weakness with ease.

How close had she come to ending all the pain? She owed her life to God—He saved her from complete devastation. And eventually her eyes were opened to the truth and she knew the problem was all Sam. She wasn't to blame for his cruelty back then. And here she was, his kidnapping victim in Jamaica.

But Sam doesn't know the new, improved Madison. Now she had God on her side. Faith. Truth. Justice. Salvation. Hope. Love. *True* love. A family in Christ. The kidnapping wasn't her fault. She might still have fears to work through, but she was not weak. She had a future worth fighting for. Maybe even a future with Luke.

Madison opened her eyes and checked outside again. The jeep was still parked at the side of their hut, so Sam must be inside. Probably scheming his next evil plan. She would have to take a chance that he either was engrossed in his work or had dozed off. Blue Eyes still hadn't shifted positions, and from the way his head leaned back, he was asleep for sure.

This could be one of a series of kidnappings if Sam develops a taste for it.

Her escape could save some other poor, unsuspecting woman from going through the same in the future, as long as Sam was arrested. Fueled by that thought, Madison stretched her legs and limbered up. This could be her longest run ever and she had no idea where it would lead. She prayed like never before and took a deep breath. With one more glance through the window to ensure everything was peaceful and motionless, she walked over to the door.

It's now or never.

She twisted the doorknob a fraction, and it creaked. She froze. Nothing. One more twist. And again. And again. Maybe the tree frogs' constant croaking outside would disguise any clicking. Madison's heart pumped like crazy and she took steady breaths before inching open the door.

With no light in her hut, she prayed nothing would attract attention to her movements. The cooler night air was a welcome relief, and Madison closed her eyes for a few seconds and allowed a gentle breeze to wash over her. Energized, she looked to the right, the opposite direction from the guys' hut, and knew that was the path out of her prison.

On tippy toes, she crept across the soft sand toward a section of lush foliage. Her hut would prevent the guys from seeing the escape initially, and after that, she would run for the trees.

Madison tasted blood and realized she was chewing the inside of her cheek.

Okay, this is where I break into a light run and get out of here.

Too afraid to look behind, she focused on the palm trees and prayed they would lead to a road of some sort. Careful not to turn her ankle on the uneven ground, Madison pumped her legs, fought back the overwhelming nausea, and soon found her rhythm.

Keep moving. Don't look back.

Relieved to be off the beach with firmer ground beneath her feet, Madison picked up her pace a little. She could keep running for a good hour if necessary, and by then she would find help. But who might be wandering around a deserted area of Jamaica in the middle of the night? She gritted her teeth. What were her options?

Her ears were pricked to recognize the sound of running from behind, or even worse, the sound of a jeep following her. The night was still. Only the chirping tree frogs and normal night sounds filled the air. Some soothing worship songs would go a long way in calming her frantic thoughts right now. What happened to her iPod? The beach at the resort—it would be buried in the sand by now.

She spotted something up ahead through the tress—a small run-down building of some sort. Abandoned, judging its current state, but it was a good indication a road was close by.

She slowed her steps to see whether anyone was inside. No chance. It must have been a fruit stand at one time but was no longer in use. A dilapidated sign and a bunch of cobwebs were all that remained. Madison leaned over her knees and caught her breath. She let out a single laugh—where did this brave Amazonian woman come from? Here she was, running through the junglelike foliage in the middle of the night in a foreign country, trying to escape her kidnappers. Ridiculous and so out of character, it was hysterical. As she straightened, she noticed a rock path leading up to a ridge. She checked behind her and then started up the path. It was a gentle incline, and at the top, she stopped for a second.

A road. Thank goodness.

The ridge brought her straight onto a paved route, and Madison resumed running at a decent speed. The moon gave enough light to see where she was going, and for the first time all day, hope welled within her. Skinny palm trees dotted the sides of the road, and lush foliage in between would provide quick cover if she needed to hide.

The road meandered for quite a distance, and Madison started to worry when not one vehicle passed by. She could be anywhere on the island, even some remote place where nobody ever visited. She may have to run all night, but that was okay. Adrenaline would take her a long way, hopefully far enough before Blue Eyes realized she had disappeared.

The door.

Madison cringed. She'd left the door to her hut wide open. The thought of it creaking again was enough to leave it as it was, but in hindsight, she should have made the effort. Bad mistake. She should have taken the time to shut it. With a closed door, the men would have no reason to suspect she wasn't fast asleep in her prison until they checked on her in the morning.

Mad at her sloppiness, Madison powered on and started praying for a route to take her off the main road. If they came looking for her at all tonight, they were sure to drive along this way.

Something flitted past her head from behind, and she screamed. What on earth? She shook her hair to make sure nothing landed on her and then spotted another flying creature up ahead.

"Bats? Really?" She tried not to cry. Instead, she focused on the road in front of her and rallied every ounce of courage she could muster. "I hate bats."

More praying, faster running, and the need to get far away from Sam kept Madison moving along the narrow road for another ten minutes or so. She didn't come across any more bats, and the ever-increasing distance from her hut boosted her confidence.

Rounding another bend, Madison's eye went straight to a small light in the distance.

Is that an actual house? They must have a phone—I can call the police and Chloe and Luke...

It was nestled among the trees from what Madison could make out, but it certainly appeared to be a house. What else would have a light on in the middle of the night? With renewed hope, she increased her pace, desperate to find someone home. A phone. Safety.

In her haste and with her eyes on her destination instead of the ground, Madison veered from the stable section of the road, misjudged her footing, and slipped on a patch of loose stones. Pain shot through her ankle. She hopped on her good foot for a few seconds, then tried to put weight on the sore ankle. Fire rocketed up her lower leg and her eyes filled with tears. She lifted her foot. *No. Not now.*

Tears leaked down Madison's cheeks, this time from desperation and frustration.

"You've got to be kidding me." She cried into the silent night. "A twisted ankle when I'm trying to escape from kidnappers? This only happens in the movies." Or was God protecting her from an even worse fate up ahead?

It wasn't injured enough to stop her, but it would slow her down. Hobbling now, she continued along the road, staying clear of any loose stones. The foot took her weight, but with each step agony shot up her leg. After a few strides, she was able to continue running. In pain.

Focus. Not much farther to go.

Madison forged ahead to the haven. Would it be safe? There could be a house full of men, or it could be a crazy party with lights on at this hour. On the other hand, it may be a kind family up with their baby. They may take her in and drive her straight back to the resort or even to the police station, wherever that might be. She decided to focus on the nice-family scenario. Wait. There were no vehicles that she could make out. Her heart sank. She would have to stay here overnight because there was no way she could run much farther. Her ankle could give out at any moment.

"Here goes nothing."

She was about to take the long, winding path down to the little house of refuge when the road lit up from behind. Her gaze darted around—where was all that foliage? She was exposed here with nowhere to hide.

Madison's heart slammed in her chest. It was an immediate decision she had to make. Either scamper down to the house, which could be going from the frying pan into the fire, or she could turn and flag down the vehicle, which could be her route straight out of here. Of course, it could also be Sam or some other night prowler. Her throbbing ankle made the choice for her. She couldn't outrun a car anyway.

"Hey, stop, please? I need help." Madison was breathless after her run, but the thought of being rescued brought a glimmer of hope. She shielded her eyes as the car slowed and headlights shone in her face.

She bent over and rested her hands on her knees while her breathing returned to normal. The car screeched to a stop. This was it. *Thank You, Lord.*

She took one deep, grateful breath and stood up to thank her hero. She pulled the sweaty hair back from her face and saw it too late—the shape of a jeep, the big guy jumping out and coming straight for her, the dragon tattoo visible from the headlights.

"*No!*"

CHAPTER TWENTY-ONE

MADISON SPUN AROUND AND LUNGED toward the winding pathway and her refuge, desperate to avoid his powerful clutches.

Three strides and he had her.

She writhed and kicked with all her might, booting Blue Eyes in the shins numerous times. But he was a beast and held her with such a grip, she could barely breathe. It didn't help that he covered her screams with his huge, bearlike paw. Again.

Adrenaline crashed, limbs like jelly. She was in trouble. No way she could escape on her sore ankle even if she could get out of the behemoth's clutches. Her attempted screams turned to sobs at the thought of what punishment might be dealt out. What frame of mind was Sam in? He never used physical violence with her before, but he reached a whole other level by kidnapping her. And there was no question Blue Eyes would use brute force if required.

Having overpowered her with ease, he lifted her from the ground as if she were a bag of flour and carried her toward the jeep. Utterly exhausted from the run and the struggle, she couldn't do a single thing to stop him.

"You're in big trouble. The boss is awful upset, you know." He spoke in clipped tones, and Madison braced herself for what might come next. These men wanted their money—who knew what they would do to ensure they received it?

Madison was shoved into the back of the jeep. As soon as Blue Eyes removed his hand from her mouth, she screamed at the top of her lungs. Would someone from the little house below hear the commotion?

Her efforts were rewarded with a hard slap on the cheek. Madison tasted blood and her whole head ached from the impact. She covered her face with her hands as the man pinned her down with one arm.

Blue Eyes snarled. "Special delivery, boss."

Boss? Madison peered through her fingers and gasped when she recognized Sam's profile in the front passenger seat. She needed to see whether it was him yet felt the urge to press her eyes shut so she didn't have to face the horrific truth.

Sam shifted around to look at her. He was calm, considering the vicious struggle playing out around him. It was unnatural and almost otherworldly, as if he observed something from afar. *Psychopath.*

"Madison."

The sound of his voice made her shudder. It was condescending and impatient, a far cry from the gentle man she once loved. He looked the same with his perfect wavy dark hair and mysterious eyes. She once found those eyes exotic and enchanting, but now as he narrowed them and bore right through her, they held a real presence of danger.

Blue Eyes jumped into the front of the jeep and started the ignition. "Home sweet home, boss?"

"You can head that way. I have something else in mind." He pulled a shiny gun from the dashboard and waved it at

Madison. "In case you have any other ridiculous ideas about escaping. You might as well sit back and relax."

A gun? Madison swallowed and then found her voice. "Sam, why are you doing this?"

"You ruined everything, Madison Grey. You didn't think I would vanish into thin air, did you? I have been working on this life plan for many years, my darling."

As they sped down the road, Madison watched the palm trees she had run past and felt the blood drain from her face. "Years? What do you mean? How many years?" A pit formed in her stomach.

Blue Eyes laughed from the driver's seat, but she needed to concentrate and hear the answer from Sam.

"Tell me. What are you talking about?"

"You only know the half of it, my darling. Your poor parents and their pathetic little plane with the mechanical issue. It was such a shame. When would Mr. Grey ever learn to check, double-check, and sometimes even triple-check his flying equipment?"

Madison gasped. She must have misheard. Even Sam wouldn't stoop that low.

He continued in a monotone voice. "Your father taught me well in the business world—I'll give him that. He took me on when I was young and desperate and gave me the tools I needed to read people and get my own way. But he was too trusting by far. It's where you inherited it, don't you think?"

"Wait." Madison shook her head. Too trusting? "Are you telling me you did something to their plane? You sabotaged their aircraft? After all Daddy did for you? What kind of a monster are you?" She couldn't breathe.

"The wealthy kind. You were an added bonus along the way, although you were so needy. As you discovered, I would have ditched you in no time. This kidnapping part of the plan is a mere inconvenience, but I'm rather enjoying it now. My muscular friend here has been a tremendous help planning with me this past year. Now all you have to do is play along and maybe I'll leave you alone to live your sad little life in comparative poverty."

Madison clung to the edge of her seat as they sped over potholes. "But why? I don't understand. What did our family ever do to deserve this?"

"Nothing at all." He adjusted the collar of his polo shirt. "I always knew I would be successful in my endeavors. I used to dream about moments like this when I was a boy. As you know, I am a patient man, and I had to bide my time and find a suitable family to help me get where I wanted to go. You were a pawn. A beautiful pawn." He reached out and touched her bruised cheek.

Madison flinched, and then her whole body tensed. "You're a murderer," she said through gritted teeth.

"And we were so close to being married. How bizarre would that have been?" He winked.

Panic welled in her chest. She had to escape. He was insane. "You won't get away with this."

"Ah, but I will. I have a new life in a new country ready and waiting for this nice little injection of cash. Added to the bonuses I gave myself from your father's company over the years, I'd say I'm set for life."

"You stole from our company as well? You really are heartless, aren't you?"

Sam examined his perfect fingernails. "Yes, I believe I am. Blame it on a crummy childhood."

Madison's head throbbed from complete exhaustion and the thought of this latest revelation. Her ankle ached. Her face stung. Could this night get any worse? "What are you going to do with me?"

"Pull over. We need to do this now." The car screeched to a stop and she watched Sam reach into a bag near his feet. He pulled out a cloth, which he passed to Blue Eyes.

Now. This was her one chance to escape. In the seconds it took for Blue Eyes to jump from the driver's seat, she pulled herself up with the grab handle and swung her legs over the passenger side. She landed on the gravel. Pain shot up from her ankle. Run.

Two steps and she was lifted from the ground. The behemoth squeezed her arms against her torso while she screamed in vain. They had her. She writhed and kicked with all her might, but they had her.

Blue Eyes laughed. It was pure evil. "Where do you think you are going, Miss Grey? The boss has somewhere special for you to go now. You won't even try escaping from there. I warned you not to run, didn't I? You hold nice and still, princess. I've got something to help you sleep." He threw her into the back seat and maneuvered his bulk above her.

"No." Madison turned her face away from him. She scrambled to the other side of the back seat, but there was nowhere to hide. He lunged after her and laughed while he flaunted the cloth.

Madison smelled the leather of the seat as she buried her head away from him, and then that obnoxious mixture they used on her early that morning filled her senses. *Not again.* Her breathing slowed and her arms stopped flailing as fabric smothered her mouth and nose. She flinched when he pressed the cloth against her stinging cheek, and then her vision dimmed as her eyelids drooped.

Heaviness covered her like a thick, warm blanket.

CHAPTER TWENTY-TWO

MADISON SIGHED. SHE LAY IN the hammock, idly rocking from side to side. It was rhythmic and soothing, and even though she must have napped for hours, she didn't want to wake up. Why was she so exhausted? *Snap out of it, girl. This is pure laziness.* But surely she needed to rest? Her body insisted. So, so sleepy.

Eyes still closed, she ran her fingers over the hammock below her. Something wasn't quite right. It felt too solid for a hammock, and why was there no wind? There was always a brisk breeze in her backyard, and this was her favorite spot under the trees, where it was cool and secluded. She did her best dreaming right here.

Weird. Why are my hands stuck together?

Madison gasped for air and sat bolt upright, eyes wide open. Still the rocking, but it was nighttime. Dark. What was she thinking? She wasn't at home in Seattle at all. She was in Jamaica. The kidnapping, her failed escape, Sam and Blue Eyes—it all came flooding back. The swaying wasn't from any hammock.

Her heart raced, head pounded. A thick cord bound both hands together and dug into the flesh on her wrists. She managed to curl her legs around and kneel up. Rubbed her grainy eyes as they adjusted to her dark surroundings.

Looking up, she saw a white canopy. She was no longer being held hostage in the rickety beach hut.

No. The gentle rocking could mean only one thing.

The hut was paradise compared with this. As she grabbed fistfuls of hair with her bound hands, the truth dawned. She was alone in her nightmare. They had dumped her in the glass bottom boat.

Moonlight provided enough visibility for her to see she was the only person on board. Completely alone. She could be anywhere on the water. Fresh air enveloped her, the ocean breeze rustled her hair, and the salt water permeated her nostrils, all confirming her suspicion.

Nausea rose from her stomach, and fear prickled her skin. She hated throwing up. *Please, not that on top of everything else.* Her breaths came in short, sharp bursts, and darkness beckoned. No way was she going to faint either. She had to be aware of her captors' next move, wherever they were.

God, help me stay conscious. She inhaled through her nose and exhaled through her mouth. In and out. Square breathing—that's what she needed to do: four seconds up breathing in, hold for four seconds across, four seconds down breathing out, hold for four seconds across. A trick she learned in counseling after her parents' deaths. She visualized the square as she repeated the exercise over and over until the shaking subsided.

This boat was an exact reenactment of the dreaded nightmare she experienced over the years since her sailing accident. Tonight was her one chance to survive it in real life and conquer the demons that refused to leave her alone. She may be powerless in her dreams, but now she had the opportunity to make brave choices. To overcome. *Lord, help me get over this fear. I trust You.*

She was able to see everything now. She stayed still and concentrated on breathing while she evaluated the situation. She knelt on a coarse blanket at the back of the boat. Holding on to a rail with a death grip, she inched forward, still on her knees.

Before her were a series of rectangular glass panels on the floor of the boat—windows to the depths below. As a young child, she always dreamed of going on a glass bottom boat, but that was before the accident, back when the ocean fascinated and beckoned.

Madison averted her gaze and concentrated on the solid wooden sides of the vessel, where long planks created benches for passengers to sit on while viewing the ocean through the glass. Careful not to rock the boat in case she was being watched, she clambered up to a bench and sat with her head between her knees and eyes pressed shut.

While she waited to fully come to her senses, she stretched out every finger and toe until she was convinced she had no major injuries. Her ankle no longer throbbed like before, although it was sore and looked puffy. Whatever they used on the cloth to knock her out, it was potent and served its purpose well. Other than thirst, exhaustion, and aches all over, she was okay. Bruised, but not broken. *Be grateful for small mercies.*

Her breathing returned almost to normal, but her wrists throbbed from the binding cord. She tried to loosen it with her teeth. Her efforts were futile. Fear gave way to anger in the pit of her stomach. How could Sam be so cruel?

Then again, anyone vicious enough to sabotage a plane and plot to steal her inheritance wouldn't think twice about using her greatest fear against her. Almost as if he hoped she'd have a major panic attack so he could watch her squirm.

A year ago, that would have been the case for sure.

I'm stronger now. Not by much, but I have a God who is all powerful. Way more powerful than Sam Kinkaid. She recalled her conversation with Sam earlier and sucked in a breath. *Wait. I'm dealing with a maniac. He killed my parents. He caused their accident...and then I loved him.*

A groan escaped from her lips. Had he laughed at her grief, knowing he was the cause? With the horrific reminder, the pain of her mom and dad's absence was as sharp as the day she had received the devastating news. She might never get over the accident, but now knowing Sam had orchestrated the whole thing—that was beyond sickening. Madison pressed her hands into her stomach. How could he? The time he spent in the Greys' home after the accident, supposedly grieving alongside Madison and Chloe, making himself comfortable in their house, and helping the girls come to terms with their loss. It was all a scam. He was a murderer. A murderer? She had loved a murderer...

It was too much to process. How would Chloe react? The rippling effect this news would have on everyone who loved the Grey family was beyond comprehension. The accident would become an open murder investigation and expose old wounds. On top of embezzlement, attempted fraud, and kidnapping. More grieving would come, but survival was first on the list. Right now, she needed to compartmentalize and prioritize her thoughts.

She looked down at her hands. Really? They were fastened together in prayer mode—a constant reminder not to rely on her own strength. Blue Eyes didn't think of that. There had to be a way of loosening the cord. Her eyes darted around to anything sharp within her reach. Nothing. That would be far too easy. The edge of the bench was going to have to suffice. She bent over and tried sawing the exposed cord against the wooden edge. Useless. *God, give me strength and wisdom.*

Madison took a deep breath and stood on weak legs. Sure enough, she was out on the ocean alone. She glanced toward the captain's chair and sighed. Even if her hands were free, she wouldn't know how to drive a boat. She peered with caution over the side of the boat and noticed a long rope attached to the dock. Her heart sank. The dock was a good distance away, meaning she would have to get out and swim for it. Sam knew she would never dream of doing such a thing. Did his cruelty know no bounds? She could grab the rope and haul herself closer to the dock but what if Sam saw the boat move? He could be watching her even now from his vantage point in the hut. Better to keep her distance from him.

She swiveled and squinted at the dimly lit beach. The moonlight enabled her to recognize her tiny prison from earlier, and a short distance along the beach she spotted the other hut, the outhouse, and the jeep. The huts had to be at least twenty feet from the shore, a hundred feet or so from where she sat in the boat. A light shone from her captors' window, and she guessed they must be inside. It didn't matter whether they were sleeping or not because she was stranded and they knew it. Sam had her right where he wanted her.

What was the point of screaming for help? No one else was here. They had chosen this location for that exact reason. There was one more dock up ahead, but it was empty. The desolate stretch of beach had one light shining from it, and that came from their hut. Madison was in no hurry to see Sam or Blue Eyes anytime soon.

She peered beyond the beach to see the hint of a road. No traffic would come anywhere close, as she had discovered from her earlier attempt to flee. How would anyone ever know to look for her here? The severity of the situation hit her again. She was alone. Just her and God on the ocean in the midst of her worst fears. She sank back onto the hard bench.

Memories of the last time she was out of her depth in the ocean came back in a flash. The transition from thrill to terror when their catamaran capsized during the crazy windstorm so many years ago. Her father's cries muffled by the pounding, relentless waves, and then suffocating darkness and the weight of water pinning her down. Burning lungs, flailing arms, then nothing. She shuddered.

The near-death experience had the potential to either make her stronger or be her ruin, and unfortunately for Madison, it had the latter effect. Through the years, she had longed to overcome her fear but never possessed the courage to see it through. Tonight could be her turning point. Or it could be her peril.

Surely, with God in her life, she could overcome anything. What was that verse? "I can do all things through Christ who strengthens me." She could do with some strengthening about now. Baby steps—Madison leaned over the glass floor from her perch on the bench. Below her, the strange window was clear and dark. It separated her from the great expanse of water, the unknown demon that haunted her since childhood. She mustered enough courage to kneel and peek through the glass. She didn't expect to see anything other than darkness but could make out underwater life of some sort. There were fish and seaweed. Something moved underneath the boat, and she froze. She couldn't do this. It was too much.

Sam must hate her with a passion to put her in this position. Defeated, she shuffled back up to the bench, putting as much distance between herself and the ocean as possible.

So much for overcoming my fears.

CHAPTER TWENTY-THREE

IT WAS A MIRACLE, NO doubt about it. Joe, the New York guardian angel, gave Luke a carrot, and it dangled before him as he sped into the dark night. So, the glass bottom boat played a major part in the kidnapping. Good to know he wasn't on a wild-goose chase. And there were only two guys involved. Phew. The thought of dealing with a larger group in the kidnapping team had batted around his imagination for the last couple of hours, and it was a possibility when he thought back to the scuffle he'd witnessed at the resort on Friday night.

"I wonder what that was all about?" He scanned the deserted horizon. "Maybe the fight was with the real boat owners or something." If it was reported to the police, no wonder the kidnappers didn't want the authorities involved. Two reported crimes at one resort would send up some major red flags.

Windblown after several long hours on the water this evening, Luke's body protested. His legs cramped, and his shoulders ached from holding the steering wheel steady against the current, but disturbing thoughts of Madison being held hostage urged him onward. Possible scenarios flitted through his mind. She could be anywhere, even off the island by now. No, he wouldn't believe that. Wherever she was, one thing was for certain. She would be petrified.

"Hang in there, Madison," he whispered into the wind.

The speedboat trawled along the coast, slowing at any signs of another vessel. Luke pulled into several smaller beaches and two larger resorts before he moored at another decrepit dock. There was a full jerrican of fuel on board, and it wouldn't hurt to fill up. He tended to the tank and tossed the empty can in the back of the boat before jumping onto the dock. He pulled out his phone and breathed a sigh of relief when the signal was strong.

"Hey, Nathan, it's me."

"Luke. You okay? Found anything?"

"I'm on the right track, but I haven't found the boat yet." Luke heard Nathan relay the information to Chloe and then continued. "I spoke with someone else who met Sam and the other guy."

"For real?"

"Yeah, they wanted to rent a glass bottom boat, and he didn't like the look of them. It was our guys for sure, right down to the icy blue eyes. Anyway, this man I spoke with brushed them off a few weeks ago, but they found a boat elsewhere because he saw them pass by his beach early this morning."

Nathan exhaled in a whoosh. "Wow. You were right. But they could be anywhere by now."

"True, they've had hours to get away, but this guy confirmed they were heading east. They must have stopped somewhere to make the call to Chloe."

"That was at two."

"Right. And think about it—they won't go far if they intend to collect their money tomorrow."

"Yeah, I guess so. Unless they split up. Blue Eyes could have Madison at some remote location and they may have left Sam close to our resort."

Some wisdom here, Lord? "No, I don't think so. Something my man said to me rings true. He called them Brawn and Brains. I don't think one could do without the other in this little scheme."

"Hmm. You could be onto something there. You must be exhausted, man. Sure you're okay to keep going? I can meet you somewhere and take over."

"No, I'm good. I'm not stopping now. It's dark, and I'm not supposed to be out, so I should continue on here, even if it's at a snail's pace."

"Is your speedboat owner going to be cool with this? What if he thinks you've stolen it and calls the police or something? You know we have to keep any sign of the cops away for Madison's sake."

"Look at you being the sensible one for a change, little brother. Relax. I left my details with them, and I warned the kid I may not be back before dark. He won't get into trouble. I'll take the flak. Plus, he'll make a great profit, which I'll bill to you, by the way. I'm a poor missionary, remember?"

"No worries. I just want everyone back safe. Without involving the police. Listen. Chloe wants a quick word. I'll pass you over to her."

Luke switched the phone to his other ear and paced the boardwalk.

55

"Luke?" Chloe's voice was strained. "I believe Madi's okay. I can feel it. But I know she's beyond scared. We can't let her get hurt. Please find her."

"You know I'll search all night if I have to. Try to get some sleep."

"That's not going to happen. But I'm grateful, Luke. You're going above and beyond here. Don't get yourself into trouble, okay?"

"I'll be careful. Don't worry about me."

There was a pause. "I've been listening to Madi's iPod."

"Yeah?" Could God use an iPod to speak into Chloe's life even tonight?

"I thought it might help me feel closer to her, like you said. Anyway, the words on these worship songs are amazing. It's like she knew I would be listening and they are written just for me."

"That's awesome." Madison would be thrilled...

"I wanted you to know. And there's something else." Her voice grew softer.

Luke strained to hear every detail. "What is it?"

"When I went back to her room earlier, I didn't find a note or anything, but I picked up her journal, and I've been reading it."

She wouldn't be happy about that. Who would? "That's awkward."

Chloe sighed. "I feel horrible about invading her privacy, but her life's at stake here. Anyway, it turns out she was freaked out by Blue Eyes this weekend like you said, but she was also determined not to give in to fear. You were right. And there's something else you should be aware of."

"Yes?" Luke braced himself.

THE GLASS BOTTOM BOAT

"I know you're a missionary and never want to get married and stuff, but my big sister is falling for you. Which is beyond huge after everything she's been through."

"I see." Luke felt the pulse in the side of his neck pumping fast.

"Do whatever you like with that nugget of information, but I thought it was important for you to be aware of her emotional state. Be gentle with her, okay? She can't handle her heart being broken again. Especially by her hero."

Luke closed his eyes, at a loss for words. Her hero? Her heart?

"Did you hear me, Luke? The line's not great."

"Yeah, I heard loud and clear. Thanks. I should go now, but I'll speak to you both later."

"Take care, brother-in-law."

Luke slipped the phone into his pocket. He couldn't move for a moment.

"Thanks, Lord, for Chloe listening to songs of hope in You. I know You can use those songs to speak deep truth into her life." He looked up into the starry night. "And, God, I'm not sure what's going on with my heart where Madison is concerned, but since it looks like she has feelings for me, I don't want to hurt her with another rejection. Am I supposed to stay single, or are my growing feelings in Your will? I need direction for my future as well as for my boat. This is crazy, but You're in control. That much I know."

He rotated his head, stretched his back, and hurtled back onto the speedboat. The moon was almost full, and it lit up the ocean before him. He had to be extra vigilant boating in the dark, and he ran the motor on a low speed while he scanned the shoreline. His eyes were acclimatized to the darkness, but the constant strain had given him a killer of a headache. The least of his worries.

A smaller resort up ahead held a beach party in full swing, and Luke recognized the sounds of a steel band drifting in the air. With nothing to pique his interest, he puttered on. There was a tranquil atmosphere between beaches, and he felt like the only person on the entire ocean. Which he possibly was at this time of night.

Unless Madison was still floating in a boat somewhere. She could be on land by now. For her sake, he hoped so. His throat clogged with emotion. Why did some people have to go through so much? This was supposed to be a week of celebration and relaxation for them all, but now? A disaster. *God, what are You doing in all this? I don't understand.*

Luke glanced down at his wrist. He wore the braided bracelet made by some of the kids at the orphanage. They presented him with it before he left and made him promise to keep it on the whole time he was away until he arrived back home. Home. Where was home anyway? Mexico or Seattle or somewhere new God might be calling him to? He touched the woven threads around his wrist and smiled. How could he even consider not going back to his beloved kids? Had he imagined the unsettled feeling in his gut when he was given his renewal papers? This time away was invaluable.

He reached into his pocket and pulled out his phone again. Only 20 percent of power left, but he needed to take one quick look. The picture of Madison at the beach bonfire filled the screen. It took his breath away. Man, she was beautiful. Not only her angel face but also her eyes captivated him like nothing else, and they reflected the grace and love that came from within. It didn't hurt that she loved babies, enjoyed traveling, and could speak Spanish. And hadn't she challenged him that maybe there was something new in his future, too?

"What, God?" Tears brimmed. "What am I supposed to do with all this? Am I imagining these feeling for Madison? Didn't You want me to stay single to serve You more effectively?"

Don't you think I can use you if you are married, son?

Whoa. Not audible words but a sentence from the depth of his soul sounded in his ears. Had he doubted God's ability? He sure hadn't meant to. Singleness had suited him up to now, but that was before Madison Grey. Perhaps his mind was cloudy with exhaustion—this might not be the most prudent time to make life-changing decisions. Although he came to Jamaica, seeking God's wisdom for his future...

Luke looked down. He held his phone next to the bracelet and glanced from one to the other. Funny how he hadn't noticed that before—they almost matched. The bright yellow and brown threads from the bracelet picked up the colors of Madison's yellow dress and chocolate-colored ringlets around her shoulders. Was it a sign?

"Tell me if I'm wrong, Lord, but I'm thinking maybe these two crazy worlds could collide beautifully."

Peace settled over Luke. He could almost feel it cover him from head to toe. His heart rate returned to normal and he slid the phone back into his pocket. *I have to go rescue my girl.*

*****

Madison attempted her breathing exercises again. What were the possible outcomes of this whole scenario? Best case—Sam would receive the money and escape, let her go back to the resort, and the ordeal would be over. But was that realistic? It sounded too straightforward, and she now knew the depth of evil Sam was capable of. With greed as his driving force, let alone whatever mental delusions clouded his judgment, he could choose to stalk her for the rest of her days just for the pleasure of knowing she'd always be looking over her shoulder in fear.

But now that she knew the truth, Sam could never go back to the States. He must have arranged a flight straight from Jamaica to some unknown destination to set himself up for the rest of his life, like he said. Unless he had no intention of letting Madison go free to identify him. After all, he'd confessed his role as embezzler and murderer in addition to kidnapper. If he ever planned on returning to the States, he would have to get rid of both Madison and Chloe and then probably Nathan and Luke as well.

Could he be that barbaric? Her stomach turned at the memory of what he had done to her parents. Even if the ransom exchange went as planned, the odds of her ever being reunited with her sister and a happy future were slim to none. *If this is it, I'll never get the opportunity to walk down the aisle to my future husband. And I'll never get to hold my own babies. I'm not ready to give up.*

Another option was even more disastrous. What if Chloe wanted to play it safe and decided to go to the police right now? If Sam found out, he might do something crazy straightaway. Her mouth went dry. If so, this could be her last night alive. The Sam facade she fell in love with wouldn't have hurt a fly, but now she'd seen his irrational side. Even last year when she discovered his intent on fraud, something edgy and unpredictable put her on high alert and caused her to get rid of every trace of him from her life. Or so she had thought. *Who knows what he is capable of now—he could even kill me and then pursue Chloe...*

Dear Chloe. Here she was, in Jamaica trying to enjoy her honeymoon. This was so unfair. Perhaps she was fast asleep after the stress of the day or pounding the streets looking for her sister. She must be frantic with worry. Hopefully, Nathan was being a rock for her. What a dreadful way to start a marriage. In an attempt to take her mind off her impending doom, Madison lowered her head to pray for the newlyweds, but as she did, something caught her eye.

The thought of having to look through the wretched glass into the ocean again gave her palpitations, but something gold glistened in the moonlight right at the edge of the window. With care, Madison bent over and grabbed it with her bound hands.

She held it up, turning it around. It looked familiar.

"No. It can't be."

She stared at a gold cuff link with the initials *N.A.* engraved in the center. Nathan Alexander. Madison's jaw dropped. Last Christmas, she had spent hours shopping in the Seattle city center with Chloe, hunting for the perfect Christmas gift for Nathan. It was a true labor of love and a test of sisterly patience, but by the end of the day, Chloe selected the cuff links and even had them engraved with his initials. Madison blinked and looked again. There was no doubt whatsoever this belonged to him. The question remained—why on earth was it on a boat belonging to Sam? But they had never met, had they? When Nathan came along, Sam was history.

Madison gasped. *Nathan isn't in on this scheme, too, is he?*

Curled in a ball on the bench, she swallowed down panic and thought back through the wedding preparations and possible conversations with Nathan that might now prove suspicious. He was eager to book this particular resort, and Chloe was happy to let him take that side of the planning, but there wasn't anything dubious about his desire to help. *Was he in cahoots with Sam all along? Does he even know Sam?*

Chloe could be in danger with her shiny new husband. The thought of Chloe being hurt brought a fresh wave of anxiety over Madison's exhausted body. Breathe. She gripped the cuff link. What if Nathan planned to scam Chloe out of her inheritance, like Sam's attempt with her last year? They could all be in it together.

No. It couldn't be. But what other explanation was there? Chloe's heart would break for sure. Madison already experienced the searing pain that followed betrayal—and the agonizing months of despair and self-loathing. But for Chloe, it would be even worse because she was married to the man. Something didn't fit, but Madison's head pounded so nothing made sense anymore. All she knew was that she had to get away from here. Away from Sam. And she had to get back to Chloe's side in order to protect her. Had to keep this piece of evidence safe.

With some effort, she slid the cuff link into the little pocket inside her waistband. Out of sight, out of mind? Her vision swirled. How had Nathan been on this boat on his wedding day? He wore cuff links—she noticed them at the wedding dinner. Nausea returned. Had Nathan sold her out to Sam? Every hair stood on end. *God, what do I do now? I can't trust anyone...*

Luke. She focused on Luke. He was genuine, wasn't he? Doubts jabbed as she imagined him with Nathan, plotting to trick the gullible Grey sisters.

No way.

In the limited time they had spent together, Luke proved himself trustworthy. God was central in his life, and even if they had no future together, he would be doing everything in his power to rescue her right now. She knew it. Whether Nathan was involved in this or not, Luke was a man of integrity and honor. Those green eyes of his were deep pools of honesty, and Madison longed to see them again. She was safe with Luke. She trusted him. Yes, she trusted him. But now it was too late. Thoughts of him in a tuxedo mingled with visions of James Bond, and then the shivering started in earnest. Fear took over and sobs erupted.

She didn't even realize she was crying at first—how could there be more tears yet to be shed? But they came, hot and fast. She let them fall, and once they were all used up, she resorted to praying out loud in the cool night air. She got over her irrational self-consciousness. She was completely alone out here, for goodness' sake, and after a while, it was as if God were sitting in the boat with her. She talked with her Father, pouring out her heart and holding nothing back.

Tears sprinkled her bound hands.

"God, help me. Help us all."

CHAPTER TWENTY-FOUR

SEVERAL MINUTES LATER, LUKE SPOTTED a commercial vessel bobbing next to the dock at another beach. No resort. One more dock ahead, but that was empty. This place was deserted. He flicked on the small flashlight and studied his map. This small beach was close to Morant Bay, and according to Nathan's list, there were no glass bottom boats here. Interesting. This boat had the familiar shape and canopy he was looking for and was attached to the dock by a lengthy rope. Maybe it had come loose and drifted, but it needed to be checked out with care.

Luke turned off his lights, as there was no ocean traffic whatsoever. He couldn't be spotted if it did happen to be the vessel in question. He got closer; his pulse raced. The sign on the side of the vessel was clear: "Glass Bottom Boat."

He surveyed the area. A couple of shacks dotted the stretch of beach, with a vehicle parked next to one of them. A jeep, judging by its angular shape. People must be here but not enough to merit having a boat like this. His skin prickled. One of the huts had a dim light shining from within. They could be sleeping or keeping watch. Extra caution was required. Luke looked down at his trembling hands. He couldn't fall apart now.

Focus over fear.

He stayed a good distance from shore and turned off the motor. Without a sound, he drifted past the beach and the boat. Something caught his attention in the silence. What was that? The sound of weeping floated into the night air. Heart-wrenching sobs belonging to a woman came from inside the boat. He strained his ears. Did it sound like Madison? It was hard to tell from a distance. And then the sobs stopped and a voice he recognized seemed to be chanting. No, she was praying.

Madison. It's really you.

Luke ached to rush up next to the boat, pluck her from the wretched nightmare, and whisk her away to safety, but it wouldn't be quite that simple. Anyone could be on the boat with her. He had to be smart and let his head rule his heart here.

A quick glance to the shoreline. Two guys, one lit hut, one vehicle. Were they both in the hut? Or was one in the boat with Madison? His stomach knotted. *Okay, Lord, I have to trust You in this. If they could both be asleep—preferably fast asleep—onshore, that would be great.*

The goal was the next vacant dock along. Not too far away for Madison to swim but far enough to avoid attracting attention.

It took a few minutes for Luke to maneuver his boat past the beach with minimal noise and attach it to the other dock. It was in rough shape, but he wasn't in a position to be picky. He secured the rope and looked back toward the glass bottom boat. The distance was nothing for him, but swimming at this depth would seem like a marathon stretch for Madison. *She's going to hate me.*

Next, one quick phone call to Nathan and Chloe. They needed to know his plan and location in case something went wrong. Which was a possibility. James Bond he was not.

He dug out the phone from his pocket and prayed once again for cell reception.

"Nathan, can you hear me?" He kept his voice down to a whisper.

"Yes, but only just. I have you on speaker phone. What's up?"

"I found Madison."

"What?" Chloe screeched, and Luke covered the phone with his hand. He couldn't get caught by the kidnappers now. He was so close. "Tell us both what's going on."

He kept his voice just above a whisper. "I'm at a little beach south of Morant Bay, according to the map. There's a glass bottom boat tied up here and it's not on the list. I passed by and heard a woman in there, and I'm positive it was Madison's voice."

"Madison?" Chloe squealed. Luke shot a look at the hut. No movement. "She's alive? Could you hear what she was saying?"

How could he tell her sister she was sobbing? Focus on the positive. "I think she's okay. I couldn't make out the words, but from the cadence in her voice, I'd say she was praying."

"Really? Do you think she's alone?"

"I would guess so. Come to think of it, I can't imagine her praying aloud like that in front of her captors, and it looks to me like the hut on the beach is occupied. The light is on, and there's a vehicle outside. Plus, if she's scared stiff because she's on the boat, I think prayer would be the first thing on her to-do list."

Nathan whistled into the phone. "This sounds like showtime, then, bro. What's the plan?"

Luke struggled to keep his voice down. "I need you to phone the police immediately."

Chloe gasped. "Are you sure? What if it goes wrong and they hurt Madi? You heard what they said about the police."

"I know I'm taking a chance here, but I believe it's the best way to go. I'm almost certain the men are in the hut on the beach, and there's zero movement, so I'm hoping they're out cold."

"What if they're not?" Nathan raised his voice. "This could even be a trap. Why would they allow Madison to be out on the boat alone? I don't like the sound of this."

"Babe, Sam knows Madi is petrified of deep water. He's relying on that fact to keep her there. If she's on the boat, he's created her own personal prison on the ocean, and there's no chance she would swim away."

Luke ran a hand through his hair. That was his fear. What if she refused to get into the deep water?

"Bro, how are you going to get her out without the dudes seeing you? Or are you going to wait for the police?"

Luke rubbed his grainy eyes. "I can't chance waiting. If they come outside to check on things, they could see my boat hitched way up on the next beach. They might get spooked and take off with Madison again. I won't stand by and watch that happen."

"I hate to ask." Nathan hesitated. "But what if these guys have weapons, man?"

Luke checked his phone battery—low-power mode. "I don't have time to worry about that. I'm going to swim to the boat and get her to swim back with me. She can make it. And

219

we'll have to slip away without a sound so the kidnappers don't suspect anything. There's no guarantee the police will make it here before we escape."

The phone was silent for a few beats before Nathan spoke up again. "There's a lot that can go wrong—"

"As soon as it's safe, I'll call you again. Now, get on the line to the cops. Make sure you tell them we're going to head straight back to the resort in the boat and they can question us all they want once we're there. I have to go. See you later."

Luke ended the call and stared at the phone for a second. For a last dose of courage, he clicked on the photo of Madison one more time. *I'm coming to save you, beautiful.* He put his phone on the seat, pulled off his shirt, and kicked his flip-flops into the corner.

Lord, I can't do this in my own strength. I need You to calm Madison's heart and help her understand what we need to do. Please keep us safe. I want to live long enough to have a future with this woman.

Careful not to make a splash, he slid into the ocean and swam in the direction of the glass bottom boat. The water was cooler without the sun warming it but not unbearable. The ocean was Luke's comfort zone, and his fear dissipated with each stroke. The familiar act of swimming cleared his mind and refreshed him for the next task, which was a big one. He could literally be saving a life.

Within a few minutes, he reached the dock and stopped to assess the situation. All was well. No crying from the boat and no movement over at the beach. A solitary light still shone through a window in the hut. Eerily peaceful.

The challenges before him made his head spin. If Madison was free and ready to escape, would she have the guts to jump off the edge of a boat into the pitch-black ocean? Was he expecting too much from her? She could have a broken leg or a concussion, for all he knew. She needed to swim back with him. Period. That would mean facing her fears head on. He gazed up at the dock he hung on to and sighed. They could chance climbing onto it and running to the beach, but then they would be dangerously close to the hut and could run straight into a trap. No way he was going to put her anywhere near those buffoons. No, the swim was their one option. *I'm so sorry, Madison.*

Luke took a deep breath and plunged down deeper into the water with huge strokes until he was below the glass bottom boat. There was only one way to make sure Madison was alone in there. And she was *not* going to like it.

CHAPTER TWENTY-FIVE

THIS IS THE LONGEST NIGHT of my life.

Fear prevented Madison from succumbing to sleep—who knew what those creeps might do with her next? The salty smell of the ocean filled her nostrils, and her stomach cramped from hunger. Two measly muffins. That's all she'd eaten in the past twenty-four hours, and it wasn't enough after the physical exertion she'd put herself through. Her body ached from exhaustion after the run and the stress and the craziness of the day. Her breathing slowed and her eyelids felt like lead. Peace. Safety. Sleep.

Rapid knocking startled Madison and she jumped.

Did I actually fall asleep?

The knocking started up again, muffled yet persistent. She gave her head a shake.

I'm losing my mind. Who would be knocking on a boat? Is that coming from underneath?

She got her bearings and peered down through the glass panel below. Too horrified to even scream, she gasped, covering her mouth with both hands. *What? How on earth?* But when the apparition didn't magically disappear, reality hit with tremendous force. Her mind wasn't playing tricks. He was swimming under the boat. It was him, for real.

"Luke?" He was here to rescue her?

Madison dropped to the floor and touched the glass with her bound hands. His dark hair was wavy in the water, but there was no mistaking the kindness in those captivating green eyes. He pressed one hand next to hers on the other side of the glass, and their eyes locked. The moment was surreal and joyous, and every butterfly in creation found its way to Madison's stomach. *Am I still dreaming?*

The next second, Luke gave a thumbs-up, and she responded likewise as well as she could with her hands tied together. Then he was gone and she was alone again. She pinched the skin on her cheek. Yes, she was awake. Madison continued staring down into the empty ocean. Had she hallucinated the merman?

A slight splash of water sounded from the side of the boat, and Madison spun around. Luke's head popped up where the ladder was located, and he grinned, heaving huge breaths. It was him. Madison scrambled across the boat and helped him over the side. She was never more relieved in her life.

"Luke." A quick glance back toward the hut. "Quickly, before they see you. What are you doing here? However did you find me?"

Luke bent over while his breathing recovered. "It's a long story, but we need to get you out of here as soon as possible."

Dripping wet, he straightened in front of her and tipped her chin up. Their eyes met again and her knees buckled. "Madison, are you okay? Did they hurt you?"

She struggled to speak. He was here. For her. "Umm, I've got a few bruises, and my ankle's sore, but it's not bad. Can you untie me, please?" She lifted her hands.

"Of course, but let's get out of sight." He checked the beach.

They ducked down, and while Luke worked on the cord, Madison's mind raced. This was one scenario she had not considered. Bizarre. She shook her head and tried to gather her thoughts.

He squeezed life back into her hands, then continued loosening the knot. "Here, wriggle your wrists for a second." He glanced down. "What happened to your ankle? It looks puffy."

"I turned it on the uneven road when I was trying to escape up the mountain."

He raised both eyebrows. "Wow."

"Obviously, it didn't work out well."

"You're a strong woman, Madison Grey."

"Look at me. I'm trapped on a boat and being held for ransom by a psychopathic murderer."

Luke broke through the last of the rope. "You're living your worst nightmare. Now, let's get you out of here."

There was only one way out. The thought of being swallowed by the ocean made her stomach twist. They may not make it. He had to know the truth. "Luke, it's Sam. He's behind all this. And Blue Eyes—you know, the guy who was following me at the resort? Sam wants the money he didn't get from me the first time."

"Yeah, we kind of thought as much. I'm so sorry."

How did he figure that out? Her mind raced. "But there's more." She took a shaky breath. He had to know what Sam was capable of. "Sam told me he caused my parents' plane to crash. And then I thought he might kill me and maybe even Chloe…" Her words ran into each other. Was she making any sense at all?

"Wait—your parents' accident, too?" Luke froze and a muscle in his jaw spasmed. "You weren't kidding when you called him a psychopathic murderer. If he confessed that nugget of news to you, I'm guessing he won't want you to be able to report him." He popped his head up and ducked back down. "We need to leave before these guys suspect anything or come to check on you. It looks like they're in one of those huts on the beach."

She nodded.

"The police should be on their way, and Sam's not going to be happy."

"The police?" Relief flooded her entire being, and then dread. The ocean. She glanced up at Luke. She trusted him. She could do this. "Okay. Tell me what I need to do."

Luke pulled her close. "We have to swim out of here. You know that, right? We can't use this dock because they could see us and it takes us too close to the huts. They could even be watching the boat right now, so we have to stay low. I'm counting on the fact they think you're stuck in here for the night. Sam knows your fear of water, right?"

"He knows." Another look at the water. Tears brimmed. "But I'm not sure if I can swim out there, Luke. Please don't let me drown."

Panic rose from the pit of her stomach. She had to hold it all together in front of her rescuer. He was putting his own life on the line for her. He was putting her first. For real. *Thank You, Lord.*

Luke enveloped her in a tight hug, and even though he was soaking wet, she pulled in closer.

"I won't let you drown. I'll be with you every second. I won't leave you. Do you believe me?"

Her heart beat a steady confirmation as she looked up into those green pools. "Yes. I trust you, Luke."

"Good. Then let's go. Take off your shoes and socks, and follow me in. We need to be as quick and quiet as possible."

Madison stripped her feet and followed him to the side of the boat. Her ankle ached a little, but swimming shouldn't be a problem. Disappearing into the inky ocean was another matter.

Luke held her hand and closed his eyes. "God, we give Madison's fear over to You and pray You will take us to safety and that justice will be served. Amen."

"Amen."

"I'll slip into the water first and help you in. You understand, honey?" His voice was a whisper.

"Sure." Madison was terrified. But did he just say "honey," as in a romantic term of endearment? Her frozen insides warmed.

"I'm afraid you don't have the luxury of sitting on the side deliberating."

"I understand. I need to get away from this place. Go ahead. I'll follow. I can do this."

The next minute, he was out in the ocean, treading water with outstretched arms, waiting for her to climb onto the ladder. She couldn't do it. Couldn't make her limbs move in that direction. There were too many unknowns, too many bad memories, too many fears.

Clear as day, Madison saw the reality before her. This trust, this leap of faith would literally save her life. *If I can take this step and leap from the "safety" of this stupid boat, which is suffocating me, then perhaps I can really live.* Placing her trust in God, knowing He would walk her through anything and everything she feared, was simple yet huge. She stared into Luke's eyes. If she took such a monumental step, maybe this young man with the open arms would be there to walk alongside her. This could be the beginning of something beautiful. There was much to lose but so much more to gain.

Madison held her breath as she backed over the edge of the boat, clung to the ladder, and lowered herself into the water. This was it—no turning back. She let go.

Luke caught her before her head sank below the surface. The water was chilly, and Madison fought to stay afloat in her initial panic, but he supported her until she gained control over her shallow breathing. *I did it.* She swallowed the cheer that welled up inside and concentrated on not splashing her arms. No noise allowed. The bulk of the boat blocked her view of the shore like a shield.

"Do we have to go underwater? I don't think I can."

"No need," Luke whispered. "We're right at the end of the dock, so we can swim above the surface all the way. Easy as pie." His encouraging smile in the moonlight steadied her nerves. "Ready?"

"How deep are we?" Madison gasped between breaths.

"Don't even think about it. Focus on our destination. Do you see the dock over there?"

Madison turned to where Luke pointed. It looked a million miles away. "Okay." Her voice quivered. "Deep is worse than distance. You pray and I'll swim."

With Luke right beside her, Madison broke into breaststroke, imagining she were in a swimming pool—a shallow, safe one. She felt warm from within, and her arms strengthened with every stroke. It wasn't so bad, as long as she didn't think about Sam. Focus. Luke's boat. Luke. Chloe. Safety.

They rounded the end of the dock, and Luke's speedboat came into view. Madison could almost taste freedom. Hope was nearly tangible and soon this nightmare would be a distant memory.

"Madison, I need you to keep calm and continue swimming all the way. Don't stop."

"Why? You're not leaving me, are you?" Madison stopped swimming and looked over at Luke. He was treading water and looking at something behind them. Water closed in above her head. *No, I can't drown now.* Her childhood dreams were front and center as she flailed her arms and legs. Where was Luke? He promised not to leave her...

In a heartbeat, he pinned her unruly limbs with strong arms and pushed her up to the water's surface. She took a large gulp of air and spluttered.

"Shhh," he whispered into her ear.

Each breath burned, but she was okay. Luke held her while she calmed down. His hands were steady and sure as he guided her onto her back.

"Shhh, you're going to be fine. Float and take deep breaths. There you go. I'm not going anywhere. Don't worry. You lost it for a second there. That's all."

Madison caught her breath and concentrated on staying above the rocking surface. "Thanks, I'm better now, I think." Inhale, exhale. "But what's going on? Is it Sam?"

"We're going to be safe in a few minutes, but we have to move faster. Someone opened the door of the hut on the beach."

Madison flipped over and launched straight into another breaststroke. "No. It can't be happening—I thought we were safe. They're coming to get me and then they'll hurt you. Luke, I'm so sorry." Her body heaved sobs with each stroke. The dock was visible. And the getaway boat was close. So close.

Luke was within grabbing reach, but she needed to do this on her own.

"We're nearly there and you're doing great." His voice was barely audible. "Please swim and breathe. Swim and breathe. You let me worry about what's going on behind us. Look ahead and keep moving."

For several seconds, they swam in silence. All Madison heard was the sound of her own breathing. And then Luke, louder than before.

"I hate to say it, but we'll be safer under the water. Do you understand?"

Dread washed over Madison. That was asking too much. Her body might be able to swim underwater, but her mind couldn't cope. The choice was hers—either trust Luke and face her demons or put his life in jeopardy, not to mention her own.

"Let's not take any chances. They're less likely to see us underwater, and if they do happen to shoot—"

"Do you think they'll shoot at us?" She remembered to whisper.

"Did you see either of them with a gun?"

Her heart plummeted. "Yes. Stay with me?"

"Of course. Keep your eyes open. I'll be right beside you. I promise. Take a massive breath."

The next moment, Madison took the deepest breath she could manage in the circumstances. Luke grabbed her hand, and the real world was left behind. Together, they plunged down and moved through the water. He was a strong swimmer and pulled her effortlessly alongside him through the deep, dark ocean.

She was okay.

They left the cruelty and the craziness above water and she willed herself not to panic. Snorkeling used to be her favorite thing to do, way back before her accident. She'd forgotten the peaceful majesty of the underwater world. A whole part of creation she had denied herself for so many years. Relax. She glanced over at Luke again and sensed he was in his natural element. Her arms burned and her lungs felt ready to explode. *Let this be over soon, please.* She pumped her legs with the last burst of energy she could muster.

Beyond the seaweed and schools of small fish, Madison spotted the underside of what must be the speedboat ahead of them. *Swim, swim, swim.*

Then Luke pulled her up to the surface, and she greedily gulped air into her lungs. He placed her fingers around the bottom of a rope ladder, hoisted himself up the side of the boat with ease, and then held out his hand for her to follow.

"We made it." His hair dripped onto her as he leaned over and pulled her up out of the water. "You're safe. You're safe." He held her in his arms as she quaked from a combination of adrenaline and exhaustion. But they weren't out of danger yet.

Shouts came from behind, and Luke pulled them down flat into the boat. Sirens sounded. Madison curled up in a ball, waiting for footsteps to march up their dock. But footsteps never came. She dared to let out her breath. Shouting voices, slamming doors. Luke poked his head up, and then—a gunshot.

Madison jumped. "*No*. What was that? Are you okay?" She pulled him back down.

"We're fine." Luke caught his breath. "You did it. Thank the Lord we're all safe. See—the police arrived in perfect time. We can leave and get you back to your sister." He pulled her up.

"For real?" Madison felt like a rag doll. Every part of her was spent, and she barely had the strength to speak. "The police? Shouldn't we stick around to speak to them?" Her teeth chattered and she couldn't stop trembling as she peered over at the beach.

Luke handed her a towel from the cubby and grabbed one for himself. "Don't worry. The police have it all under control. We don't have to hang around. I guessed that if this worked, you would be anxious to get back to Chloe. Nathan should have explained the plan to the authorities, and so they'll be expecting us back at the resort." He jumped up to untie the boat from the dock. "I'd rather get going before the police decide to chat with us here instead. I'm afraid it could be a long night."

She craned her neck in an attempt to see what was going on back at the shore. "I want to be certain they have Sam. What if he made a run for it?" Would she ever quit looking over her shoulder if he was on the loose?

Luke stepped back into the boat and pulled a pair of binoculars from the cubby. He held them to his eyes. "Trust me—they have both guys. I don't know who was shot, but there doesn't appear to be anyone on the ground." He offered her the binoculars.

She shook her head. "I'd rather take your word for it." She'd seen enough of Sam and Blue Eyes.

He put an arm around her shoulders and she fit perfectly against his side. "You're going to freeze if we hang around here any longer. Let me get things ready to set off here." He turned to check the gauges. "Help yourself to my phone—it's on the seat. See if the signal's strong enough to give your little sister a call before I start the engine. I don't have much battery left, but Nathan is on speed dial."

Madison bit her lower lip. Was it over? Was she safe? She reached across and grabbed the phone.

One click of the button and she had service. "Nathan, is Chloe there?"

"Madison? Yeah, we're both here on speaker phone."

"Madison?" Chloe's voice broke.

"Chloe, it's me. I'm with Luke and we're both safe." Squeals and hollers ensued while Madison explained the situation amid tears of joy. "Chloe, we need to get moving here, but we'll see you at the resort. We can answer all the police questions there. I have so much to tell you."

"How long will you be? I can't wait to see you safe and sound."

Madison looked at Luke. "How long?"

He tipped his head to one side. "An hour or so?"

Chloe said her goodbyes, and Madison handed the phone back to Luke. He retrieved two water bottles and handed one to Madison. She guzzled the contents in seconds while Luke started the motor.

"I'm guessing Chloe's relieved?" he shouted above the rumble of the engine. "I'll have you back with her as quickly as I can."

He backed the boat away from the dock. Madison stumbled with the sudden movement. She gasped. Her swollen ankle. Adrenaline must be fading.

Luke idled the motor and was at her side in a flash. "First, let's prop your ankle up before it inflates like a balloon." He helped her to the captain's chair and lowered her into it. He placed her foot on the next seat and padded it with his T-shirt. "Better?"

Madison nodded.

Luke waved to the police, and they waved back. They were on their way.

Wind blew the hair from her face as she looked up at her hero. "Luke, you risked your life for me." She had to shout over the boat noise.

Luke stood at the steering wheel and shrugged. "It was nothing." He let out a laugh. "Sorry. That was a complete lie. I'm not in the habit of rescuing beautiful, kidnapped women."

He called her beautiful. "It's not a regular occurrence in Mexico?"

"No, can't say it is." He turned and tapped her nose. "But I would do it all over again for you in a heartbeat. You have no idea how worried I've been."

Madison gulped. "You know you saved my life, don't you?" Her voice was husky, the magnitude of his sacrifice overwhelming her. She cleared her throat. "Somehow I knew you wouldn't leave me. I don't even know where to begin in the gratitude department. You're my knight in shining armor. Come here a second."

He bent down to her level and she planted a quick kiss on his cheek.

His eyes widened and dimples appeared on his cheeks. "I think we have some talking to do." He straightened and turned back to the wheel, half watching the water, half watching her face.

"Do we?" Madison's heart swelled. What about his whole singleness thing? Had something changed?

"I think so. At least, I do. Let's say God opened my eyes to a whole new realm of possibilities."

Was their conversation just yesterday? What had they said? *"Maybe God has something exciting planned for you which you know nothing about yet."* She allowed the words to sink in deep like a promise. "I like the sound of that." She smiled and shivered.

"You need some help keeping warm?" His green eyes filled with concern and he settled in the chair next to her. They would have to sit close together all the way to the resort. She could live with that.

Madison didn't say anything but rather tucked herself under his arm, shut out the night, and reveled in her newfound freedom. Freedom in the water. Freedom in love.

CHAPTER TWENTY-SIX

WHEN THEIR RESORT CAME INTO view, Luke cut the boat's engine. This whole crazy ordeal was almost over, thank goodness. Soon, Madison would be reunited with her sister, but first he had questions he needed to ask her. "Can we talk for a few minutes in private before facing the barrage of questioning?"

Madison sat up straight. "Of course."

He held one of her hands as they sat side by side. He twirled her signet ring around and around on her finger. This was going to be awkward, but he needed to know. "I want to make sure I heard you correctly back there. Did you say Sam was responsible for your parents' death?"

She nodded. "That's what he told me." He strained to hear her whisper. "He also said he'd been pilfering money from Dad's company for years. This scheme has been a long-term plan, and I guess when I busted him last year, he couldn't let it go." She wiped a stray tear from her cheek. "How can I live with myself, knowing I fell in love with and almost married my parents' murderer?" She gasped after saying it aloud.

Luke longed to take her pain away. He angled her face to look right at him and stared into her eyes.

"You were innocent in all this. You have to remember that. Sam is out of control, and you have to cling to the truth. You and Chloe are both alive and safe in spite of his plans. I guess your father didn't see through him, either. You can't blame yourself. It's in the past, and it'll take some working through, but look at what you endured and survived tonight."

"I know. It's going to be so hard breaking that piece of news to Chloe. It was painful enough coming to terms with our parents dying in a freak accident. I have my faith, and I know God will get us through this mess, but I'm worried about Chloe." Her shoulders sagged. "And there's something else I need to tell you."

There was more? "Okay. Go ahead."

Madison pulled away. "Back in the glass bottom boat, I found something, and I'm not sure what it means." She sniffed and retrieved a small object from the waistband of her shorts.

Luke held out his hand. "What is it?"

"It's a gold cuff link, and I know who it belongs to." She closed her eyes.

Luke inspected it. *"N.A.* You think it belongs to Nathan?" His mouth fell open. What did that even mean? Why was she carrying around a cuff link belonging to his brother? "Wait. You said you found it in the boat?"

"I'm sorry. I can't believe it myself, but I know for a fact it's his because I was with Chloe when she bought it for him last Christmas."

Nathan? He didn't want to even touch it. He handed it back and raked his hand through his windswept hair. What on earth? "And it was in the boat? Are you positive? I don't understand. I've only ever seen him wear cuff links on his wedding day. I don't even know—"

"Yeah, I'm positive. I love your brother to bits, Luke. I do. But do you think he could have been involved in any of this? I don't think he even knew Sam."

Nausea crept up from Luke's stomach as he looked out over the pitch-black ocean. "I think my little brother has some explaining to do. He already told Chloe and me that he met Sam earlier this year."

"What? No. Poor Chloe. How could he?"

Luke touched her hand. "Hear me out a second. He didn't realize it was Sam at the time. He said he wouldn't know him from Adam because there are no photos or anything at your place, which is understandable."

"That's true."

"We believe Sam set him up with the resort and even tied the boat into the scheme. There's a lot of information to sort through, but I know he would never, ever intentionally put you or Chloe in any danger." *God, he wouldn't, would he?* "He's not that kind of guy. I guarantee it. I don't understand the details, but I trust my brother. Do you trust me?"

Madison gazed up with tears in her eyes. "With my life."

"Then let's wait and talk with Nathan so we can figure everything out. Okay?"

"Yes, you're right. There has to be some logical explanation." She slipped the cuff link back into her pocket and looked ahead. "Since we're nearly here, would you do something for me?"

Luke stroked her still-damp hair. "I think you know by now I'd do anything for you." *Lord, this feels so right...*

She gripped his hand. "Pray for us?"

They bowed their heads. "Heavenly Father, how do we begin to thank You for leading me to Madison in that boat? For helping us escape? For the police arriving in time? You are sovereign and we are in awe. But, Lord, there is still so much we don't understand, and we desperately need Your wisdom. And we pray for our siblings in this, for Nathan and Chloe and their brand-new marriage. And we pray for our relationship, too." He paused and peeked down at their entwined fingers. "Father, that it might blossom and grow, if it's Your will. In Jesus's name we pray. Amen."

Madison squeezed his hand in response. They were in this together.

"Amen." Her voice was loud and clear. So was the message. His heart soared.

He started the boat back up and steered it in the direction of the resort. As he approached an empty spot between two speedboats on the main resort dock, a massive sigh of relief escaped his lips for many reasons. Madison was safe—that was his mission and it was accomplished. He hadn't freaked out while on the hunt for her and even came away with zero injuries—bonus. Chloe and Nathan would be able to continue their honeymoon, as long as this cuff link business was cleared up. His stomach churned at the mere thought of his brother being involved with such lowlifes. No way. But he needed answers. And until then, he needed to keep Madison safe. And Chloe.

He pulled Madison in close beside him. She must be emotionally spent. This was surreal. He was opening up his heart to the most wonderful woman he could have dreamed of. The peace radiating from his inmost being was confirmation; this was so right. And what about Mexico? Seattle? How did he and Madison make a relationship work on the mission field? They had a great deal to talk about. But not today.

He waved at Nathan and Chloe, who stood together at the end of the main dock. First things first—they had questions to answer, a kidnapping to wrap up, and a mystery to solve regarding a certain cuff link.

CHAPTER TWENTY-SEVEN

MADISON RELISHED THE WARMTH OF Luke's body beside her as they shared their final seconds on the boat. It felt right and good. What a night. How did this relationship develop at such breakneck speed between two souls intent on not opening up their hearts? In the dingy hut and again on the scary boat, she prayed for her life to be spared, and now she faced more potential happiness than she had ever imagined possible.

Luke was serious about her. The words he prayed moments ago, they were real. She wasn't dreaming. Something changed in his heart and she was falling hard for her rescuer. Tonight, she swung from the lowest of lows to the highest of highs in a matter of hours. Both her head and her heart were ready to explode.

Please, God, let the truth about my kidnapping be revealed so I can start living again. Preferably alongside this particular missionary.

"Madi? Madi!" Chloe waved both arms in the air.

They pulled in, and while Luke secured the tie lines, Madison stepped off the boat and was engulfed in a tight hug from her sister. She cried and laughed and held on to the dearest family member she had left. Chloe made no sense as she bawled into Madison's shoulder. It was good to be together. They pulled back and wiped their faces.

Madison moved farther onto the dock to allow Luke to jump from the boat. Chloe took both of his hands in her own. "I don't know how I'll ever repay you for this, but you are hands down the best brother-in-law ever." She glanced at Madison. "Thank you so much for bringing my sister back. You'll never know how much it means to me."

Madison grinned at Luke as he shifted from one foot to the other. "Anyone would have done the same. Especially for this young lady."

"I don't know how you did it, man." Madison spun round at the sound of Nathan's voice. He stepped forward and slapped his brother on the back and then resorted to a bear hug and plenty of whooping. "I guess your God really does answer prayers, eh? You're pretty awesome. You know that, right?"

Luke laughed, but it sounded forced. "I've always told you God answers. I'm glad you believe me, at long last. But you'd better stop with all this gushing. I'm not used to receiving actual compliments from my brother."

"Yeah, I'm done now. Gotta keep you humble." Nathan smirked.

Madison caught Luke's eye and attempted a reassuring smile. They needed those answers sooner rather than later.

Chloe linked arms with her sister. "I thought I'd lost you forever. I even prayed, and you know I'm not into that."

"Your prayers worked, then?"

"Yeah, I guess. Are you sure they didn't hurt you? I heard the thug slap you when we were on the phone. I've been so worried, imagining the worst..." A sob choked her voice.

"Hey, I'm fine. I think I sprained my ankle, but it's already feeling better than it was."

"But you were on a glass bottom boat?"

"On my own." A shudder ran through her body. But not as bad as before.

Chloe cringed. "Like in your nightmares. However did you cope?"

"It was worse than I imagined. But I knew God was with me and I prayed like crazy. Then this merman came along..." She winked at Luke.

"What?"

Their conversation was cut short when the resort manager joined the foursome at the end of the main dock. He was taller than the guys by at least four inches and looked like a stiff wind could blow him over. Judging by his disheveled shirt and crooked tie, he had been awakened for the occasion. He was the manager they reported to on Saturday night. Perhaps now he would take them seriously.

"Hello again." He turned to Chloe and Nathan. "My name is David, and I believe we have some serious business to attend to tonight, ladies and gentlemen." He checked his watch. "Or should I say 'this morning'?"

Madison had lost track of time. "Is it morning already?"

"It's one o'clock, miss," David said. "But don't worry about that. Our main concern is the well-being of our guests, and we want to make you comfortable while the authorities help sort it all out. Why don't you come with me to one of the meeting rooms? I've been informed that the police are on their way and need you to answer questions, of course." He narrowed his eyes when he saw the boat. "I don't know who that belongs to, but we'll worry about it later on."

Madison caught Luke's grin and his hand as the entourage followed David across the beach while he continued talking.

"Are you all okay? Hungry perhaps? Any injuries? You seem to be limping, miss. I can call our first-aid administrator if necessary. I'm afraid I don't know much about this incident, other than the kidnapping."

Madison shrugged. "I'm exhausted. A few bruises, a sore ankle, and a headache, but other than a dry set of clothes, some ice, and a painkiller, I don't think I'll need anything else. My stomach's not up to food right now, but thank you."

"Of course. I'll see to it." David glanced at Luke. "And your husband?"

"I'm fine—thanks. But I'm not her husband." Luke ran his free hand through his hair.

Yet. "He's my hero." She squeezed their clasped hands. With Luke on one side and Chloe on the other, her heart was full.

"Good. Here we are." David ushered them all through the deserted lobby and into a small room. A large rectangular table took up most of the space and was surrounded by formal padded chairs. "Excuse me while I round up some supplies for you." He rushed back out toward the lobby.

Chloe released Madison and fell into Nathan's arms. They both looked exhausted and took two seats on the far side of the table.

Luke led Madison to a chair and let go of her hand. She collapsed into it, her narrow escape sinking in, her adrenaline crashing fast.

Luke claimed the chair beside her. "You all right?"

"Just bone weary. I can't think straight anymore." She glanced over at her sister, who was deep in conversation with Nathan.

Luke followed her gaze and lowered his voice. "Do you want to tell Chloe about Sam's involvement in your parents' accident or ask about the cuff link before the police arrive?"

Madison leaned both elbows on the table and rested her head in her hands. "Half of me wants to forget I ever found the stupid cuff link, but what if Sam implicates Nathan? I can't bear the thought of Chloe hearing about it that way, but she also needs to know the accident wasn't an accident."

"Did I hear my name?" Chloe chimed into the conversation. "What's up, sis? Can I get you anything?"

She sat up straight. This was not going to be easy. "Listen, guys. This is super awkward. I'm so grateful to be back and overjoyed nobody was hurt in the process, but there's something I need to tell you." She bit her lip.

Luke shifted his chair closer to hers and put an arm around her shoulders.

"What's wrong?" Chloe's blue eyes were like saucers.

There was no way to candy-coat this piece of news. "Sam told me he caused Mom and Dad's plane to crash."

"What?" Chloe's mouth flew open. "How can that be? They did a full investigation, didn't they?"

"Yes, but it was inconclusive, remember? A lot of evidence was compromised in the lake, and we had no reason to suspect anyone would ever try to tamper with Dad's plane."

"I can't believe it. They were...murdered? I didn't think it could get any worse. And Sam? We let him into our lives. We were nice to the guy who killed our parents? No, it can't be true." Chloe buried her face in her hands.

"I know." Madison took a deep breath. "I nearly married him, remember?"

"I can't believe this."

"There's more to his scam than we ever imagined. He also said he'd been pilfering money from Dad's company for years and saw the plane accident as a means to getting to me and, in turn, the major money."

Chloe almost choked. "But we welcomed him into our home, and he never broke a sweat. He sat there and comforted us while we grieved. He helped us both through a horrible time and he weaseled his way into your heart. How could he?"

Madison shrugged. She had already cried over the realization, but this was fresh news for her sister. "He played us all. Even poor Dad."

"That's absurd." Nathan pulled his chair closer to his wife's. "This guy's got nerve. To be that close with your family and have this whole master plan going on." He squeezed Chloe's hand. "Actually, Madison, this is going to sound crazy, but I have to tell you something, too."

Madison stared across the table at Nathan's green eyes. He looked down. "Really? Because there's something I need to ask you about. I found something on the—"

"Good morning, everyone."

Their conversation was cut short when three Jamaican policemen entered the room and filled the space. They wore flat black hats, which they removed when each took an available seat around the table.

The eldest policeman spoke again. "I'm Officer Peters, and these are Officers Stephens and Johnson." He looked at the bedraggled group leaning over the table. "It appears you have all had a traumatic day. I'm sorry for your distress."

"Yes, sir." Luke spoke for them all. "We're glad to have the whole situation behind us. Are the two men in custody?"

"Yes, I can confirm they are both in custody." Officer Peters pulled a notebook and pencil from his breast pocket. "We'll be contacting the US Embassy and the police force in Seattle straightaway. You're safe now."

Madison exhaled and closed her eyes. "What a relief." Her eyes flew open. "Was anyone shot? We heard a gun go off back at the other beach."

"No, miss. I would say it was a warning shot. Nobody is injured."

Madison nodded. The need to see Sam receive justice was at the top of her list of priorities after today. Being shot to death seemed like an easy out. Her parents deserved justice.

Officer Peters took his time staring at each of them around the table, landing on Nathan. "You must be the brother who phoned us?"

He nodded. "That was me. And I have the note I mentioned right here." He dug into his shorts pocket and set the ransom note in front of the officer. Madison's chest tightened. She didn't want to read it. Not right now.

"Good." He scanned it and scribbled in his notebook before looking at Madison.

"We will need you to tell us everything that happened today. I know this will be hard and you are tired, but I must insist. We will record this interview. Okay?"

She wanted the whole thing over with. "That's fine."

One of the other officers took a small tape recorder from a briefcase and placed it on the table.

The manager entered the room with fresh robes for Madison and Luke, and he was followed by a young lady who set a pot of steaming coffee and mugs on the table and some ice and a bottle of painkillers with four glasses of water.

The aroma of coffee was heaven. Madison smiled her thanks and slipped into the robe's warmth. She swallowed the pills and reached for the coffee to warm her insides and give her enough caffeine to concentrate on the interview. She rested the ice pack on her swollen ankle. Instant relief.

Officer Peters's finger hovered above the recorder. "Are you ready, Miss Grey?"

She took a deep breath and nodded. *I can do this.* Starting with Friday night in the lobby when she had first spotted Blue Eyes, she relayed every detail she could remember. Luke interjected with observations of his own, further explaining his role in the rescue. Between them, they covered everything. It was grueling, especially when the officers interrupted with even more questions. An hour later, a yawn split her face.

Chloe spoke next. "Officer, my sister is exhausted. And I think she needs to get home as soon as possible. If I can find flights, I think we should leave tomorrow."

Officer Peters shook his head. "I'm afraid we'll need you to stay in the country until we get this all figured out. I'm sorry."

"That's fine." Madison fought another yawn. "I need to rest and recover, and I can do that right here, so let's stick to our original plan. I'm safe now. I can't imagine having to pack up and get on a plane tomorrow. Really, Chloe, I'd rather recuperate on the beach. And you guys have a honeymoon to salvage."

Officer Peters cleared his throat. "There is one thing we need to discuss as a matter of importance, even though I know you must all be tired."

"Go ahead." Luke offered Madison another coffee. She shook her head, in danger of a caffeine overload at this hour. He poured himself a cup.

"Evidence was found at the scene where we picked up the alleged kidnappers—incriminating documents, chloroform, a gun. But the suspects were also forthcoming with some information they thought we would find interesting, and it concerns one of you." His eyes darted to Nathan.

Nathan's mouth fell open. "Me? Why?"

"Mr. Sam Kinkaid implied you were involved in this scam, Mr. Alexander. He is willing to write a statement confirming you knew about the planned abduction in the boat several months ago and that you met with him and Mr. Holloday on numerous occasions."

"What? Mr. Holloday?" Nathan shook his head. "I don't know any Holloday."

Madison heart lurched. She took one hand from the table and touched the cuff link, still tucked in her waistband.

Luke rubbed his chin. "That must be Blue Eyes."

Madison looked from Luke to Nathan. "How well did you know Sam? Luke told me you'd met him."

Nathan groaned. "This is such a mess. I met them both when we were planning the wedding, but he used another name. He called himself Steve Jacobs." He paused while Officer Peters scribbled down the name. "I had no idea he was your ex, Madison. I had nothing to do with this sick scheme. I swear. It was only after the ransom note that I started to piece everything together and we realized Steve Jacobs was Sam. Why would I put my fiancée—my wife—through this turmoil?" He put an arm around Chloe as tears trickled down her cheeks.

The officer tapped a pencil on the table. "How did you happen to meet these men?"

"They posed as photographers, and then Sam came to me later with a great deal on this resort. We met a couple of times, but he made me uncomfortable, and so I shook him loose as soon as I could. Haven't heard from him since."

"Why did he make you uncomfortable?" Madison stared into Nathan's eyes, so like his brother's. She had to know the truth. It had to make sense.

"He kept going on about how we should incorporate this glass bottom boat idea into the wedding. Now I realize why, but at the time, it was plain weird. And he asked a lot of questions about you, Madison." He squeezed Chloe closer. "More than about the bride, which is kind of suspicious, in hindsight."

She lowered her head and blinked away tears as Luke put an arm back around her shoulders.

Officer Peters cleared his throat. "So, you're saying you had nothing to do with today's kidnapping."

"Of course he didn't." Chloe threw her hands in the air. "Why would he? For goodness' sake, he married me and is entitled to half my money anyway. It wouldn't make any sense. There's no proof, only what that loser is trying to pin on Nathan."

Madison chewed on her thumbnail. She vacillated between keeping the whole cuff link business a secret or exposing Nathan and seeing what answers he might have. But how could she live with herself if he did something wrong and Chloe was put in danger or had her heart broken later on? No, the truth was going to come out. It had to, for them all to move on from this.

She reached into her waistband and pulled out the cuff link. A quick glance at Luke. He nodded, his expression grim. She placed it on the table without saying a word.

"What's this?" Officer Peters pointed with his pencil.

Nathan reached across the table and held it between his thumb and forefinger. "My cuff link. Where did you get this?"

Madison swallowed the lump in her throat. "It was in the glass bottom boat."

"What?" Chloe's hand flew to her mouth. "Nathan? What's going on?"

Officer Peters's gaze flitted from Chloe to Nathan and then to the other policemen in the room.

Nathan stood. His chair fell over behind him. "You all need to believe me on this. I haven't worn my cuff links in months. Chloe, have you seen me wearing them recently? I thought I'd lost one of them, and I didn't have the heart to tell you because I knew you'd be mad. You bought them for me at Christmas."

"Oh, Nathan." Chloe grabbed a tissue from her pocket and dabbed at her red-rimmed eyes. "Why have you been so secretive? I don't understand any of it." She looked at the officers. "But it's true. I haven't seen him with these cuff links in a long time."

"Wait." Luke pointed at his brother. "Is that why Mom bought you a new pair for the wedding? Does she know you lost Chloe's pair?"

"Yeah." Nathan shrugged. "You know what Mom's like. She insisted on buying me a similar set, hoping Chloe wouldn't notice. She didn't want me to get myself into trouble."

Chloe grabbed his hand. "Of course I noticed—I'm the detail queen. When you said you wanted to wear a pair your mom bought you for the wedding ceremony, I thought it was sweet. You could have told me you had lost one of mine."

Luke stood eye to eye with his brother. "Don't you see? That's good. I knew there had to be some explanation. It proves you lost them beforehand. Right, Officer?" He looked to Officer Peters.

"I'm not sure the word of his mother would clear him. Kind of biased, wouldn't you say?" He tapped his pencil on the table.

"I have the other cuff link back at home, but it's not much good on its own." Nathan collapsed onto his chair.

"What?" Luke smacked his own forehead with the palm of his hand. "Duh. Sometimes I wonder about you. Why didn't you say so in the first place? And why on earth would you have one lone cuff link with you if you were on the boat in Jamaica? Who wears one cuff link on its own? If the other is safely in Seattle, it looks to me like this one was stolen and planted and proves you've been framed. Right, Officer?" He sat back down.

The three policemen conferred in hushed tones while the others sat in stunned silence. Madison's headache was fading, but so was her energy. The past twenty-four hours were catching up with her. She massaged her temples and avoided eye contact with anyone, struggling to keep her tears from spilling over.

Officer Peters stood. "It would appear that you were framed. Are you sure you can lay your hands on the matching cuff link at home, Mr. Alexander?"

251

"Yes. I know it's in my top drawer. I saw it there when I was packing for this trip. The jerk must have stolen one, but I can't think when. He could have been following us all for weeks and even snooped around my apartment, for all I know. This gets creepier by the minute." He dragged his fingers through his hair. "Am I off the hook, then?"

"Thanks to your additional information and testimony, we will be questioning Mr. Kinkaid and his associate at length. We'll keep you up to date, Miss Grey, and you can rest assured the two gentlemen in question won't be going free. I hope you are all able to enjoy what's left of your vacation on our island."

One of the other officers switched off the recorder and stowed it in his briefcase.

Madison cleared her throat. "There's something else you need to speak about with Sam Kinkaid." Luke squeezed her hand. "He confessed to me he tampered with my father's plane and caused their fatal accident two years ago in Seattle."

She couldn't keep the sobs at bay any longer. Exhaustion was kicking in hard and fast. Luke folded her into his embrace and she buried her head in his chest.

One of the other officers made a note, and Peters looked surprised at that piece of news. "It's a shocking addition to the charges. We'll be sure to include this in the questioning, Miss Grey. I'll have someone from the US Embassy come over first thing. We'll be in touch later today for you to come in for written statements."

She pulled back from Luke and dried her eyes on the sleeve of her robe. "Of course."

He nodded. "Good night, everyone. We'll leave you all to get some rest. Once again, I'm glad you're all safe."

There was an audible sigh of relief when the two couples were left alone in the room.

"I'm so sorry." Nathan wiped a hand over his stubbly face. "I've messed up big time not being open with you all. Honey, can you forgive me?" He lifted Chloe's delicate hand and kissed it.

She sighed. "I love you. Yes, I forgive you. We were all fooled, but we're okay now. How are you doing, Madi? You look drained."

Madison blinked. Even that took a great deal of effort. Sleep would be bliss about now. She clambered to her feet and stretched. "I need a hot bath, and then I'm falling into bed. We can talk more tomorrow. I mean, later today."

"Do you want me to stay with you?" Chloe rushed around the table and gave her a hug. "Nathan won't mind. Right, babe?"

"Madison, I feel so awful for everything you've been through. I don't mind. Heck, I'll stand guard outside your door if it helps."

"No way." Madison took a deep breath. "You two have a honeymoon to enjoy. I'm going to sleep like a baby. I promise. No more nightmares about glass bottom boats either." She reached a hand out to grab Luke's. "Thanks to this guy, I think I've conquered that fear. I'll catch up with you later, okay?"

Chloe shook her head. "I can't believe what you've been through in the past twenty-four hours."

"I'm fine. I will be fine. Truly." Madison glanced at Luke. "More than fine."

*****

253

Luke put an arm around Madison. She trembled from exhaustion and needed to rest. "You two can go on ahead. I'll walk Madison to her room since I have a feeling she might even need carrying at this point. And I'll keep my phone on tonight so she can call me at any time if she's worried."

"Your phone is still in your room on the bedside table. I checked it earlier." Chloe kissed her cheek. "Sleep well."

Nathan punched his brother in the arm. "Hero to the end."

"Thanks." Madison leaned against Luke's side as the newlyweds left. "I think I hit a wall. Could you be my knight in shining armor for a while longer?"

He grinned down at her. "I think we could consider making that a long-term arrangement." He swooped her up in his arms with a surge of energy that belied his own exhaustion and carried her to the elevator, then all the way to her room.

"Thanks. You can set me down while I dig out my key." She kept her voice to a whisper in the silent hallway.

Luke lowered her to her feet. "I can't believe you still have your room key." Why hadn't he thought to check with Chloe?

"Right? I hope it still works." She smiled up at him, and his heart hammered in his chest. How was she still so beautiful after everything she had experienced in the past twenty-four hours? "I'd forgotten it was even in here." She pushed aside the hotel's robe, then unzipped the small back pocket of her shorts and slid out the plastic key before glancing up at his face. "Are you staring at me?"

"Just thinking how amazing you look." He leaned against the doorframe.

She raised a brow and smoothed her hair. "I feel gross. A mixture of salt, sweat, and sticky. But thanks for the sentiment." She pushed the door open.

"Mind if I come in and check everything?"

"Be my guest." She flicked on the lights while Luke checked that the French doors were locked, saw her phone charging on the nightstand beside the bed, and poked his head into the bathroom. "Can I run you a hot bath? Everything will feel better after that."

"Thanks. That sounds perfect."

He emptied a small container of something with a delicious lavender scent into the steady stream of water. It was the least he could do to make her feel better. Would her skin smell of lavender when he saw her later on?

He cleared his throat. "Sure you're not going to fall asleep in the tub?"

Madison stood at the bathroom door and chuckled, a small pile of clothes in her hands. "I promise. I'll make it quick—the bed is my ultimate destination. Thanks for bringing me in, but I think I've got it from here."

"Sounds good." He left the faucets running and joined her. "I'm done in, too. Give me a call if there's any problem at all?"

"Don't worry. You're my number-one hero go-to guy from now on." Her smile was wobbly but her eyes shone with truth.

It warmed his heart. "Promise?" He stroked her silky-soft cheek.

"Yeah. I think I do, missionary boy." Her voice grew husky.

Luke turned to the door. "I should go now." He knew his cheeks were flaming. "Get some decent sleep and call me when you want some company for breakfast."

"I will. Thanks again, for everything. Sleep tight."

Madison shut the door behind him, and he waited until he heard the lock turn. He could hardly put one foot in front of the other. He yawned and stretched his arms above his head on his way to the elevator and punched in the floor number for his room. The doors slid open, and he entered, then slumped against the side of the elevator. Up two floors.

As he ascended, peace washed over him again. This all felt so right, the whole Madison situation. He wanted to protect and cherish this woman always, not only in Jamaica. *This is the real deal, isn't it, Lord? This is what I've been waiting for.* A holy *Yes* resounded in his chest.

The corridor was deserted as he plodded toward his room. He glanced down at the woven bracelet on his wrist and smiled. *I'm coming home, kids. And I think you're going to like the new house mama I have in mind...*

CHAPTER TWENTY-EIGHT

MADISON SOAKED IN THE WARM sun and breathed in the salty air. How was it Friday already? She glanced over at Luke's strong profile and sighed. Talk about surreal.

This was the most bizarre week imaginable—and one she would never forget as long as she lived. Had she really survived a Caribbean kidnapping ordeal a few short days ago? That didn't happen to regular people. To high-school teachers from Seattle.

She touched her wrist and then her upper arm. The bruises from being bound and manhandled were almost invisible, thanks to a deepening tan. Earlier this morning, she had walked along the beach with Luke, and her ankle didn't even twinge. Every part of her was healing. Especially her heart.

The past few days, Chloe and Nathan had made an occasional appearance, and Madison was relieved to see them salvage at least part of their honeymoon. It was not the ideal start to a marriage, but in some ways, the scare had brought the couple even closer together. They would have no secrets from each other in the future. Madison smiled. She had shared some special conversations with Chloe since Tuesday, when she returned the journal and iPod. Her sister may not realize it, but she was searching spiritually, and God was already working in her life. This was just the beginning for the newlyweds.

And it was the beginning for her and Luke. Unbelievable. Most of this week, Madison spent precious time with him. Together, they laughed, cried, talked, and shared about everything including the kidnapping ordeal. Madison worked through any lingering worries and was able to bring closure to every part of her life involving Sam.

Now she dreamed of a future with her brother-in-law's brother. Didn't see that coming a week ago. When she arrived in Jamaica last Friday, love was the furthest thing from Madison's mind. Her priority had been to create a magical wedding for her sister and keep her old ghosts at bay. She had been purely in survival mode. She went into the vacation skeptical and licking her wounds—until a certain missionary caught her eye. Thoughts of Mexico swirled in her mind, and she realized she had memorized the name of almost every orphan at Luke's home. Learning Spanish was not accidental. There was a plan all along.

God works in mysterious ways. She had always wondered about that little gem of a saying and now she understood the depth of its meaning. Mysterious, all right.

Tomorrow, the four of them were due to fly back to Seattle for Chloe and Nathan's wedding reception. Madison bit her thumbnail. "Luke, do you think all this has been in the papers back home? I hate to think of the reception being tarnished or overshadowed by the kidnapping."

"Honey, there's nothing we can do about it from here. We'll keep a low profile when we hit Seattle. I know Mom and Dad have kept it quiet. It was all Dad could do to stop Mom flying out and pampering us to death. Fortunately, she's going out of her way to ensure every detail of the reception is perfect. Try not to worry about it. Let's enjoy our last day in paradise."

Madison leaned back against his shoulder. "You're right. But you don't think they'll transport Sam and Blue Eyes on the same flight as us, do you?"

Luke stroked her arm. "Already sorted out. No chance of that happening."

"Do you think the media will try to crash the—"

"Madison." He voice held a smile.

"Yes? I know. I'm a worrier. It's what I do."

Luke turned to face her and took off his shades.

Madison melted. Would she ever grow accustomed to those green eyes?

"I love you, worries and all. But what's our verse again? 'Do not be anxious about…'"

"'Anything.'" Madison laughed. "You're going to have to be patient. This one doesn't come naturally to me. But I'm working on it."

"And that's fine. Believe me—I've got plenty of my own issues to work on. But I'll help you. You know that now, don't you?"

Madison ran her fingers through his thick, wavy hair. "You've helped me with so much this week, it's ridiculous. First, you saved my life. That was rather a big one. Then you had me snorkeling, and you taught me to pray without ceasing, give my worries over to God, and on top of everything else, you've stolen my heart. Not bad for a missionary."

Luke kissed her cheek and pulled her sparkly pink sunglasses from her face. Never thought she'd see those glasses again.

"I've fallen in love with you, Miss Grey. Unconditionally. You turned my world upside down. I know God was keeping me single because I had to wait for you."

"Luke, that's beautiful."

"It's true. I've never been more certain of anything. Now I'm the one who's out of my depth, so we have to help each other stay afloat to make this relationship work. You do trust me, don't you?"

"I do. I'm ready for whatever comes next. Chloe's happy and excited to start her life with Nathan. And I'm ready to start using my Spanish in a practical capacity anytime you like."

"For real? Are we talking Mexico?" His eyes sparkled as brightly as her sunglasses in his hand.

"Hmm. I've been praying and I think I could be persuaded." Madison batted her eyelashes. "Especially if I get to meet a certain little baby named Sophia."

"It can be arranged. And I was kind of hoping there would be other babies on the horizon..."

"Green eyes and chocolate-brown ringlets?" Madison raised a brow.

Luke fiddled with the yellow-and-brown woven bracelet on his wrist until it came loose.

She gasped. "What have you done? Didn't your orphanage kids make you promise you'd keep it on the whole time you were away?"

Luke didn't reply at first. He took Madison's delicate wrist and tied the bracelet around it, fastening it with a tight knot.

"Somehow, I don't think they'll mind that I found a beautiful girl to put it on—if there's a chance they'll get to meet her." He slipped his phone from his pocket and snapped a picture of her adorned wrist. "There we go. Proof for them."

Madison gazed at the bracelet and reminded herself to exhale. Was this happening? She grabbed Luke's hand. "Tell them I promise to keep it on until they can see it for themselves."

"They'll hold you to it, you know."

"I know."

Luke moved closer, and they watched the fluffy clouds float across the turquoise Caribbean sky in comfortable silence. Today was the final hurdle of all the fears she faced during her stay in Jamaica. It felt good. Amazing even. Nestled in the arms of the most wonderful man imaginable, she rocked on the ocean in a glass bottom boat.

What a week of miracles.

Luke cleared his throat. "The Alexander brothers are known for their short engagements, you know."

Madison closed her eyes and took a deep breath, memorizing this spectacular moment.

"I'm counting on it, missionary boy."

Her life would never be the same again.

ABOUT THE AUTHOR

Laura is a published Christian author with a heart for inspiring and encouraging readers of all ages, with books for children, teens, and adults. Originally from the UK, she lives in British Columbia, Canada, as an empty-nester. Laura is a mom of three, married to her high school sweetheart, and is passionate about faith and family—and chocolate.

www.laurathomasauthor.com